For testimonials from law enforcement,
visit Carolyn Arnold's website.

A nail-biting crime thriller packed
with heart-pounding twists

CAROLYN ARNOLD

Sometimes the past should stay there...

VIOLATED

A Brandon Fisher FBI Thriller

HIBBERT & STILES
PUBLISHING INC.

Hibbert & Stiles Publishing Inc.
hspubinc.com

This is a work of fiction. Names, characters, places, and incidents are the products of the author's imagination or are used fictitiously. Any resemblance to actual events, locales, or persons, living or dead, is entirely coincidental.

Names: Arnold, Carolyn, 1976
Title: Violated / Carolyn Arnold.
Description: 2021 Hibbert & Stiles Publishing Inc. edition. | Series: Brandon Fisher FBI Series ; book 5

Identifiers: ISBN (e-book): 978-1-988064-71-0 | ISBN (4.25 x 7 paperback): 978-1-988064-73-4 | ISBN (5 x 8 paperback): 978-1-988064-70-3 | ISBN (6.14 x 9.21 hardcover): 978-1-988064-74-1

Additional formats:
ISBN (large print editon): 978-1-989706-36-7
ISBN (audiobook): 978-1-989706-66-4

VIOLATED

To Chelsea…

"Life can only be understood backwards;
but it must be lived forwards."
—Søren Kierkegaard

PROLOGUE

Monday, August 24th, 11:10 PM Pacific Time
Canyon Country, California

The mark was in his forties, had no kids, and worked a white-collar job. Average height, average looks. Nothing was truly memorable about him except for his uncommon first name, and that was only because it belonged to a character from a popular eighties movie.

Ferris Hall.

She had followed him to some honky-tonk in Canyon Country, an unsavory location at any time of day, but factor in the late hour and it was even worse. But Ferris had chosen this dive as his hunting ground. Women were easier to lure in with a little chemical persuasion, and that was easy to pass off around here.

He entered the bar with head held high, his back straight, the tease of a smirk on his lips—the end of the evening a foregone conclusion in his mind. He was sipping on his first bourbon, though he was acting as if he was on his third by slurring his words and talking loudly. He'd even thrown a sway into his swagger. Somehow he always managed to make his eyes look bloodshot, too, furthering the charade. And the women would come. And the women would fall for his tricks.

Tonight, she'd be that woman, but she'd be his last. He had to learn there was a price to pay for his actions.

She was sitting down the bar from him. Occasionally, he'd pass her a look—the predatory kind that made her blood boil. She smiled at him, doing her best to convey carnal hunger with her gaze, smearing on a seductive curve to her lips. She dipped her finger into her manhattan and sucked on it—the cherry juice sweet, the whiskey bitter.

Ferris was off his stool and sidling up her to within three seconds.

The ruse worked every time. It also helped that she exploited what nature had given her—a slender frame and shapely legs. High heels accentuated her well-defined calf muscles, and men stared when she walked into a room. When she paired even higher stilettos with a short skirt and crossed her legs, men's mouths tended to fall open. She utilized all these virtues tonight.

She flashed another sultry smile, and he lifted his glass toward her before tilting his own back and draining it. He set it back on the bar and knocked on it to get the bartender's attention.

"I'll have another on the rocks and—" he rolled his head toward her "—get the lady whatever she'd like."

Time to feign innocence and flattery.

She waved a dismissive hand in his direction. "I really shouldn't."

She saw the quick look he gave her glass before meeting her eyes again. "Nonsense. Please, it would be my treat."

If she stripped his voice of its candy-coated tone, his words were pushy and controlling.

"Well"—she angled her glass, showing how little of her drink she had left—"only if you're sure."

If she had actually been given a chance to prove her acting skills, she could be living in a sprawling mansion by now.

"Absolutely. What will it be?" Ferris asked, a grin teasing his lips as he tugged down on his left earlobe. It wasn't hard for her to figure out what was going on. Ferris was asking for something "special" to be added to her drink—the "special" being some kind of date-rape drug.

She lifted her glass to the bartender. "Another manhattan."

"Coming right up." The tender left to make their drinks, and she watched him, taking the time to calm her heartbeat and flow of adrenaline.

"I like a woman who can handle her whiskey." Ferris was looking quite comfortable beside her now. He was fully facing her, his left elbow perched on the counter, and he wasn't discreet about his drifting gaze, which gravitated to her thighs.

"What can I say? I'm a little whiskey girl." The words from the country song rolled off her tongue, cinching her gut, but she had to do what was necessary to pull him in.

"Toby Keith," he said.

"Pardon?"

"Toby Keith." He pointed to a speaker on the ceiling. "The singer who sings that one."

"Ah, yes." And here, she thought she was doing well by knowing it was even a country song. She smiled at him again. He truly thought of himself as a woman's man.

Pathetic.

"Have I seen you here before?" he asked.

She dipped her head.

"I knew it. I never forget a beautiful face. So what's your name?"

"Names really aren't important, are they, baby?" She extended her hand, her long, narrow fingers bowing before him in feminine elegance.

"Oh, she's mysterious. I like it." He kissed the back of her hand, and she was proud of herself for not rolling her eyes.

The bartender returned and placed their drinks in front of them. "Here you go."

From her observations, Ferris seemed to keep a running tab here. Rape now, pay later?

Oh, and Ferris would pay...

"You never told me your name," she said, falling into her role.

"Oh, I can tell you mine, but you can't—"

"Uh-huh." She sucked on the tip of her finger again.

"Ferris." He still held onto her other hand, and she pulled it back shyly.

"Are you from around here?" she asked, resorting to the necessity of small talk.

"I just fly in from time to time for business."

"Ah." She'd have to call upon her acting skills for this performance. She knew he lived less than three miles away from this place. "What business?"

He tapped his jacket pockets, then slid a hand inside one. "How embarrassing. I don't have any cards with me. Besides, I don't really want to bore you. Why don't we talk about you?" He leaned toward her and lifted his rocks glass. "To a fun night."

"To one we won't remember."

They toasted, and he took a long pull of the amber liquid. She pressed her own glass to her lips and pretended to take a sip.

"Wow, this is good stuff." She licked her lips and hopped off the stool.

"Hey, where are you going?"

"To the washroom. Wanna come?" She knew he'd decline. He liked to carry out his acts of violation in privacy.

"Nah, but I'll be waiting here for you."

I'm sure you will.

She grabbed her glass and sauntered off to the restrooms. "A girl can never be too careful," she tossed over her shoulder to him.

The bathroom reeked of cheap perfume and urine. Grime was embedded in the tile, which was likely unredeemable even if someone used a heavy-duty scrub brush on it.

She dipped her fingers into her glass, splashed the whiskey on her neck as if it were a fragrance, and dumped two-thirds of the drink down the drain. Afterward, she studied her eyes in the pitted mirror, but she dared not to look too deep or she'd get swallowed by the darkness in her soul. Her irises swirled with pent-up rage from a lifetime of heartbreak and betrayal.

She left the restroom and staggered back toward Ferris. When she saw him watching, she bumped into an unoccupied table. She went to set her drink down on the surface but let go of it. The glass rolled across the table, stopping shy of going over the edge, but the alcohol spilled. She grabbed the table to right herself and saw that Ferris was hurrying over.

"How embarrassing. Whiskey goes right to my head." She slapped her forehead and laughed huskily.

"It is good for that." He put his hands on her sides, copping a feel of her breast while "helping" her straighten up. There was no apology for the grope—not that she expected one.

She ran her hands along her skirt. "How about we get out of here?"

"Sure thing," he said with a wink.

"Wonderful." She touched his brow, brushing back a strand of his hair with her fingers. Then she leaned in toward him, his arm around her, and they left the bar.

In the parking lot outside, Ferris helped her into his car, and before she could buckle her seat belt, he had his tongue down her throat. It was time to pretend she was enjoying this and somehow manage not to throw up in his mouth.

Minutes later, he pulled back, breathless, his eyes narrowed in arousal. "So what do you say? Should we take this someplace else?"

She narrowed her eyes. "Why not."

He peeled out of the lot, wheels squealing on the pavement, and not long later, flickering orange lights announced they'd reached their destination: Motel. It was a seedy place where rooms were rented by the hour.

He parked in view of the lobby and went in while she stayed in the car. She watched him hand over some cash, and he was quickly on his way back to her. His steps were lighter now, and any pretense of feeling the alcohol was gone. As far as he was concerned, the show was no longer necessary.

She leaned against the headrest and lolled her head toward him. She pretended that she wanted to smile but couldn't quite form the expression, giving the impression that the drug was setting in. He helped her out of the car and into the room.

Inside, she could make out a double bed across from a dresser and TV. A couple of chairs and a round table barely big enough for two were in front of the window that faced the parking lot. The curtains were already drawn, and when he hit the light switch to the left of the door, she winced and covered her eyes.

He laughed. "A little bright for you? Come on, let's sit on the bed."

Yeah, let's sit.

She slipped out of her heels and pretended to stumble a bit as she headed toward him. She was giggling as she dragged her purse by its strap behind her.

He patted the mattress. "Come on, baby."

"Why don't you take your clothes off, and I'll—" She sucked on a finger.

"Don't have to ask me twice." He wasted no time tossing aside his clothing and lying back on the bed. His white body obviously never saw the sun, and his erection was already full. She swallowed the bile that rose in her throat. Even though violators like Ferris normally preferred to dominate liaisons like this, most men couldn't refuse the offer of a blowjob.

"How about a little bondage?" She eyed the barred headboard. This would be too easy...

"Nah, let's just—"

She pulled out a pair of cuffs from her purse and snapped one end on his wrist and the other to the headboard before he could protest.

"Hmm, you like to be in charge? Well, so do I." He whipped his body off the bed as far as he could and yanked on her hair with his free hand, pulling her to him, mouth to mouth—all tongue and domination. She pretended to like it for a few seconds and then pulled back, teasing him.

"Let me see your tits." His eyes were narrowed slits, and a mischievous grin twisted his lips.

She was still standing, and she rocked on her feet in an attempt to break free of his hold. She stumbled backward, but he never let go of her hair and pain seared her scalp.

"Get naked." His tone held impatience now.

She needed to fully restrain him before she could put the rest of her plan into action. Body size alone indicated that he could overpower her. She was about five foot nine and 130 pounds, and Ferris was six foot two, 220. At least one wrist was already bound to the headboard.

He let go of her, and she stepped well out of his reach. His swipes at the air to reach her kept coming up short. She ducked and picked up her purse again.

"Please, just a little patience. I promise it will be worth the wait." She walked around the end of the bed and pulled out another set of cuffs.

"This is not fucking cute anymore." Anger coated his face, wrinkling his brow and darkening his eyes.

"I get you off, and then you can do whatever you want to me."

"I say that happens now."

"Lie back on the bed again. Please." She played coy and teasing, tossing in another deep-throated suck on her index finger just for the hell of it. Men were so simpleminded.

Ferris relented and got back into position.

She moved stealthily around the other side of the bed and secured his other wrist to the frame.

Any hint of modesty now gone, she assumed the role of dominatrix. "Are you sure you can handle it?"

"Oh, I can handle you." He thrust his hips forward and clenched his jaw with hunger. "But can you handle me?"

The sound of his voice was nauseating. She couldn't wait to silence him.

With both his arms pinned, she returned to the end of the bed.

"Take your fucking clothes off!" he barked.

"Why rush things?" She pulled out two more sets of cuffs. The chains on these ones were long enough to reach the bedframe. She restrained his legs, even as he squirmed.

"Now, take your fucking clothes off," he hissed.

"First things first." She took a roll of duct tape out of her purse and ripped off a strip.

"What the—" His impatient squirming had turned to resistant bucking, but she got the tape in place.

She casually looked at him from the end of the bed. His erection was softening, his eyes finally showing fear. And she hadn't even given him anything to be afraid of.

Yet.

It must have been something in her energy and what she was communicating without words. It would have been clear by now that she wasn't drugged, that she was actually the one in control here.

She drew her knife from its sheath and studied the blade.

He was trying to say something, but from behind the tape, it came out as mumbling. He jerked his body as if pure determination would free him. His eyes widened, and fear transformed into outright panic.

"Let's get on with this night we won't remember, shall we? Or should I say you won't remember it, because you'll be—" She thrust the blade into his testicles. His screams weren't much more than a whisper behind the tape, though tears streamed from his eyes, terror streaking through them.

She stabbed him a few more times and then, with one swipe, rid him of what had been his weapon. It would take him awhile to bleed out, but she was prepared to stay with him until the end.

CHAPTER ONE

I'd never understand women—at least not one woman in particular. But I wasn't about to admit it out loud when my job with the FBI Behavioral Analysis Unit required that I successfully assess other people's states of mind. For the life of me, though, I couldn't figure out what had gotten into my colleague and ex-lover Paige Dawson or why she'd decided to take off and go to California with a man she hardly knew. But I sensed there was more to it.

I knew she'd recently lost a childhood friend, but it wasn't a tragic accident that had suddenly claimed her life. Really, she'd been merely existing as it was, as her life for the past twenty-some years had consisted of being hooked up to a ventilator. It wasn't until a couple of weeks ago that the woman's mother decided to pull the plug. I could only guess how Paige was feeling, and maybe a getaway was exactly what she needed to process it all. It wasn't like she discussed her emotions with me anymore.

We'd decided to end our romantic relationship—if it could be called that—not long before she took up with what's-his-name, actually. Speaking of what's-his-name, she was probably snuggling up to him at some bar while I was buried in paperwork from the last case. Murderers killed people *and* trees.

"How's it coming along, Brandon?" Zach asked.

I hadn't even noticed that he had returned from lunch. It was a rarity that the senior profiler even took one. His desk was about three feet from mine. That meant zero privacy, but it did encourage open communication.

Thinking of being posted behind a desk made me feel useless, as if my time could be put to no better use. Here we were, stuck pushing paperwork while as many as fifty active serial killers targeted their next victims.

I looked over at Zach. "I assume you're referring to all these reports?" I splayed my hand over the paperwork, and he nodded. "Oh, it's coming along *wonderfully*."

"You do know sarcasm is anger's ugly cousin, right?"

"It's also a sign of intelligence."

Zach smirked, a spark lighting his eyes.

I narrowed my gaze at him. Something was different. "Who is she?" I asked.

His eyes widened, a subtle blush coming to his cheeks. "Excuse me?"

"The woman you're seeing. I take it by your bright-red lips, you've either taken to wearing lipstick or you've been kissing. *Heavily*." I was the one smirking now. Zach, however, was stark serious.

Maybe I shouldn't press my luck. I had just become a full-fledged agent, having only passed my probationary status last month. But it was too much fun to tease him after he'd done it to me for so long with that damn nickname he'd had for me, "Pending." He certainly couldn't call me that anymore.

"Brandon, mind your own business," he snapped.

"Ah, so it's serious... That's why you don't want to talk about it."

He shuffled some papers around on his desk with no apparent purpose. "I never said that."

"You never denied it." I paused for a second, but he never continued. "Redhead? Blonde? Brunette?"

"I like how you started with redhead." He locked his gaze on mine, an obvious dig at me for having a thing with Paige.

I shrugged. "That's in the past."

"So you two keep telling me. But I guess it must be true if she's on vacation with Sam, huh?"

Zach might be a genius and older than my thirty-one years, but at times he had the maturity of a college student.

The glint in his eyes—in addition to his words—hinted that he hadn't expected me to know.

I flicked a glance at him, then back to my work. "I'm well aware."

That's as far as the conversation went. I couldn't afford to concern myself with Paige's love life. Besides, I was seeing someone myself. I met her during a previous case. Her name was Becky, and she was a police officer for Dumfries PD. It was nothing serious, but we enjoyed each other's company.

Zach chuckled, and the tapping of his fingers on his keyboard told me I was free from any further teasing for the moment. There were times I could strangle the guy. He had the tendency to push buttons and then stand back, awaiting a reaction. Maybe it had to do with him not having any siblings to torment while growing up. However, I was an only child and I turned out perfectly fine.

I turned my attention back to thoughts of Becky. We had plans to meet for drinks at the Earth and Evergreen Restaurant near her place, which was about twenty minutes north of Quantico. And if everything went according to plan, I'd be spending the night with her and coming back in the morning.

I conjured up the smell of her perfume and the softness of her skin beneath my fingers—

My cell phone rang, breaking me from the beginnings of my fantasy and wresting me back into the real world.

"Agent Fisher." I had answered without checking the caller ID, but the ensuing silence on the other end of the line had me pulling back the phone and consulting it now.

Santa Clarita V.

That tells me nothing...

"Hello? This is Special Agent Brandon Fisher. Can I help you?" I looked for Zach, but he was gone again.

There was no verbal response on the other end of the line, but I heard a distinct exhale, followed by more deep breaths.

Santa Clarita... Where was that? It sounded Californian. And I knew only one person in California.

"Paige?"

There was a jagged intake of breath. A sob, maybe?

"Oh God, Brandon." It was Paige, and she was definitely crying. And Paige didn't cry. I'd witnessed the odd tear fall when our relationship had ended, but this was different. Something was very wrong.

I leaned on my desk and looked around, but no one was nearby.

"What's going on? Are you okay?" I asked. I gave her a few seconds to respond. She didn't. "Where's Sam? Is he okay? Talk to me, Paige."

"Shh. I don't want everyone to know."

"What's going on?" I was starting to get annoyed that she was avoiding my question. She was the one who had called me.

"I'm in trouble," she began. "Big trouble."

"What kind of trouble?"

"I'm in...jail," she ground out.

Her words struck me as a physical blow. I even stopped breathing for a second. I sank back into my chair. "You're what?"

"There's been a misunderstanding is all."

I'd hope so...

"Where is Sam?" I asked again.

"Please, Brandon, don't tell Jack or Zach."

Another aversion tactic. "I don't know much to tell." My concern for her was quickly morphing into irritation. "Where's Sam?" I repeated a third time. Maybe I should record myself and just hit "play."

Another deep exhale into the receiver.

"Talk to me," I entreated.

"He doesn't know."

"What? How can he not know you were—"

"Shh! I can't explain everything over the phone. I need you to get me a good defense attorney and send him to the Santa Clarita Valley Sheriff's Station. Have them ask for Detective Grafton or Mendez."

A *good* defense attorney?

"What are you suspected of?"

"I don't want—"

"You called me, remember?"

She sighed. "Something I might be regretting…"

"I'm sorry, but you asked me to get you—"

Jack came up next to my desk. He ran a hand along his throat, indicating my call needed to end. Now. And based on the way he was staring me down, refusing him wasn't an option.

"Where's Zach?" he asked.

"God, is that Jack?" Paige whispered. "Brandon, you can't say a—"

I cupped the receiver portion of my cell phone and held it away from my ear. "He'll be back," I told Jack. "He probably just went to the bathroom."

"Hang up," Jack demanded. He never tolerated personal calls on the job, but this was going overboard. Besides, this particular one wasn't personal. Or was it?

And why did Paige call me and not Sam? Was it just that I was familiar, or did she not want to give the new guy a bad impression? I dismissed the idea of her still harboring feelings for me before I even considered it, but whatever it was, I wasn't sure I was completely comfortable with it.

I got up from my chair and walked away from Jack, taking my cell phone with me. I had it pressed to my ear again and could tell Paige was still on the line. I could feel Jack's eyes watching me, but so far, he wasn't following.

"I will do what you asked," I said into the receiver, "but it would help to know what you're...you know." I didn't want to say *being charged with*, seeing as Jack was still within earshot.

"I don't want to get into it with you, Brandon. Hell, I probably shouldn't have even called you. I just thought I could trust you."

"You can." The words had come out of their own volition.

"Thank you. I just need a defense attorney who is good at getting the innocent off—" Someone spoke to her in the background. "Yes, I know... Fine," she said, her voice muffled, probably from her hand over the receiver. Then back to me. "I've got to go."

"I'll get you someone."

"Remember, Detective Graft—"

"Grafton and Mendez. I got it."

"One more thing, Brandon. Please let Sam know I'm okay."

"And what about the part where you were..." I couldn't elaborate as Jack was now literally breathing down my neck.

"You can't tell him I've been arrested."

"Yeah, okay."

"Can I trust you or not?" she asked impatiently.

I nodded even though she couldn't see it. "You can."

"Sam's at the Hyatt Regency, room 328." Then she hung up. With the conversation over, I was left to face Jack, and based on his epic scowl, I was going to have explain why I didn't hang up the second he had told me to.

"I need to make another phone call," I said.

"Not right now you don't," Jack replied.

Zach came back to his desk, a confused look on his face when he saw the two of us, and Jack gestured for us to follow him into his office.

I was pacing in front of Jack's door, not wanting to go in because I needed to get Paige that lawyer ASAP.

Jack gripped my shoulder with a firm hand. "Go inside."

"Uh, yeah. On it." I pressed on a smile and went into his office.

Jack shut the door and didn't bother to take a seat. Neither did Zach or I, but the two of us kept looking at each other for a clue as to what this was about.

"Paige has been brought in as a murder suspect." Jack delivered the statement as if it were any other case—direct, punchy, and succinct.

I swallowed roughly, my throat so dry I wondered if my mouth was even producing any saliva. I sought out one of the chairs that were positioned in front of Jack's desk.

Jack's gaze followed me until I sat down. "That was Paige on the phone with you, wasn't it?"

"Yeah," I choked out.

His jaw tightened. He shook his head. "Unbelievable."

I wasn't exactly sure what he was referring to—Paige's arrest or my consorting with the…enemy?

Jack closed his eyes. "She just couldn't leave it alone."

"Leave what alone?" Zach asked.

Jack let out a heaving sigh, met my eyes, and then turned for the door. "Come on, we're going to California. I'll explain on the plane."

CHAPTER TWO

It was earlier that morning and Paige was standing in the window of the hotel room, looking down on the town's streets and watching people carry on with their lives. Sam was still asleep, and last she looked, he was on his back with one leg under the sheets, one over. It felt good to get away from her job, but this vacation wasn't really for pleasure. Sam had tried to convince her they could also have some fun while in Valencia, but Paige had only one thing on her mind: confronting the man who had destroyed her friend Natasha's life.

It had happened twenty-two years ago when they were on spring break in Mexico, but the repercussions had lasted a lifetime. Natasha had been gang-raped by a group of four guys they had met at the resort. It had led to a suicide attempt a year later that resulted in Natasha losing all brain activity, and after all this time, Natasha's mother had finally decided it was time to say good-bye to her daughter. The funeral service was unbelievably rough on Paige, but it provided her with the one lead she needed to find the group's leader. That was the real reason she was in California…

"Paige?"

She turned to find Sam lying on his side now, braced on his elbow. She walked over and sat next to him.

He placed a hand on her back and maneuvered to look at the clock. She followed the direction of his gaze. "What are you doing up so early?" he asked.

"I couldn't sleep." She wasn't going to get into everything with Sam. Like how she had slipped out last night and took a trial run past the rapist's house, how she had followed him... Some things were best left unsaid.

"You don't have to see this Ferris guy, you know. I would understand if you changed your mind."

She pressed her lips together and nodded. "I know, but we've come all this way."

He took her hand and tapped a kiss to her fingertips. "It's never too late to just turn this into a fun vacation."

The words stung. *A fun vacation.* She felt as though she had cheated him. They each only had a few weeks of vacation time a year, and she'd talked him into using his to follow her out here. "I never should have asked you to—"

"Hey." He struggled with the sheets a bit as he sat up. "I wanted to come. Remember?"

She stared into his eyes, trying to determine if he was telling the truth, reliving the moment when she had asked him to come along. Maybe she had been wrong to include him in this. He was relatively new to her life; they'd met only a couple of months ago, and with the distance between them—him living in North Dakota and her in Virginia— they had only spent a few weekends together.

"You didn't make me come here," he reiterated. "And I'll be by your side the entire time."

Paige rose from the bed and crossed her arms. It was warm in the room, but suddenly chills rippled through her. After bringing him all the way here, how could she tell him that she had changed her mind and wanted to approach Ferris on her own? But maybe he'd find relief in being left out of this. She'd do what she needed to do to get closure with Ferris, and then they could have a normal vacation.

"I think this is something I need to do alone," she said, watching for his reaction.

Sam's brows lowered in consternation, and he swung his legs over the side of the bed. "Do you really think that's smart? Safe? You know what this guy is capable of." His words were hot and fierce.

"What he was capable of over two decades ago anyway. He could have changed." She wasn't going to tell Sam that Ferris had served thirty-six months in prison for sexual assault just seven years ago.

He angled his head to the right. "And you and I know the likelihood of that is slim."

"Maybe he wasn't the ringleader I thought he was. Maybe he was pressured by the others to…" For some reason, she couldn't bring herself to say the word *rape*. Being this close to Ferris was almost too much for her to handle. All those years of trying to track him down just after the rape, of learning a foreign language and even returning to the Cancun resort, and it was all coming to an end.

He came up next to her and took her hands in his. "I understand that you feel you need to see him."

She took her hands from his, looking away. When she returned her gaze to him, she saw his concern. Where there was once conviction, there was now doubt. "You don't think I'm taking this too far?"

He splayed his arms to take in the room. "I'm in California, nearly two thousand miles from home. With you."

She smirked. "Fine. Stupid question."

"Damn right, it was a stupid question, but I'll allow you the one. Any more and I'll need to take it from your hide." He wrapped his arms around her waist and placed his mouth on hers, his tongue probing, teasing, claiming. She lost herself in the moment, and as he led her back to the bed, she could think of nothing but him. She teased, touched, caressed. She leaned back against the pillow and arched her back as he trailed kisses from her neck down to her breasts.

Her breathing became heavy, her desire burning, as Sam began panting, his jaw tight, his energy possessive. When he thrust into her, she let out a moan and she was lost.

Sam rolled to the other side of the bed. As the heat of sex cooled, Paige stared at the ceiling, her hands laced over her stomach, thinking about her goal. No matter how much he didn't like it, she'd stick to her conviction to see Ferris on her own. Given the guy's history, maybe she was being foolish and rash, even naive to think she could handle the situation herself. She was emotional enough already and not even face to face with him yet. But she was a trained FBI agent. She had brought down many psychotic unsubs. She had firearms training and could shoot a target from a thousand yards out, easy. She had strong hand-to-hand combat skills and had defended herself against those hell-bent on keeping their secret lives just that, so how was Ferris any different? From a black-and-white perspective, Ferris was no different, except for one thing. With him it would be personal. Her blood chilled even as the warm pulse of adrenaline flowed through her.

She turned to face Sam to find him staring at her.

"You're beautiful, you know that?" He twirled a strand of her red hair around his finger.

She intercepted his hand and held onto it. "I know you're not happy about this, but I need to confront him on my own."

"No." He jumped from the bed, shaking his head. "God, I was hoping you had temporarily lost your mind."

"Gee, thanks."

"You can't go there by yourself. I mean, you *can*, but I wish you wouldn't."

She had hurried around the bed and stood in front him. "I need you to trust me. Please."

He took her hand but shook his head, his jaw tight. "You're crazy to do this alone."

She kept her eyes locked on him. "I've made up my mind."

"Fine. If that's what you want." He stepped back, snatched a bathrobe off a nearby chair, and wrapped it around him.

"It is."

He wasn't looking at her anymore, just pacing around the room.

"You could hang out at the hotel," Paige added. "Get a massage, use the pool."

"Throw in a mani-pedi and I'm sold." He met her gaze and then rolled his eyes.

"Listen, I know you're not happy about—"

"You're right. I'm not."

"It will be broad daylight. I'm not going inside his place. Besides, I'll have my Glock."

His gaze was hardened steel. "I'd say that's a smart idea."

"The gun or staying outside?" she teased.

"Both." His tone was serious, and based on the jut of his jaw there was nothing she could say to soothe his worry. The only thing that would make him comply was his desire to please her.

"You know what confronting this man means to me…"

After seconds of silent eye contact, he said, "I'll agree to this stupidity on one condition."

"Name it."

"You have breakfast with me first."

She smiled, but it dulled before reaching her eyes. "You got it."

CHAPTER THREE

Tuesday, August 25th, 8:45 AM Pacific Time
Canyon Country, California

Sam had hardly said a word at breakfast, which made Paige wonder why he even asked to share the meal with her. Maybe he was hoping that she'd magically change her mind and let him tag along when she went to Ferris's house, but that wasn't going to happen.

She'd taken the rental car and followed the GPS, even though she remembered the way from last night. About a block out from Ferris's house, the laughter and screaming of children playing in a local park filtered through her open window. They were enjoying the summer months the way kids used to, before televisions became babysitters. It was good to see that some kids were still *kids*. She passed abandoned bicycles in driveways and chalk drawings on sidewalks, indicating the area had a lot of families.

She parked the car in front of the correct address and walked to the sidewalk, where she stood and looked at the place Ferris called home. He lived in a newer townhouse with each building consisting of five units. Ferris's was on the end of one such group. A chain-link fence capped the end of his property, and a public walkway trailed between his building and the next.

She walked to the front door and stood there, doubts swimming in her mind.

Did she possess the courage to follow through, to push the past in Ferris's face and make him acknowledge what he had done? She'd come all this way to do just that, and it certainly wasn't time to back down now.

Her arm felt heavy as she raised it to the knocker. Her fingers grasped the brass, her heart beating so fast, she felt light-headed.

She glanced up and down the street again.

She heard a door open and shut, and a female neighbor from the adjacent unit bounded down her front steps and hurried toward her sedan. She was probably trying to make it to work by nine. It was 8:45.

Did she know that she lived next door to a rapist?

The woman was off without a look toward Ferris's house.

Paige was still holding the knocker, though she hadn't yet used it. Her thoughts were still tumbling over one another in her mind. Would Ferris recognize her? Would his eyes widen in fear if he did? Would he know that it was time to account for his actions, or in the very least own up to the fact that he'd destroyed a young woman's life?

Natasha's face flashed in her mind, and Paige couldn't allow herself to turn away.

She slammed the knocker against the wood.

No sound from inside.

She wanted to get this confrontation done and over with—now. She didn't want to come back again.

Since Ferris had a garage, it was impossible to gauge if he was home based on the lack of a vehicle in the drive. Was he inside and ignoring her, or had he not heard her? All she knew was that she wasn't about to leave without making absolutely sure he wasn't there. If she could get into his yard, there might be a back door she could try.

Her heart bumped off rhythm. Was she really considering going into his backyard?

She knocked again and waited. More silence.

She bit her lip and looked around the neighborhood. All the activity still seemed to be at the park.

Without giving it another thought, she stepped down from his front steps and headed toward the sidewalk between the two buildings. She glanced at the end unit of the neighboring building, doing her best to be inconspicuous. All the curtains were closed.

She glimpsed over her left shoulder, then her right. She wanted to pick up her pace but managed to retain a casual saunter. Going slightly past the corner of Ferris's lot, she surveyed his yard. It was a small patch of grass with a shed that took up a third of the property. A wooden fence butted up against the building and ran to the back of the yard, separating him and his neighbor. While the woman had left that unit, it was still possible someone else was at home. The divider would provide some privacy, but she didn't really want to explain to anyone why she was in Ferris's yard in the first place. She couldn't see her persistence to reach him standing up against scrutiny.

The flipside was that if Ferris was home and tried anything, no one would be able to help her. But that was ridiculous. She was a skilled—and armed—FBI agent. Where were these moments of self-doubt coming from? Still, nerves had her putting her hand over her holster.

"Karen, wait up!"

Paige jumped and turned in the direction of the young voice. A girl of about seven was racing along the path to catch up to another girl about six years her senior, who smoked past Paige on her bicycle. The younger one seemed to be all legs and not getting anywhere fast on her bike. Streamers hung from the handlebars and spoke beads accented her wheels, catapulting Paige back to her childhood.

Memories of youthful innocence reengaged Paige's focus. She was outside the house of the man who had taken so much from her friend when she was in her early twenties, at a point in life when she was finally coming into her own.

Yet, while he had destroyed Natasha's life, he had set Paige's on another course. She came to realize life wasn't easy and it wasn't fair. The optimist in her hadn't wanted to admit defeat and accept that philosophy, though. But now, as an FBI agent, she had the power to at least do something about all the evil in the world. The murderers she caught paid for their crimes, and she prevented further killings from occurring.

Her gaze returned to Ferris's house. All she was going to do was see if he was home. She lifted the latch on the gate and, with one deep breath, entered his yard.

CHAPTER FOUR

Paige stepped onto Ferris's deck, keeping her steps light as she moved across the wood to the patio door. Fence or no fence, ethical or not, it had taken years to get this close to Ferris, and now that she was outside his home, she couldn't just turn around and accept that Ferris wasn't here and move on.

The vertical blinds on the patio door were drawn open, but that wasn't all Paige noticed. The sliding door was partially open, too.

"Ferris Hall?" she called through the crack.

She didn't hear any sounds or movements coming from inside. Her FBI training was telling her that something wasn't right, that people didn't usually leave their doors wide open in the middle of the morning, but that same experience told her she couldn't go inside without justification.

Paige pressed her face to the glass and held a hand to her forehead to cut out the glare. Directly inside was a dining room with a table and four chairs. Beyond that she could see an L-shaped kitchen, and to the left of the dining area was the living room. Everything appeared to be neat and tidy. Even the counters were relatively clear except for a toaster, coffeemaker, and a bottle of Aleve.

There were no visual signs of an altercation; therefore, no real basis to enter. Except her gut was knotted with a foreboding sense that someone had broken into Ferris's house. Despite the edge of the door and the frame not appearing to have any damage, without something blocking the inside track, a patio door made an easy access point for breaking and entering.

A burst of giggles came from behind her, and she turned quickly to see more children racing along the pathway. None of them paid her any attention.

When they disappeared from view, she turned back to the house. She stuck her head through the opening and called out his name again. "Ferris?"

Straining to listen, she was again met with silence.

Why would his back door be open if he wasn't home, other than a B&E? Surely, he wouldn't have forgotten to close the door behind him if he'd left.

She gnawed on her lip, trying to find a rationalization for her to enter. If something had happened to Ferris in there, would she even be inclined to help him, though? The man had essentially taken her friend's life. If she found him dead, would she feel any pity, or would she just feel as though Karma had been repaid?

But she was curious to see how this man lived his life, how he carried on despite the fact he destroyed lives.

Still, she was an FBI agent, she argued with herself—not above the law but an advocate of the law. Could she defend a decision to enter without any sign of a true disturbance? She calmed herself with the thought that if she entered and found nothing amiss, no one even needed to know she'd been there. And if something *had* happened, she'd admit to the truth.

She called out a third time, and when he didn't respond, she swallowed, about to step inside.

"Excuse me," a woman called out in a curious tone. "Who are you?" Based on the direction of her voice, she must be standing on the pathway to Paige's right.

Coolness blanketed Paige's flesh as heat burned her insides. She blew a strand of hair off her cheek and turned her face toward the woman. She was wearing dark sunglasses and dressed in shorts and a collared tee. One hand was on her hip, and she held the other to her forehead, shielding her eyes from the sun.

"What do you think you're doing?" Her curious tone had quickly turned accusatory, and the woman moved closer to the fence.

Paige had one option: lie. The question was just whether she was going to simply distort the truth or completely evade it. She could say she was an FBI agent and add that she was here to speak to Ferris. That actually would have been quite accurate. But that would lead the woman to believe that he was suspected of a crime and being questioned concerning one. If there *was* a situation inside, it would give her something to fall back on if she had to report a crime, but it would also get the Bureau involved.

"I'm a friend of Ferris's," Paige blurted out before she could really formulate her plan. At the same time, she made sure that her holster was tucked under her shirt. Thankfully, the woman was on her right and the gun on her left.

The woman lifted her shades up and rested them on her forehead. "I've never seen you before. And it still doesn't explain why you're at his back door."

Think, Paige, think.

"I feel so stupid." Maybe if she played the distraught and somewhat crazy one-night stand... Paige stepped across the deck, closing the distance between her and the woman. "I spent last night with him and left my purse inside."

The woman was through the gate in an instant. *Oh God.* She hopped up the three stairs onto the deck, stopping short of Paige. She pointed toward the open door. "Did you do that? Are you breaking in?"

"No, no." She hated lying, but in this case it was necessary. "He...he gave me a key."

The woman arched a penciled brow but relaxed as Paige maintained eye contact. Her expression eased into a smile. "Oh, I've been there before. You have everything under control, then?"

Paige mustered a smile for her in return. "Yep. I think I do."

"All right, then. I'm off. Things to do." The woman hopped off the deck and into the grass as if the four-foot elevation was nothing and waved over her head. "Have a good day," she said with one last glance over her shoulder at Paige.

Paige returned the wave and slipped inside Ferris's house. She took a moment to catch her breath, supporting herself on a dining chair. It turned out trespassing wasn't that easy on the heart rate. She abruptly jumped back as she realized she had let the distracting neighbor mar her better judgment. She had to approach this as she would a crime scene, and her fingerprints would be all over the top of the chair now. She pulled on the bottom of her T-shirt and wiped the surface with it. Then she covered her fingers with her shirt to slide the door closed.

Being inside Ferris's home like this felt as if she were violating him—an odd emotion given what he had done to her friend. She'd breached brick and mortar; he had transgressed against flesh and blood.

She made her way through the main level, cognizant of her surroundings. So far, as she had concluded from peering inside, nothing indicated a struggle or altercation. In fact, it was the opposite. The place was immaculate and carefully organized.

In the living room, three remotes were laid out side by side on a tray. Sports magazines were fanned out on a coffee table, as if it were part of a waiting room at a doctor's office.

The place got cooler the deeper inside she went, and that meant Ferris relied on an air conditioner. Her mind went to the patio door. It must not have been open for long if it was still so cool in the depths of the townhouse.

Thank God she had her gun. She stopped moving to listen, but was met with only silence again.

With each step, her conscience condemned her as a trespasser while her training urged her to investigate and her curiosity taunted her.

She cleared the first floor and basement. She almost touched the banister on the staircase to the second level, but realized just before making contact and pulled her hand back. The last thing she needed to do was leave any trace or fingerprints.

Her heart raced, its beat thumping in her ears.

On the upper floor, there was a bathroom, one bedroom, and an office.

She stepped into his bedroom, imagining what might take place here, assuming he was stupid enough to bring the woman home. But it was unlikely. Still, to be where he slept, where he got a good night's rest...

She spotted a plain wooden box, the size of a small jewelry chest, on his dresser and was drawn to look inside.

Using the fabric of her shirt again, she opened the lid. What she saw made her momentarily lose her balance. She lifted out the necklace...

"Paige, look what I got." Natasha was smiling and dancing around Paige, one arm held up in the air, her other hand pointing to her neck and the silver necklace that adorned it. Dangling from the chain was a heart-shaped pendant with the letter N *engraved on it.*

"Where did you get that?"

"From one of the merchants set up by the pool."

"Why do I sense there's more to this story?"

Natasha smiled and winked at Paige. "A guy bought it for me."

"What did you do?" Paige asked, admiring the piece of jewelry.

She laughed. "I was just me. Isn't that enough?" Natasha beamed and grabbed Paige's hand. "Come on, let's go have a drink."

Paige blinked the tears from her eyes. It couldn't be. She wiped her wet eyes, her gaze not leaving the necklace in her hand. The chain was a common style, but the heart pendant and the letter *N*...

Still, it didn't mean this one had been Natasha's...

Paige swallowed. But she remembered when Natasha had realized she'd lost it. She had dropped on the end of the hotel bed as if all the weight of the world were piled on her shoulders. It was the morning after the rape.

Tears now fell freely down Paige's cheeks. There was no doubt in her mind that the necklace she now held had been Natasha's.

Paige cried as the past washed over her and continued to do so until rage replaced her sadness.

Somehow, she would make this son of a bitch pay for what he had done. She was past the point of keeping within the shades of the law and would circumvent legal means if that's what it took to hold him responsible.

She clasped the necklace around her neck. Had Ferris kept it as some sort of sick notch in his bedpost? If so, that showed a psychology to him that confirmed he was a repeat offender. And if that was his mentality, prison wouldn't have rehabilitated him, and that meant there were likely date-rape drugs here to prove it.

She stormed from the bedroom and toward the bathroom.

Beyond the point of caring anymore if she left her fingerprints behind, she emptied the contents of the medicine cabinet, and his toiletries now filled the sink.

Nothing.

She rushed back to his bedroom and tore it apart. The drugs were here somewhere. A man like Ferris wouldn't stop raping…

Several minutes passed as she searched, and when she was finished, his bedroom looked like a tornado had struck. But still no pills.

Maybe she was being ridiculous, hoping to find something where there was nothing. And even if she found the drugs, what did she hope to accomplish? While possession of date-rape drugs was illegal, her means of getting them would make them inadmissible in any court. But she couldn't stop. All she could see was her friend's body in that casket—the way her face, even in death, showed her tortured existence.

She hurried downstairs to the kitchen. There was no way she was stopping now.

She searched each cupboard and drawer, pulling out items and rooting to the back. She had one place left to look, and as she opened it, she saw that it was a catchall drawer. Stuffed with anything and everything from a meat thermometer, to sandwich bags, to tin foil, to… She pulled out a sleeve of pills. She flipped them and read the stamp on the silver backing. Allergy pills.

She continued working through the contents of the drawer until she reached the last item. It was an Aleve bottle. That was an inconvenient place to keep a pain reliever… She opened it and looked inside. It was only the medication. She was still holding the bottle in her hand when she recalled the one on the counter. She exchanged one for the other, not about to give up. Just because the bottle was labeled one way… She twisted the lid.

Police sirens wailed somewhere nearby, and she paused. Her instinct told her to leave this alone and get out of his house immediately. But it was too late, the whooping sirens were on top of her now, and then the patio door slid open on the other side of the dining room. Two police officers entered the house, guns drawn.

"Santa Clarita Sheriff's Department! Put your hands on your head!"

"What's—" The strength drained from her legs, and her head spun. *She* was under arrest?

Oh God. That woman must have called the police.

"I said, put your hands on your head!" the same officer shouted.

Another officer went around behind her, stripped her of her gun, passed it off to the second officer, and proceeded to cuff her. "You have the right to remain silent—"

"This isn't what it looks like."

"It looks like you're ransacking the house of a dead man."

A dead man?

"I'm an FBI agent. I can explain—"

"You can do that down at the station."

CHAPTER FIVE

Jack, Zach, and I were on one of the FBI's private jets headed to California. I had already called Becky to let her know I would be out of state working a case. I didn't tell her it involved Paige for a couple of reasons. One, she'd worry, and two, she'd worry—only they'd be for different reasons. She was aware of my former relationship with Paige and, for some reason, still thought I had feelings for her.

Zach and I were seated across a table from Jack as he began to brief us.

"I received a phone call from Detective Grafton of the Santa Clarita Sheriff's Department," he said. "Ferris Hall was found murdered in a motel room at eight this morning. Time of death was placed between ten and midnight last night. His car was found in the lot."

"How does Paige tie into that?" I asked, confused.

Jack clenched his jaw before continuing. "Paige was found in his home."

"And who is Ferris Hall exactly?" I still didn't understand the connection between Paige and this man.

"Hall was one of the men who raped her friend when they were on spring break in Cancun. She must have tracked him to California."

"I didn't think anyone could be held legally responsible for the rape," I said, remembering that Paige had told me the rape hadn't been reported to the police in Mexico.

Without that measure, there was nothing that could legally be done. "You said that Paige was found in Hall's home?" Maybe I was sounding like a parrot right now, but none of this was making sense.

Jack patted his shirt pocket—craving a cigarette, no doubt—but there was no smoking on the jet. "Local detectives believe Paige killed him."

"Why?" Zach asked, eyes wide.

"Evidence found at the murder scene points to a female killer. And the last person seen with Hall was a woman with long curly hair fitting Paige's age and appearance."

I scoffed. "That's his *evidence*?"

Zach slid me a glance. "I'm with Brandon on this. There has to be more. Where was this woman seen?"

"An employee at the motel where his body was found saw her. And before you ask, the place has no cameras." There was a pulse tapping in Jack's cheek. "Grafton, the detective in charge, isn't saying much of anything, but I can only imagine that once they discover Paige's history with Hall and the fact she chose the same city he lived in for her vacation, it won't look good for her. Add in the fact that she chose this week, the week he shows up dead, and it will seem too coincidental. That's not even mentioning that she was in the middle of ransacking the place when she was found this morning."

"She was...what?" I choked out, the words dry in my throat.

"If they think she killed Ferris, then why do they think she went to his house the next morning? That doesn't make sense. Why not leave things alone?" Zach asked.

"More questions that need answers." Jack was pissed if the look in his hardened eyes was any indication. "And I intend to find out those answers."

I could hardly believe we were doing this—setting out across the country to defend Paige against murder charges. "What did you tell the director?" I asked, my curiosity ratcheting up my courage. FBI Director Myron Hamilton wasn't someone you wanted to mess with. I couldn't even imagine Jack risking getting on the man's bad side.

"I told him the truth: one of our own is being accused of a murder she didn't commit, and we're going to investigate."

I glanced at Zach, then back to Jack. "And he was all right with that? He authorized all of us to—"

"I also told him that I believe Ferris Hall's murder was the work of a serial killer."

"And he accepted that without proof?" I spat out, wondering how far Jack exaggerated things to warrant the director's approval.

Jack glared at me. Right, Jack was above questioning...

He produced a curled folder from an inside jacket pocket. "Now, there's not much here yet seeing as this investigation was just opened, but this is what we've got." He opened it and pulled out some photographs, sliding them across the table to me and Zach.

I picked up the one closest to me. It was a close-up of Hall. He was naked and bloody, laid out on a bed. The shot captured from his thighs up to the wall by his head. His arms were spread as if fixed in the motion of making a snow angel, nothing binding his wrists. And on his chest was a... I looked closer.

"Is that a pill on his abdomen?" I asked, meeting Jack's gaze.

He nodded. "Rohypnol."

"A date-rape drug," I said, unnecessarily stating the obvious as I exchanged the photograph for another. Bile instantly rose in my throat. I swallowed roughly. "Is that what I think it is?"

"If you're thinking that's a severed penis, then yes," Jack said. "The rest of Hall's genitalia was also mutilated. And all this was done while he was alive."

The way Jack had just laid it out there like that, one would think we came across this exact sort of depravation all the time. If Jack had presented these photos to the director, I understood why he could accept a possible serial killer at work.

"His—" Vomit reached my mouth now. Ick.

"The killer also urinated on Hall," Jack said.

Apparently the killer wasn't worried about leaving any trace…

"They can determine sex from that." Hope filled my voice, but the look in Jack's eyes stamped it out.

"And we'll make sure they do."

"What actual evidence do they have against Paige?" I asked.

"Yeah, Boss, evidence seems to be something they are short on," Zach added.

"As I said," Jack began, "This Grafton guy refused to part with much. We just have the eyewitness who saw the woman and there was a tube of lipstick at the scene—the same brand Paige uses."

"You're serious? That's all. He's got to be withholding. What about comparing DNA left on the lipstick to Paige? Fingerprints? Maybe it's because she's an FBI agent. He could be using her to build himself up." I realized I might be jumping to a large conclusion here, but it was no secret that tension existed between the police and the FBI. "We can't let him make a case against her."

Jack narrowed his eyes at me. "That's why we're on a plane headed to California."

There were a few moments of silence.

"What was the cause of death?" Zach asked.

"Exsanguination. I have Nadia looking for any murders in California that fit the MO," Jack replied and then got up and headed to the bar fridge, where he grabbed a soda.

Nadia Webber was stationed at the FBI headquarters in Quantico and was our go-to person for everything from backgrounds to updates on forensic findings when we were on the road.

Zach had picked up the file and was reading the few pages we did have. Meanwhile, I must have appeared to be staring mindlessly into space, but I was actually deep in thought. Why would Paige go all the way to California to see the man who had raped her friend? There was no way I'd accept that she murdered the man. Paige was subject to a temper—a stereotypical, yet accurate, quality inherent with red hair as I, too, should know—but she'd never kill an innocent person.

But he wasn't *innocent.*

I dismissed the doubts creeping in that would make me wonder if she was capable of meting out her own justice.

All I knew was that those photographs didn't lie. Whoever had killed Hall was motivated by deep-seated rage. But until we had the proof that a serial killer had murdered him—or in the very least, presented a more viable suspect—Paige's innocence remained in question.

CHAPTER SIX

Paige was taken back to the Santa Clarita Sheriff's Station and tossed into an interrogation room after being carted through the station like a prized trophy in cuffs. They had a murder suspect in custody, and she was a fed. No one was talking to her; they talked *around* her. Her question about what made her a murder suspect had so far gone unanswered. She'd be able to provide an alibi, but they obviously weren't ready to hear it.

The buzz of the fluorescent light dangling overhead droned steadily. The white brick walls begged for a splash of color, and the table was a veneer top with silver metal legs. There was a plastic bucket chair on each side of the table. She pressed her fingers to the tabletop as she took a seat, and the table wobbled. Shifting her weight, she tried to find a comfortable position, but it was impossible. The seat bit into the back of her legs, cutting off her circulation.

But she refused to stand and let the detectives witness her discomfort. She guessed there were probably at least three sets of eyes on her from behind the one-way glass—the two detectives from Ferris's house and their sergeant. They'd surely be discussing how she was found in a dead man's home. But it wasn't like Ferris's body was in his house. All she was really guilty of was trespassing. If they'd just listened to her, she could put this sordid mess behind her.

She glanced at the walls for a clock but there wasn't one. How long had she been in here? An hour? Or did it just feel like that?

She knew what they were doing, as she often played the same game in her career. Delaying an interrogation was a tried-and-true method. Toss the suspect into a dank room for long enough, and even the innocent would start to doubt their innocence. But these detectives were foolish if they thought they could manipulate her. She had nothing to hide.

The door opened, creaking on its hinges, and she tucked the necklace beneath her collar.

Two men entered the room. There was a stark age difference between them, and the lead detective was easy to identify. He was in his fifties with silver hair, while the rookie was in his late twenties—tops—and had a thick mop of dark hair and bushy eyebrows.

She should ask for representation, but something about doing so would make all this more real. Surely, she'd have an alibi to provide. She just needed to know Ferris's time of death and location.

She swallowed, wishing away any motive she'd have for killing Ferris. Maybe the time she had spent sitting in here actually *was* playing with her mind.

The senior detective slapped a file folder on the table and made a show of opening it while keeping his greenish-gray eyes on her. His gaze was cold.

The rookie walked behind her and stood to her right. He emitted a cocky assuredness that seemed fueled by the need to prove himself, and he would use her flesh to advance his rank.

Rule one, don't speak first. It would prove that their tactic had weakened her, and she needed to retain all the power she could.

"I'm Detective Grafton, and that there is Mendez," said the older one. The fine lines around his eyes seemed more dominant as he narrowed his gaze on her, and his wrinkled brow indicated a rough life. The leathery appearance of his skin suggested either a health condition or an alcohol dependency.

Grafton sat in the chair across from her, leaning back casually and clasping his hands in his lap. His eyes locked on hers, assessing, trying to get a read on her. But while he analyzed her, she did the same to him. She recognized the lick of flame in his gaze. He was hungry for a conviction—and to stick it to a fed probably only made her more appetizing.

After letting the static build between them for about a minute, Grafton spoke. "According to your background you're an FBI agent. Is that correct?"

"Yes." He had asked a question he knew the answer to, as he'd stripped her of her ID and badge at Ferris's house. This was a detour, and she wanted to get things moving and get out of here. "I can explain why I was—"

Grafton held up his hand and settled farther back in his chair. The shift in weight caused the cheap plastic to groan against its metal frame. "I'm sure this was all a misunderstanding. You were at Hall's house because he was the suspect of a crime?"

It didn't surprise her that Grafton would approach things this way. It was probably another reason the detectives had taken so long getting into the room—they were debating strategy.

"But that wouldn't explain why he was found murdered this morning," Grafton continued. He gave it a few seconds. "Do you have anything to say about that, Miss Dawson?"

"Where was Ferris found? It obviously wasn't in his home," she said, trying to rush the detective along.

"Oh, we'll get to that." He was scowling now. "You weren't there for a case."

An expertly laid-out accusation to tempt her to speak. Dirty cops really ruined it for the good ones who fell into question. Like criminals, law enforcement officers accused of a crime were also presumed guilty.

"I can always call your supervisor"—he tapped his hand on the file—"Jack Harper."

The threat was to elicit a reaction from her, panic or guilt or anything, really. And it almost worked… Her mouth fell open, but she snapped it shut.

"Huh, nothing." Grafton directed the comment to Mendez, who was still standing behind Paige.

Paige glanced back at him. His face was relaxed, his features stoic.

Grafton smacked the table. Paige didn't even flinch.

"What were you doing in Ferris Hall's house?" Grafton barked.

"If you had listened to me earlier, you'd know his back door was already open, and I was concerned about his safety."

"Come now, Miss Dawson, one LEO to another… You must have had a good reason to be at Hall's house. Your record is impeccable." He referred to the file. "A total of seventeen years with the FBI. I wouldn't even guess you were old enough." Grafton gave it about twenty seconds and then went on. "A total of eleven years with the office in New York, then one year as a training instructor at the Academy, and for the last five you've been with the Behavioral Analysis Unit." He peered up from the report and met her eyes. He had managed to soften his gaze, as if he'd found some empathy for her, but she knew better than to accept this display as genuine.

"When was time of death?" she asked.

"You really do like getting right to it."

She shrugged.

"Last night between ten and midnight."

Her pulse quickened as anxiety started to fill her. That was around the time she had followed Ferris. She'd have no alibi.

"And why were you there in the first place? Did your being there have something to do with this?" Grafton waved Mendez over, and Mendez handed him an evidence bag with the Aleve bottle inside. Grafton dangled it in front of her. "Why were you holding this when we found you?"

She had two options: come clean as to why she was in his home, or call a lawyer. But it was the *why* that she wished to avoid. It would only make her look guilty. It was getting hard to breathe. Each pump of her heart seemed to be in slow motion while at the same time it was rapid-fire.

"I see it in your eyes, Agent."

She lifted her chin, trying to act confident even as her palms were sweating. "What is it you see exactly?"

"Panic."

"You're not very good at reading people, then."

"Hmm."

She just had to keep it together. She had to get this wrapped up before her vacation was over—and with zero involvement from Jack. And preferably none from Sam. God, what would his opinion of her be when he found out his new girlfriend was suspected of murdering the same man she'd traveled all this way to confront?

"See, I think you went to Hall's to hide evidence," Grafton continued. "Things could have started there…"

Instinctively, she felt herself wanting to look at the Aleve bottle, but if she did, Grafton would notice.

"Did Ferris Hall rape you?"

He had no idea how close he was to the truth. Her eyes snapped to his. "That's what he does."

Grafton shrugged. "He served his time."

If he was trying to make her angry, it was working.

"So I'll ask you again: did Ferris Hall rape you?"

Tears of indignation wet her eyes.

"He did, didn't he?" Grafton's voice was just a tad softer, but she detected the hunter in his tone.

She just had to keep quiet for a little longer. Maybe it was time for that lawyer. He obviously wasn't going to listen to anything she had to say without twisting it.

Grafton slapped a bunch of photographs on the table in front of her. He fanned them out and then layered them. Paige had seen countless photos of murder scenes in her life, but this was beyond grotesque.

Ferris's body was laid out on a bed and a glimpse of the nightstand and headboard implied a cheap motel. Blood was pooled on the sheets, most of it concentrated around his thighs and genitalia. His testicles were shredded, and his penis was next to him.

She glanced away for a second. Normally her constitution was one of steel, but they thought she did *this*?

"He died of blood loss," Grafton began, "a slow and agonizing way to go. Only relief he'd have was that he likely passed out pretty quickly." He watched her for a reaction. She gave him none. "Now, see this—" Grafton set a close-up of Hall's chest in front of her on the table. He pressed the pad of his index finger to the white pill sitting on Hall's chest. "That is a date-rape drug, more specifically Rohypnol. But you know that already, don't you?"

She didn't give him any indication she'd heard a word he said. Her mind was on Ferris Hall. The way his body was laid out, how it had been mutilated, the pill on the abdomen. It smacked of the work of a serial killer, but it could also be an isolated incident. Nothing more than a woman extracting revenge. Still, if the case was the latter, with this level of violence, she was dangerous and likely to kill again.

Grafton glared at her. "You killed Ferris Hall because he drugged you, then he raped you—"

"And how could I kill him if I was drugged?" she countered quickly.

"Someone's a smart-ass. But how much do you want to bet that if we get our hands on the rental's tracking device, it will lead us to the motel where he was murdered? We know from the GPS on the dash that you punched his home address in last night."

"I want a lawyer."

Grafton leaned forward. "Somehow, I thought you would."

CHAPTER SEVEN

Tuesday, August 25th, 4:45 PM Pacific Time

Paige dropped her face in her hands. She was sitting on a bench in a holding cell and couldn't stop revisiting her decision to call Brandon instead of Sam. But her relationship with Sam was too new, and the impression she'd make on him with all this wouldn't be a good one. And how would he respond when he found out she had gone to Ferris's the night before?

Her stomach twisted with guilt. While she was here thinking of him, he was probably trying to reach her, worrying about her. But the police had confiscated her cell phone the second they had patted her down on scene. They were no doubt sifting through it for evidence.

Against me...

She felt the silver necklace around her neck and squeezed the pendant. She wondered what Natasha would think of the lengths Paige had gone to. Not that Paige knew what happened after death, but a part of her had to believe her friend went on.

Paige's gut compressed tighter. The detectives would find out about her motivation for coming here and the e-mails that included all Ferris's information. It's not like she said she wanted to kill him in any of the correspondence, but she'd look obsessed.

If only she could figure out who killed him, she could get the spotlight off her. He'd likely hurt many women over the years... But it wasn't as if she were free to investigate.

No, all she could do was wait and think.

. . .

Paige was pacing the cell when Detective Mendez approached the bars and had an officer unlock the door.

"Your legal rep is here," Mendez said.

She followed Mendez through the corridors, wishing that she had been honest with Brandon and told him she needed defense against murder charges.

Murder charges.

The thought of all this happening to her was like a nightmare. There was no way she'd kill the man. The fact that she'd taken life before was a job hazard. Killing for personal retribution was something else entirely. She didn't even enjoy taking down unsubs with lethal force. The flashbacks would lessen over time, but ending a person's life had a way of imprinting on the soul and haunting you forever.

But was Ferris Hall that much different from the men she hunted for a living? He might not have killed, but he stole life from the living. What she had to acknowledge was that despite the brutality of his murder, she felt no sympathy for him—not when she looked at the crime scene photos or now. Ferris deserved what had come to him, hadn't he? Of course, she'd keep those dark thoughts to herself.

Mendez stopped outside an interrogation room. "Here you go."

Paige rounded the corner of the doorway but came to a standstill when she saw Jack sitting at the table facing her. What was he doing here? She wanted to leave, but it was too late; he'd seen her.

"Jack? What…what are doing here?"

"Sit." He didn't gesture to the chair across from him, but it was plainly implied.

She glanced over her shoulder, almost preferring that the eager detective stay. Instead, Mendez shut the door, sealing her in the room with her boss.

"You better start talking," Jack said.

Each of the six steps to the table—yes, she counted—were hard to execute. Why was Jack here? Had Brandon told on her? Did he really think Jack was who she wanted to help her? If she had wanted Jack to come, she would have called him. But then the simple answer presented itself.

"Detective Grafton called you," she concluded.

"Sit."

She followed his repeated directive.

"Now talk." He blinked slowly, and based on his grimace, he was mostly up to speed.

"You obviously know that I'm a murder suspect. The victim was Ferris Hall, one of the men who essentially took my best friend's life." Her voice cracked. She reached to her neck and held the pendant in her hand, as if it could give her the strength to get through this.

Jack pointed to the silver chain. "Where did you get that?"

She let go of the pendant and looked down at it. When she felt confident enough to trust her voice, she spoke. "I found it in Ferris's house. It was Natasha's."

"So you stole from him."

"He stole from Natasha," she ground out. "I'm sorry, Jack, I didn't mean that to come out so harsh." She met his gaze, and her voice lowered. "How am I supposed to feel sorry about what happened to him?"

"No one's saying that you have to."

"Jack, I didn't mean for this to happen."

"For what to happen, Paige? Did you kill the man?"

His question stole her breath as if she'd been punched in the gut. "You have to ask that?"

He hitched his brows.

"No. I. Did. Not. Kill. Him." She could honestly say she had never even considered it. Not feeling sad about his murder and attributing some justification to it was far from taking action.

He remained silent, but there was something in his eyes, in his energy—maybe his somewhat laid-back demeanor— that made her think he knew more than he was letting on.

"Do you know something I don't?" she asked.

"Talk and we'll find out."

"You know that they found me in Ferris Hall's house?"

Jack nodded. "What were you doing there?"

"I went to his place with every intention of confronting him. I admit to that. Hell, my friend is—" She couldn't bring herself to say *dead*. Emotion welled up in her throat, and she wasn't sure whether to scream or cry. "There was no answer at his front door. I'd come all this way…" She paused, assessing his eyes, but they were blank. "I went into his yard, thinking I'd try the back door, but it was open."

"It was open when you got there?"

"Yes, and I told them this." Her eyes went to the one-way glass, but there would be no one watching or listening. With Jack serving as her legal representation, they had no right to do so.

"You went inside because there were signs of a struggle?"

She swallowed. "Not exactly. But something wasn't right. No one responded when I called out. I had to go inside."

"You *had* to go inside? Paige, why not call the police and let them handle it?"

She shrugged and bit on her lip. "I was curious, Jack, but not so much because I worried about his welfare. I started thinking about how he lived with what he does to women. Once I was inside, I wondered if I could find proof that he was still drugging women. Stupid, really. I couldn't even use it against him if I found any. But at the time all I could think was that he…needed to pay."

"It seems that he did."

She took a staggered inhale. "I didn't kill him, Jack. Besides, what punishment is there in death? Please, you tell me." She heard the hysteria in her voice. "Wouldn't it have been worse for him to live with the consequences of his actions? If I could have shown him what he had done to Natasha, how he had stolen her life…"

"He likely wouldn't have cared. And you know that. You know how people like him are."

She put a hand to her aching heart.

"Your personal history will be used against you," Jack went on. "Now, is there anything else I should know?"

There was no way she'd expose Nadia for helping her track Ferris Hall down. Even she knew that would look like conspiracy to commit murder.

"Paige, I asked you a question."

She looked Jack in the eye. "No, nothing else."

"Are you certain?"

She licked her lips. He'd come all the way here to defend her. The least she owed him was honesty. "I went to Ferris's house last night."

"Why?" Disappointment and incredulity drenched the single word.

"I don't know… A trial run, I guess, to get a feel for how he lived, what his neighborhood was like."

"You could have done that on Google Earth."

"Shit, I don't know." She ran her hands down her face and then back through her hair. "And I followed him."

"You what?" Jack spat out, acid lacing his voice. "What the hell were you thinking?"

"Well, I wasn't thinking about killing him," she spat back.

He clenched his jaw. "Where did you follow him?"

"Down the street, but not all the way to wherever he was going."

"To where *exactly*?"

"I turned around in a motel parking lot."

"Budget Motel?" Jack sounded like he was going to be sick now, and nothing much swayed his emotions.

"Don't tell me that that's the same—"

He was just staring in her eyes.

"I would have been there within the time of death window. This doesn't look good, but—"

"Damn right it doesn't."

"Jack, I went back to the Hyatt right after that."

"And Sam can vouch for that?"

She hesitated a little too long.

"Paige?"

"Not exactly. He was snoring when I left, and he was still out when I got back. The time difference is only two hours for him, but the jet lag hit him pretty hard."

Jack's eyes glazed over, and it was as if he were looking through her. "So Ferris didn't pull into the Budget Motel at that time?"

"No, he kept going."

There was a brief lull of silence, which she broke. "What else do you know?" She was almost afraid to ask again.

"Not sure how far you got with the detectives, but there was a tube of lipstick left at the scene. It matches the brand they found in your purse."

She felt her face pale. "Well, it wasn't mine, Jack. I'll give my DNA, whatever it takes."

"I'm hoping we don't even have to go there."

CHAPTER EIGHT

We had picked up two rental cars once we'd landed in Burbank. There was a local FBI field office in Los Angeles, but right now we wanted to keep this situation quiet. Jack was going straight to the sheriff's station while Zach and I were headed for the hotel in Valencia. Both were thirty-minute drives. I was thankful for the delay, too, as I really didn't look forward to facing my replacement and telling him that his new girlfriend was the prime suspect in a murder investigation. I hadn't really liked the guy when I'd met him a couple of months ago. But it was possible that my perception of him was tainted because he had his sights on Paige. At the time I couldn't have her, but it didn't mean I wanted someone else to, no matter how selfish it sounded.

The lobby was full of guests milling about and checking in. The marble flooring and the thick round columns were impressive, but nothing when compared to the centerpiece of the space. A chandelier was suspended from a recessed panel in the ceiling, pale blue lighting making it appear as if the light fixture came out of a pool of water. We passed under it, going straight for the elevator bank.

"I can't believe Paige is suspected of..." Zach looked around, taking into account all the people. "You know what."

"Tell me about it. It's as if we fell into another dimension."

Zach raised his brows. "Sci-fi? I wouldn't have pegged you as the type."

We reached the elevators, and Zach pressed the "up" button. The doors dinged immediately, then opened, and Zach and I boarded without any stragglers. I selected the third floor.

I carried on as if there'd been no pause in our conversation. "You know what I mean. It's just so odd." I wanted to ask him if he thought she could have killed the man but realized how traitorous I'd appear if I did. It was one thing to consider Paige killing a man in my head and quite another to verbalize it. That wasn't even giving consideration to her mutilating his testicles and cutting off his penis. Shivers laced through me. I actually pitied the guy. No one deserved to go out that way. "Do you think Nadia's going to find any related cases in the system?"

"It's hard to say, but given the thought and planning, not to mention violence, of Hall's murder, it wouldn't surprise me."

"Same here. I mean, obviously Jack thinks this unsub has killed before or he wouldn't have Nadia looking into it. The killer would have had to get Hall to the motel, too. Was it by strength or manipulation or threat?"

Zach shrugged. "Well, remember a motel clerk saw a woman with Hall. If anything, I'd say manipulation."

"Very true," I said. "It's unlikely that she overpowered him, anyway. Maybe she sedated him after luring him into the room. A drug was found on Hall."

"We still don't know if any drugs were in his system."

"That's true, too," I admitted.

"We really need more information before we can make any real guesses. All we have are the basics and some crime scene photos."

I cringed. "And no man could forget those."

"Nope, a man's worst nightmare." We were quiet for a moment. Then Zach asked, "How do you think Sam's going to take the news?"

"Guess we'll find out." And his reaction would tell us a lot about the man and if he deserved Paige.

We unloaded and followed the signs to room 328. I knocked. We waited. No answer. I knocked again.

"It's Brandon Fisher," I called out.

Yeah, that ought to get him running to answer the door.

No sound came from inside.

I knocked again and then held my ear to the wood. I drew back and shook my head. "He's not here."

"Well then where the heck is he?"

"That's a good question." I hadn't even prepared for the possibility that he wasn't sitting around waiting for Paige to return. But then again, if it were me and I knew Paige was confronting a man who had ruined her best friend's life, I never would have let her go alone in the first place.

CHAPTER NINE

At least Sam had gotten Ferris's address from Paige before she'd left him that morning. He climbed into the back of a cab and told the driver where to take him. His phone still in hand, Sam redialed Paige and again was met with her voice mail.

He clicked off, as he'd already left two messages. The first had been weighted with anger while the second was more concerned. She'd left him at about eight o'clock that morning and it was nearing five in the afternoon. He'd been patient, assuming that she went somewhere to clear her head after seeing Ferris. But that didn't explain why she wasn't answering her phone, or why she'd been gone for *so* long. The detective in him told him something was wrong.

He debated calling the local sheriff's office to see if any accidents had been reported but had decided against it. His gut was telling him she wasn't in one, which only intensified the tingles of suspicion and paranoia that something worse had happened.

The GPS in his phone indicated that Ferris's townhouse was around the next bend. He leaned forward, his forehead near touching the passenger-seat headrest, as if by doing so he'd reach his destination faster.

Police cruisers were in front of a townhouse, their lights spinning. Still about five units away, Sam counted down the numbers.

They had cordoned off Ferris's house!

"Stop the car!" Sam barked.

He gripped the handle and cracked the door open, preparing to jump from the moving vehicle if need be.

"Hey, what are you do—" The vehicle came to an abrupt stop, thrusting Sam's shoulder into the back of the front seat. He tossed a fifty to the cabbie before leaping out of the vehicle. He heard the taxi's wheels squeal as the driver sped away.

Sam ran to a deputy who was standing in front of Ferris's driveway. "What's going on here?"

The officer tucked the clipboard he had been holding under an arm and lifted both hands. "Stop there. This is an active crime scene."

Sam's heart was thumping wildly. He reached for his badge, cursing with the realization that he didn't have it on him, and he shouldn't have had any reason to need it. *Some vacation...*

"I'm a detective with Grand Forks PD. What happened?"

"Grand Forks? I haven't heard of it. I'm going to have to ask you to step back."

"North Dakota. Listen..." Sam extended his hand toward the deputy, who stepped back out of reach. Sam held up a hand to convey he wasn't a threat. "It's my girlfriend. She was coming here earlier today. Is she—" He couldn't bring himself to ask if she was okay. Paige might have only entered his life a couple of months ago, but women like her—independent, sexy, *and* intelligent—were hard to find. He knew this for a fact from all his failed attempts to find them.

The deputy's gaze met Sam's eyes but looked through him. "This is an open investigation."

This is ridiculous.

"Paige!" Sam screamed.

"Sir, I'm going to have you forcibly removed if you don't coop—"

Sam plowed past him. The deputy's clipboard hit the pavement, but Sam didn't slow down. He kept moving toward the house.

An officer—likely a detective based on his stance of authority and lack of a police-issued uniform—came out the front door.

"Stop right there!" Given both his tone and the edge to his eyes, he meant business. His hand hovered above his weapon, ready to draw it, looking for one good reason to.

Sam briefly surrendered again. "I'm Detective Barber." No point bringing up his locale as it obviously didn't matter. Valencia was a light-year from his jurisdiction.

"And I'm Santa Claus." He looked around Sam to the deputy. "What the hell is this guy doing here?"

"I'm sorry, Grafton." The deputy yanked on Sam's shoulder, but Sam wasn't going to budge until he found out what the hell was going on.

"I'm not going anywhere until someone talks to me."

"Are you looking to be arrested?" A veiled threat if the underlying curiosity in Grafton's eyes was any indication.

"My girlfriend… She came here earlier. Is she all right?"

Grafton remained silent, staring at Sam. Sam shrugged the deputy off his shoulder, and the man complied. "She came by to see him this morning, and I haven't heard from her since. Is she all right?" He expelled a deep breath.

"It depends. Who's your girlfriend?"

God. Does that mean a woman was hurt—or worse—in this house?

"Paige Dawson," Sam rushed out. "Now answer my damn question! Is she okay? What happened? Please tell me she is okay." His clear emotion may as well have met with a brick wall for how much it seemed to affect the detective. But there was a glint in the man's eyes that told him Paige was just fine. "What is it?"

"Why don't you come with me? Name's Detective Grafton, by the way."

Got that already.

"Please, tell me what's going on," Sam said, softer this time.

"Well, Miss Dawson is a murder suspect."

"A...what?" Had he heard that correctly? "That's impossible. And *ridiculous*. She's an FBI agent."

Grafton shrugged. "FBI or not, she's looking guilty for the murder of Ferris Hall."

He was going to be sick. "You're going to have to enlighten me."

"Actually, I don't." He paused a few beats. "But I will. Your girlfriend was found inside the house, ransacking the place. We caught her rummaging through his kitchen drawers."

There was no reason for the detective to lie, and rage curdled throughout Sam. She had promised to stay outside. He'd have to curb his anger right now, though, and he did his best not to let it show, peacocking his stance. There was no way Paige would have killed Ferris Hall. Was there?

He hated that even an infinitesimal bit of doubt crept in. But he knew how angry she was about what he had done to her friend. Still...murder? Was that why she had wanted to come alone, to leave him out of it?

"I see it on your face, *Detective*... You're wondering if she might have done this."

What is this guy? A fucking mind reader?

Sam met Grafton's gaze. "I have no doubt she's innocent."

"Huh." Grafton smirked. "Either way, you're coming with me."

"Happily. I'd love to clear up your clusterfuck."

CHAPTER TEN

It felt like Paige was in the room with Jack for an hour or more before the door opened, and Grafton entered with Mendez trailing him.

"Time's up," Grafton announced. "You've had enough time to confer."

Jack stood behind Paige. She wished she could open her eyes and have all this be behind her. But no such luck. This was reality.

Grafton tossed a file folder on the table and remained standing. Mendez hung back by the perimeter of the room once more, observing the senior detective.

"Special Agent Harper."

Grafton extended a hand toward Jack, who just crossed his arms.

"You will be releasing Miss Dawson. She is innocent," Jack said.

"And you know this how exactly?" Grafton asked, raising his brows. "Were you by her side last night between ten and midnight?"

"Miss Dawson is a respected FBI agent. She's worked with me for seventeen years, and in the time I've known her, she's acted only in accordance with the law."

Grafton angled his head, his gaze on Paige. "I'm surprised this is who you chose for counsel. The personal connection could hurt you."

She glanced at Jack, and he placed a hand on her shoulder.

Jack glanced sideways at her and there was a pulse tapping in his cheek. He didn't want any surprises. He wanted the full truth. While the thought of the woman had crossed her mind, how could Paige have known she would come forward? She condemned her foolishness in thinking otherwise. She reached for Natasha's necklace, but she dropped her hand before making contact.

"She said, and I quote…" Grafton lifted a sheet from the file and read aloud. *"I asked her what she was doing, and she said she was with Ferris the night before and left her purse in the house."*

Seconds passed in silence, and rendering Jack speechless wasn't an easy thing to do.

"Miss Dawson," Grafton said, raising his voice, "was with Ferris *the night before.*" He waited for that to sink in.

God, she should have been honest. Or at least have stretched the truth to say she was investigating him for a crime. Anything else but the lie she'd told.

"To make it clear, if it's not already—" Grafton dragged a pointed finger from Paige to Jack "—the night before, last night, was when Ferris was murdered. Miss Dawson told a third party that she was with Ferris at that time. And you know that the GPS reading in the car showed she reached her destination at ten oh five."

She almost wanted him to follow through on the warrant for the tracking device that the rental company would have placed on the car. He would see that her travels took her to the motel, but it would also show she wasn't there long enough to kill him and that she kept moving. But the detective would probably find another way to twist things.

Grafton curled his lips. "Neither of you have anything to say to that? Huh. Interesting." He turned to Mendez. "Would you like to share what else we do have so far?"

Mendez gave a smirk. He was obviously pleased that Grafton was passing the conversation over to him. "Miss Dawson, is it true that you had originally booked a flight and a resort for this week in Cancun, Mexico?"

"Yes," she answered.

"And is it true that you canceled that reservation?"

"Yes." She'd keep her responses short and simple without room for misinterpretation.

"Then you booked tickets to Valencia. Is that correct?"

"Yes."

"Why?"

"Why? Really, that's your question?" Jack mocked the detective. "Miss Dawson changed her mind. She wanted to come to California for her vacation instead. That hardly means anything."

"My point is, *Agent*, that Miss Dawson decided to come here because she found out this was where Ferris Hall lived. We all know what he did to her friend, giving her motive. She tracked him down—opportunity and means. We'll get it all stitched up." Mendez reached into his pocket and pulled out Paige's cell phone in a plastic bag.

Shit! This was really happening. She should have removed all "evidence" of Nadia's involvement from her phone. But in her defense, how could she have ever guessed she'd wind up suspected of Ferris Hall's murder?

Jack turned to her, but she couldn't bring herself to look him at him.

"There is correspondence on here between Paige Dawson and a woman named Nadia Webber. I'd ask if you know who she is, Agent Harper, but I know you do."

Paige dared to look at Jack now, and it was his turn to avoid her gaze. Nonetheless, betrayal was in the set of his jaw.

She had to say something.

"There is something I need to confess—"

Grafton smiled. "You confess?"

She glared at him. "I confess *only* to coming out here to see Ferris Hall."

"Just to see him? You had twenty years of anger built up inside of you. No one can blame you for wanting to get some sort of payback," Mendez said. "Actually, your friend, she's dead now, isn't she?"

Tears filled her eyes, and she fought the urge to cry. She hated herself for showing the vulnerability. "I didn't kill him."

Jack faced her. "You need to be quiet. Now."

"Jack, I haven't done anything wrong."

His cheeks reddened, and his eyes were blazing. He started to pace, rubbing his chin.

She straightened in her chair, facing the two detectives again. "I showed up at his house—"

"His? Please be specific, for the record," Grafton directed.

Surely, she was making things worse in her head than they would be if she just told the truth. If these detectives heard her side of the story, they'd relate and understand. It would tide her over until the forensics exonerated her.

"I showed up at Ferris Hall's house," she restated. "I knocked on the front door. No one answered, so I went to the back door."

"I'm sorry, Miss Dawson, but I'm not following your reasoning. No answer at the front means you go around back? That you enter his house?" Grafton quirked an eyebrow.

"I told you this before. Are you going to listen if I continue now?"

Grafton waved her along.

"His door was already open." She paused, as if expecting to be interrupted as she had the last time she'd said this. No one spoke, so she went on. "It was open, and at first, I wasn't sure whether I should go in or not."

"But you obviously did. That is where we found you," Mendez pointed out.

She ignored his chiding. "There wasn't an obvious sign of a struggle," she said matter-of-factly.

"Yet you entered anyway. Why?" Mendez asked.

Paige turned around. Based on the energy in the room, and the fact Mendez's jaw snapped shut, he wasn't supposed to address that part yet.

"Go on, Miss Dawson. Why did you enter? You said there was no sign of a struggle," Grafton prompted.

She didn't want to get into all her internal motivation, which ending up including finding proof that Ferris was still up to his old tricks. She also didn't want to expound on her interaction with the neighbor and add credibility to what the woman had stated on record.

"See, I'm finding the discrepancies piling up," Grafton said. "You told a woman you were with Ferris the night before."

"That was a lie."

"So you were lying then, but you're not lying now? How do you know what the truth is, Miss Dawson? Can you distinguish the difference?"

"Enough." Jack's voice boomed through the room. "You will release Agent Dawson to my care."

Grafton scoffed. "You want me to let her go? I will do no such thing. We are well within our rights to hold her for twenty-four hours without formally charging her, and I intend to do at least that. Seeing as she's suspected of murder, I may apply to hold her for up to ninety-six hours."

At least twenty-four hours as a prisoner? It wasn't like she didn't know the law, but this was her they were talking about here. She could almost cry thinking about sleeping in a cell tonight. She wasn't even going to consider this nightmare lasting any longer than that.

She looked at Jack as he squared off with Grafton. She hated putting Jack in the position of defending her. And from Jack, her mind went to Sam. She didn't want him involved with this mess, either, but it was likely unavoidable. As soon as the detectives found out about him—and they would, if they hadn't already—he'd be dragged in for questioning. If she was forthright about him, maybe it would help things.

"I came to California with someone," she told the detectives. "Talk to him."

"Sam Barber? Yes, we know," Grafton said.

Jack clenched his jaw, then ground out, "I'm going to need a minute with Paige."

"Sure, whatever you need." Grafton's voice was smug. "Oh, and one more thing, Miss Dawson. Just so you know, the pills in the Aleve bottle were just that. I'm assuming you expected to find Rohypnol."

CHAPTER ELEVEN

The door had no sooner shut than Jack turned on her. "What the hell were you thinking?"

"Jack, I can—"

"You're going to tell me that you can explain? I asked you if there was anything else I should know and you said *no*." He jabbed a finger toward the door. "But there is. An eyewitness? But what bothers me the most… Nadia helped you find Ferris?"

Her chest was so heavy, it hurt to breathe. "I'm sorry."

"You're sorry?" He bashed the top of his fist against the table. "You misled me into thinking you told me everything. Tell me why I shouldn't kick you off the team right now."

Her stomach knotted mercilessly, and if she had anything in there, she'd throw it up. "Please listen to me."

Jack splayed his hands but didn't say a word.

"Ferris killed Natasha."

Jack glared at her. "Why involve Nadia in your personal vendetta?"

"It's not that simple. And it's not a vendetta."

"Simplify it," he said coolly. "I had to clear this by the director."

"So he knows—"

"About you being accused of murder?" Jack nodded. "That and the fact that Hall's murder seemed methodical and so violent—"

"You told him it might be the work of a serial killer?" She leaned forward on the table, resting her forehead in her hands.

"I can't believe I'm saying this, but I hope for your sake—for my sake—it is. Now, tell me how we got to this point, Paige. What were you thinking?"

"I just…" She dropped her hands and sat up straighter. She knew verbalizing her reasoning to Jack would make it lose some of its strength, its potency weakened by the repercussions. She fidgeted with her hands. "When it first happened, Natasha lived in denial, talking as if she could handle what had happened to her. She was raped the night before we were to fly home, but she only told me at the airport when we were about to board. See, we'd been sharing a room, and when she didn't return from the club with me, I didn't think…" She sniffled and wiped away tears that fell. "I was young. I should have known better. I thought it was all fun and games. Nothing in my world had ever been dark like that. For lack of a better analogy, it was all sunshine and lollipops." She paused, glancing up at Jack. Her heart ached so much, she thought it must have fractured in her chest. "She was always the life of the party. I should have looked out for her."

"What happened wasn't your fault."

"It was." She met Jack's gaze. The reflection in his eyes mirrored hers, and the condemnation was fierce. "If I had been a better friend, I would have watched after her more closely. If I had been thinking, I would have noticed…"

"Noticed what?"

She swallowed roughly. "There were a few guys hanging around her." She'd never admitted to observing this before now. She was even afraid of confessing it to herself.

"Ferris and his friends?"

"Yeah." She worried her lip.

"There's no way you could have known their intentions."

"I wish I could believe that. All four of them raped her, Jack. It was my fault." The weight of the confession grounded her to the chair, rendering her paralyzed.

"None of this was your fault." His voice was soothing. He was trying.

She shook her head. "Nope, it was." More tears came, and she let them fall freely. She spoke through sobs. "When I found out she was raped, I did everything I could to help her. Natasha refused to get help or go to the police so I went on her behalf. But since she didn't report the rape in Cancun—"

"There wasn't a legal stand."

Paige nodded. Tears were dripping off her chin now. "There was nothing the local police back home could do. Natasha was gang-raped and she'd have no justice." Her eyes snapped to Jack. "But I didn't make it, Jack, not this way. I didn't kill Ferris."

"I know."

She expelled a breath, deflating her lungs, but her chest remained heavy as if a weight were pressing down on it. "Back after it happened, I returned to the resort. I even learned Spanish. I tried to deal with it over the phone, but with the language barrier, it was hard to articulate exactly what I needed from them. I was trying to get the guys' information. I don't even know what I thought would happen once I found them. I just wanted them to know that I knew—other people knew—what they had done. I found Ferris and wanted him to know that he had an FBI agent watching every move he made. Ferris actually used his real name when we met him, too. He was such a flirt. I should have known." She was shaking her head but stopped when she felt Jack's hand on her shoulder. She looked up at him, and when they locked eyes, she started to bawl.

"Come on." Jack summoned her to her feet for a hug.

"You don't have to..." He wasn't the hugging type, but maybe his mother's death a couple of months ago had triggered something in him. Paige doubted any changes would be permanent. "I'm sorry for all this, for dragging you into it."

"Hug me. You'll feel better." Jack rolled his eyes, but there was the hint of a smirk on his lips.

She complied, and the embrace felt wonderful. She remained there until the natural time had passed, and then she released him. She pulled back and wiped her cheeks.

"Better?" Jack asked.

She nodded.

"Good. Maybe there's some credit to what people say about hugs. But don't let my saying that out of this room."

She managed a smile and half laugh and shook her head.

"Now, tell me about Nadia," Jack said. "And anything else I need to know."

"I shouldn't have gotten her involved."

He gave her a pointed look, resuming the role of her boss again. "No, you shouldn't have."

"When we returned from the case we worked in Grand Forks, I visited Natasha. Not that she knew I was there... I hated seeing her that way. She was basically imprisoned in her own mind. She couldn't talk, but she was able to communicate *yes* and *no* by blinking." The tears blurred Paige's vision, and she took some time to breathe through her emotions.

Jack touched her forearm briefly.

Paige composed herself enough to continue. "I'm just happy that I saw her one last time...before the funeral. But that's where I saw the photograph."

"The photograph?"

Paige nodded. "It was one of Natasha, me, and some other people in Cancun. But it included Ferris. At first, I thought my mind was playing tricks on me and I was just seeing things I wanted to see. I have no idea why I'd never seen that picture before. I admit I hadn't been the best of friends to her. I hardly visited her. It's just…" She choked back more sobs.

"We all do the best we know how."

Jack's encouragement had her angling her head.

"Don't say I never offer advice."

"Oh, I never would." She managed a small smile. "It's just unbelievable. Her mother had no idea that one of her daughter's rapists had been in front of her the whole time. She still doesn't. I wasn't going to tell her. I just made a big deal out of the picture, saying how I wished I had a copy, and she let me take the photo with me after the service."

"So this photograph is how Nadia factors in? She aged him?"

Paige nodded. "I knew from my visit to the resort in Cancun that Ferris lived in California, but that was as far as I was able to get. A first name and a large state doesn't exactly narrow things down. But after Nadia aged his photograph, she ran it through criminal databases. That's when I found out about Ferris's record. From there, it was easy to get his address…" She made eye contact with Jack. "I had no idea things would turn out like this."

The room fell silent for a few seconds before Jack's phone vibrated.

He unclipped it and checked the caller ID. "Speaking of Nadia."

"Please, don't—"

"Nadia," Jack answered his phone.

Paige watched as Jack listened. He seemed to be avoiding eye contact with her, his gaze cool. He was focused on every word Nadia was saying.

Seconds later, he hung up. He hadn't spoken one word to Nadia about what she had done to help Paige find Ferris.

Paige swallowed. "Thank you, Jack."

"Don't be thanking me yet." Now he aligned eyes with her. "It seems our killer may have struck before, so we might be looking for a serial killer after all."

Paige sat up straighter. "Good for me, not for the world. So you can get me out of here?" The hope was lit.

"Not quite yet."

She frowned. "What? Why?"

"Ferris and the other victim weren't mutilated in exactly the same way. There are some differences."

"But they're connected, right? You just said—"

"The evidence in this other case pointed toward a male killer."

"Okay, then why would you think the same person murdered Ferris?"

"You do trust me, Paige?"

"Yes, but—"

"Let us review everything in the two cases tonight." Jack tapped Ferris's evidence folder on the table.

"I have to spend tonight behind bars?"

Jack met her eyes. "Trust me."

"But when they find out my car was at the Budget—"

"Timeline, but there's something else we can do. You said you went right back to the Hyatt? What time was that?"

"Ten forty, give or take, but that still falls within the time of death window."

"The hotel will have cameras in their lobby."

"What are you thinking?"

"We prove when you returned to the Hyatt and narrow down the timeline."

"And if that doesn't work?"

"We need to find the real killer."

CHAPTER TWELVE

When Zach and I told Jack that Sam wasn't at the hotel, he directed us to get a couple of rooms. We texted him to meet us in the room under Zach's name. That's where we were now. I was pacing the room while Zach sat on the bed and channel surfed, not settling on one program for longer than a minute. We had ordered a large pizza from room service but had hardly touched it.

The knock on the door was hard and impatient. It had to be Jack. I snatched the remote from Zach and turned off the TV before going to the door. Jack stormed past me, heading toward the window, obviously deep in thought. He wasn't silent for long, though, and spun around to face us.

"Nadia found another murder similar to Ferris Hall's. It took place six years ago in Los Angeles," Jack began. "The victim's name was Kyle Malone. I had Nadia send me the file. I've already forwarded it to both of you. Zach"—he handed a file folder to Zach—"I need you to read this right now. It's on Ferris Hall. See if anything's been added since earlier today."

"Of course."

Calling Zach a speed-reader wasn't a true enough label. Suffice it to say, the man could read—and remember—everything at alarming speed.

Both Zach and I had already looked at what Jack had e-mailed us, and that probably explained why the pizza was hardly touched.

"In Malone's case, the killer cut off his penis and—" I burped up the little I had eaten "—jammed it up his anus." *Yep, we were looking for one sick bastard.*

"You make it through a case where the murderer is grinding up human intestines, and this makes you squeamish?" Jack asked.

Leave it to Jack to bring up Salt Lick, Kentucky, dredging up the memory of the ten bodies ritualistically killed and buried.

Zach closed the folder and tossed it next to the photos on the bed.

It had taken him all of two minutes, if that, to read the case file on Ferris Hall.

When Jack was certain he had our attention, he spoke. "The unsub, like in the case with Hall, urinated on Malone. A dose of Rohypnol was also found on his abdomen."

"Sticky residue was found on Malone's face, too," I said.

"And there's an indication that hair was pulled from around Hall's face. It's possible it was from duct tape, but it's still to be determined," Zach added. "The knife used on Malone was a non-serrated blade, same with Hall."

I didn't envy the coroner when it came to determining that aspect. That particular area of the body would have been so bloody and mangled…

"Both murders were also motivated by extreme rage," Zach said. "Both seem driven by retaliation, but especially Malone's case, as Hall's body wasn't violated in the same way. I'd wager this unsub may be making a stand against rapists, though, based on the date-rape drug left at each scene, and mutilated genitalia. We'd have to find out more about Malone and see if he was a rapist."

"Malone didn't have any assault charges or accusations against him," Jack explained. "We'll speak with Malone's closest friend from the time, though."

I nodded. "Sounds like a plan."

"Uh-huh." Jack gave me a look that communicated he didn't need my agreement.

"Something else I find worth noting," Zach said, "is that Malone was HIV-positive. We'll need to see if Hall was also carrying the disease. It could be part of the victimology profile. As a side note, the urine on Malone contained DNA."

"Which is unusual for a healthy person," I said.

"Correct. So it makes me wonder about our killer's health—at least in Malone's case," Zach stated. "And we'll want the urine left at Hall's scene fully analyzed as well."

I listened as Zach talked, but I was also stuck on the differences in the cases, the main discrepancy being that one case indicated a man and the other a woman. Then there was the placement of the severed penis. It seemed to somehow be related to homosexuality to me. We'd have to find out Malone's sexual preference when we spoke to his friend.

"Now, the file indicates that Malone wasn't drugged," Zach said, "but that just a pill was left. The unsub wanted him to experience the pain."

Lovely thought...

"We should know tomorrow if Hall was and hopefully get some of our other questions answered," Jack added. "As for the autopsy, I'm the only one cleared to attend. We need to connect the two cases before bringing Malone's up to the detectives. While the two of you get started on that, I have to speak with hotel management about something."

CHAPTER THIRTEEN

Sam was asked to sit in a meeting room that felt more like an interrogation room, and his request to see Paige was denied. The space had wood-paneled walls and a laminate table with eight chairs. A credenza on one end had a fake plant in a pot, its leaves dusty as if it hadn't been washed in months. Framed prints on the walls showcased officers holding awards. After twenty minutes, he was sick of looking at their faces. And now it was going on a couple of hours.

His insides were jumping with rage. They were probably pressuring Paige to confess to a murder she didn't commit. There was no way he'd give real consideration to her killing a man. Even if the victim was Ferris, she wasn't a killer. All she had wanted was for Ferris to know that his actions all those years ago had consequences and that she'd be watching his every move. Sam hadn't for one second questioned her stability. For her to cross over from confronting him to murder… No, he wouldn't accept that. What he didn't understand was why she had ransacked the place. That deserved an explanation. But he could only imagine how scared she was facing this on her own. Why hadn't she called him? Surely, she was given her one phone call.

The door opened, and Grafton entered.

"What the hell is going on?" Sam barked. His hands were gesturing wildly. "She should have been allowed a phone call."

"She was."

Sam stared at the detective in shock. All he could do was blink and breathe, albeit shallowly. Who had she called? He pushed his distress and vulnerability away. He wasn't going to let the detective see that side of him.

"There is no way Agent Dawson killed anyone." He used her formal title without thought, but it was appropriate. She was a federal officer with a solid record. She wouldn't destroy it over a personal vendetta. The cost would be far too high. He knew what the Bureau meant to her.

"No matter what you believe, the evidence doesn't look good for your girlfriend." Grafton was cool in his delivery as he took a seat at the table.

Sam sat back and clasped his hands. "I assume you have proof?"

"She was found in the victim's house the morning after his murder. Do you know why she was in his house?"

Sam remained silent.

Grafton let at least a full minute pass, leaning back in his chair, his arm extended across the table, his hand flipping back the corner of a piece of paper.

"If Paige was inside, it was for a good reason," Sam finally said. "Maybe she thought Ferris was in danger."

"That's exactly what she said. Did you rehearse this?" A sly smile lifted the corner of Grafton's mouth. "He wasn't killed in his home, though."

"Okay, now you've lost me."

"He was found in a motel room." Grafton pulled a crime scene photo from a folder.

"Oh." Sam covered his mouth and turned away. In his entire career as a detective, he'd never seen anything so horrific. "When was he found? Time of death?"

"Found at eight this morning at the Budget Motel by a maid. Before you ask, she's been cleared."

"Eight is early for a maid."

Grafton shrugged.

"Time of death window?" Sam repeated the question.

"Between ten and midnight." Grafton paused. "And a woman with long curly hair was last seen with Ferris."

"Well, it wasn't Paige."

"You sure?"

"She'd never do something like that. I know her."

"Is that true? You've known her a long time, then?"

"Long enough."

"Come on, now, Detective. A week, a month, years?"

Sam's eyes shot to Grafton's. He didn't care for the way *Detective* came off the man's lips, full of disrespect and belittlement. It meant that Grafton had no bounds when it came to his fellow officers in law enforcement. He'd grind any of them if it served his purposes. And Sam recognized what that meant for Paige. There was already an underlying dislike, or competitiveness, between most state and federal officers.

Sam made certain to meet Grafton's gaze. "You're only after her because she's an FBI agent."

"She had reason to kill Hall."

It was there in the glint of Grafton's eyes. There was a lot of "evidence" Grafton was holding back. Sam also had a feeling that they had uncovered the true reason for the trip to California, so he'd be revealing nothing new by being honest. "She was going to let him know what he had done to her friend. That's all."

Grafton leaned forward. "Yet, it seems she did more than that, didn't she?"

Sam gritted his teeth and looked up at the ceiling, trying to restrain himself from punching this guy right in his stupid grin. "I want to see her."

"As I said before, that's not going to happen." Grafton leaned back in his chair again, leaving one arm extended and resting on the table. "So let's get the mundane out of the way, shall we?"

"By all means."

Yes, let's get this over with and free Paige, you stupid bastard.

"Paige Dawson was found in Hall's home. She claimed she found the door open."

Sam felt the pressure lift from his chest. "Then she had a reason to enter."

"That can't be proven."

"Yet her murdering him can?"

"All in due time."

"Fuck all in due time," Sam spat out. He could feel the large vein in his forehead throbbing.

But his outburst had no apparent impact on the detective. Grafton just continued in a calm voice. "A witness says that Paige told her she was with Hall last night."

The tidbits of information seemed to be packaged in pairs now. A witness? "Last night? What does that have to do with anything? She went to see him this morning. And last night, she was with me."

Grafton locked eyes with Sam. "Was she?"

"Of course she was. We got in on Saturday night and haven't been apart since, except for this morning when she went to see Ferris."

"And you let her see this man—a man who raped her friend—alone?"

Sam wasn't going to answer that. He detested the accusation that he was a crappy boyfriend. As if he didn't feel like shit enough on his own. He never should have let her go by herself. It was his fault she was sitting behind bars. But based on Grafton's hunger to convict her—and even his possible beef with the FBI—Sam knew Grafton would hold her for at least the full twenty-four hours. The bastard might even apply for an extension.

"What about last night between ten and midnight?" Grafton asked. "Was she with you?"

"I told you we hadn't been apart since Saturday."

"And you're sure you don't want to change that answer?"

"Positive."

"You rented a Toyota Camry, yes?"

"She did, but what does that—"

Grafton held up a hand. "The GPS showed she arrived at Ferris's house at ten oh five."

The nausea came on quickly, blanketing over him and threatening to suffocate him. None of this was making sense.

"As I said, did you want to rethink your answer?" Grafton pressed on a smug smile that Sam wanted to wipe off permanently, but he was at a loss. He had no defense for Paige.

"We've already started the process to get a warrant for the tracking device on the rental."

Sam tightened his jaw. "You told me she used her call?" He didn't add, *I hope she contacted a damn good lawyer.*

"She sure did, and Jack Harper, her boss, is her legal representation. I believe he and his team are here, actually."

The way the detective phrased his response—*She sure did*—and his tone of voice told Sam these were separate instances, and if that was the case and Paige hadn't called Jack, who had she used her phone call on?

He didn't need to think about it for long—Brandon Fisher.

So much for past flames being just that.

CHAPTER FOURTEEN

It was nearing eight o'clock and the three-hour time difference was starting to drain me, but there's no way I could sleep until my body gave out on me. I owed Paige that much.

"We know that motive—at least at face value—is damning against Paige," Zach began. "Add that to the GPS in her rental, the time of her excursion, the fact that a woman was last seen with Hall, and none of this looks good."

"Well, the woman last seen with Hall wasn't Paige," I said in her defense. "And hopefully Jack can get his hands on the Hyatt's surveillance video." Jack had filled us in on what he was after before he left the room.

As if on cue, the door opened and Jack came in. "They'll have the video ready for us to watch at eleven tomorrow morning."

"The morning? But that's not—" My jaw dropped slightly when I realized what that meant. "Shit, Paige has to be in jail all night?"

"Afraid so."

I felt bad for my quick reaction given how dejected he sounded. He'd been gone for a couple of hours, likely fighting with the hotel staff the entire time. Given the circumstances, he'd have to go about things without a warrant.

Jack took a slice of pizza from the box on the table and took a large bite. After swallowing, he pulled out his phone, dialed, and put it to his ear. "Nadia, I want you to pull the background on Detective Maxwell Grafton." He clicked "off" and returned his phone to its holder.

"Tomorrow, hopefully, we'll get the results of several other items recovered at the scene, like the tube of lipstick found under the bed," I said. "Surely the DNA will clear her."

"If only it were that simple." Jack tore off another chunk of his pizza. Obviously he was in no mood to be cheered up.

"There were smudged prints on the headboard," Zach added. "Deep bruising on Hall confirms he was bound to the bed, and the markings indicate four sets of cuffs, probably metal. None were found on scene or on Paige."

I let the silence sit for a while. "All right, so we know the GPS in the car doesn't look good for Paige, but why do they really think Paige was in the house? By extension, what could the possible motivation have been for the killer?" I wondered aloud.

Jack bobbed his head. "Good question."

"I wish we could get into Hall's house and just have a look around."

"That's not happening right now. We'll see what tomorrow brings. Maybe forensics will bring us something that undoubtedly ties Malone's murder to Hall's."

We could only hope...

Jack tossed the rest of his slice into a garbage can. "Paige told me she didn't think she was far behind whoever had entered Hall's house. She said that as she went deeper into the house it got colder."

"So the door wasn't open letting in warm air for long before Paige arrived," Zach concluded. "We just have to figure out who was there and why."

"I'd also like to know what police found in Hall's house to get them so worked up about Paige's presence there," I added.

Jack's hands formed into fists, and he was glaring with his focus on nothing in particular. "I don't care if they like it or not, we will be getting into Hall's house."

There was a knock on the door. I glanced at Jack and Zach before padding across the room. I looked out the peephole to find Sam. I let him in, and he bypassed me, going straight to Jack.

"Whatever you're up to, count me in."

CHAPTER FIFTEEN

"Grafton let me go as soon as he realized I had nothing to do with Ferris's murder. It only took about three to four hours out of my day by the time all was said and done." Sam paced the room. "God, I know some things make it look like she…"

"Take a seat," Jack said, gesturing toward one at the table.

But Sam headed straight for the minibar and pulled out a miniature bottle of whiskey. He held it up to Jack. "I'll pay you back."

Jack dismissed him with a shake of his head. "What did Grafton say to you?"

Sam snapped the lid off and tossed back the alcohol in two gulps. He wiped his mouth with the back of his hand. "Some shit about Paige leaving me last night."

Jack nodded. "All right, we know about that. We're working on it."

"Working on it?" Sam's eyes widened, and he pointed toward the door. "She's spending the night in jail."

Jack's eyes glossed over. He really wasn't one for repetitiveness. "Until you spoke to Grafton, you had no idea that she stepped out last night?"

"None. Hell, I still don't want to believe it." Sam's gaze went around to all of us. "Now what? I know she didn't kill this guy, and you guys do, too." His gaze settled on me. Anger and a tangible sadness emanated from him. I wondered if he knew that she used her call on me.

"We believe that Hall was the victim of a serial killer," Zach said.

"What just happened to a good old-fashioned murder?" Sam asked. "Are all murders because of some deranged psychopath? Is that the only way you're programmed to think?"

"I'm sure Paige had a good reason for going out last night," Jack said, but I didn't detect any conviction in the tone of his voice.

Sam heard what Jack had said, but he was having a tough time accepting it. What good reason could she possibly have had? In fact, part of him was doubting everything, starting with their relationship.

"Last night, after dinner out, we stayed in the room." He so wanted to look at Brandon and rub it in. Sam hadn't liked Brandon much from the moment they'd met. And as Sam got to know Paige and found out about her previous relationship with Brandon, he liked him even less. "It was a low-key night, really. I was still jet lagged, and went to sleep around nine." He'd still know if she'd left his side, wouldn't he?

Apparently not.

But he had to keep his cool and cooperate with these three men. Aligning with them was the best shot at getting Paige back sooner rather than later. And he saw how they worked and trusted that they'd get her off the charges. He also had no doubt that they'd find the real killer.

"So you had no idea she left the room?" Brandon asked.

It had been an innocent enough question, but coming from Paige's ex-lover, it felt more like a stab to the solar plexus.

"I didn't." He hated the admission, how incompetent it made him feel, both as a detective and as her lover.

"It doesn't matter," Jack said.

His tone was resolute, and if Sam were open to feeling any better about the situation, the man would have helped him in that. But what was niggling at him the most, though, wasn't that she had left his side—and it wasn't the why—but it was the fact that last night Paige had talked as if she'd had every intention of taking him with her to Hall's house, and then this morning, she had come up with this ruse as if she had just decided to go by herself.

CHAPTER SIXTEEN

Eleven o'clock—it had been twenty-four hours since she took the power of judge and executioner into her own hands, though she wasn't so concerned about accomplishing something for the higher good. It really was all about her, her own experiences and how life had been flipped on its head so many years ago. However, she'd be remiss to deny that watching him bleed out had been spiritual in a way. Those who hurt others deserved to feel pain.

She closed her eyes, basking in the vindication of her actions.

The flashbacks to last night kept coming, and with each revisit, they became clearer. She relived each moment repeatedly, taking in the smells, the feel of the blade going through his flesh, the penetration…

He had kept passing out, and she had needed to slap him awake several times. She wanted him to be aware of the pain, of every drop of blood leaving his body, of his life draining away. The sheer terror in his eyes, knowing that these were his last few moments alive, had been sublime.

Now she sat in her studio apartment. It was small but all she could afford. Right now.

The kitchen cabinet doors were cheap laminate; one even hung on an angle from its top hinge. She had never bothered to fix it, but she wasn't going to live in this squalor forever. But when she wasn't hunting the violators, she was usually sleeping. The drugs had a way of knocking her out.

But when she was here, and awake, she favored the living room because it had the only window with any sort of view. The other one in her apartment faced the brick wall of the next building.

She opened the window overlooking the street, and a delicate breeze blew into the apartment. A neighbor was playing music, its bass thumping through the night air, and lights cast shadows on the pavement below. A few people wandered the sidewalks. Lovers held hands and those alone seemed in a hurry to get to wherever they were going.

She sat back in her recliner, her feet perched on the windowsill.

On the side table was a glass of water and a prescription bottle. She wished there were a drug that numbed her emotional pain, but they all let her down and only made her feel worse once they wore off. And she didn't have the money to chase bliss.

No, life had forced her to face—and embrace—the cruelties worked out on her. But she had to believe that they had brought her to this point for a reason.

She snapped the top off the pill bottle and peered inside. There were only twelve tablets left. She needed more money, and fast. The pharmaceutical companies were the worst kind of drug dealer. They raised their prices without justification. Those on the street kept their prices roughly on an even keel. They especially never went up 5,000 percent!

She poured out two pills and washed them down with a mouthful of cheap whiskey. She closed her eyes, wishing to float away and no longer care. About anything.

But as her mind drifted, Ferris's face morphed into that of the bartender from Wild Horse bar. She knew exactly who he was now, but it had been a long time since she'd seen him before last night. He didn't even seem to pay her any attention. It would soon be time to get reacquainted.

CHAPTER SEVENTEEN

Jack didn't like people who tried to read his mind, and he especially didn't like people telling him what to do. The fact that Grafton had said Jack was the only one allowed to attend Hall's autopsy secured the detective's spot on Jack's bad side. But there were a lot of things about Grafton that Jack didn't like. Yes, there might be some "evidence" that pointed to Paige, but the man's drive felt personal. Hopefully the detective's background would shed some light on his motivation for being so intent on putting Paige away for murder.

When things get personal, that's when everything goes sideways...

It was why Paige was in this mess to start with. If agents let their actions become personal, motivated by emotion, things always went wrong. Emotions needed to be compartmentalized. It's why he had succeeded in his career, first as a soldier and now as a supervisory special agent. While emotions were intrinsic to the human race, he had yet to figure out their true purpose. From his standpoint, all they caused was friction, from the slightest disagreement to world wars.

Jack clenched his jaw. He hated to think that Paige had spent the night behind bars, but there wasn't anything he could have done about that. If she had acted more logically, she would have called the police when Hall didn't answer the door. Heck, she wouldn't have been at his house in the first place if logic had been guiding her.

She was supposed to be on *vacation*. When the hell had the line between relaxation and work become so blurred for her?

But whether he liked to admit it or not, he had a soft spot for Paige. Ridiculous, really. And it had nothing to do with the fact that she was in a career heavily dominated by men or that she was the only female field agent on his team. He'd had women report to him before, but he never had a bond with any of them like he did with Paige. And there was no way in hell he'd let her go to prison for a murder she didn't commit. Spending a little time in a cell to learn a lesson, though? Well, he didn't really have much choice but to allow it at this point.

And he'd dragged his entire team into this with him, all the way to California. To make matters worse, he may have exaggerated things to the FBI director to make him believe there was a solid reason to think the murder was the work of a serial killer. In fact, at the time, he didn't know of any other victims besides Hall. Maybe Jack had even acted out of emotion this time…

He stepped into the coroner's office and was given directions to the morgue. The door swung wide as he pushed his way through.

"What have we got?" He didn't care about greetings and introductions. It was time to get to the point. And to get this over with. The longer the case was focused on Paige, the longer the real killer was free.

"Wow, Agent Harper. All business this morning, I see," Grafton said. He was standing with Detective Mendez next to the gurney. On the other side of the gurney was a gray-haired man with round spectacles perched on his nose. They gave him a comical appearance and reminded Jack of Geppetto from *Pinocchio*.

Geppetto stepped closer to Jack, his hand extended.

Jack stared at the man's hand for a moment before taking it.

"FBI Special Agent Harper," the coroner spoke on Jack's behalf, not bothering to give his own name.

Jack took his hand back and pointed to the body of Ferris Hall lying on the gurney. "The autopsy?"

Death had turned his skin bluish, except for the deep maroon that stained his pubic region, and decomposition had made his abdomen swell. His eyes were milky and open.

"Those feds are all business," Geppetto borrowed from Grafton's earlier words and went back to the gurney, seemingly undeterred by Jack's disinterest in establishing any sort of professional comradery. The man even had a bounce to his steps. He was too happy considering he worked with the dead.

The autopsy would start with the external examination and then proceed to the internal. Each step and its findings would be cataloged in detail along the way. Most medical examiners and coroners Jack encountered recorded themselves as they worked through the process, and then they—or their administrative staff—typed it up afterward.

Jack would be staying for as long as it took to get solid answers. If that required him to stay for the entire autopsy, so be it.

"I've already conducted the external, and we have some forensic findings," Geppetto began. "The victim was alive when the killer...uh...um...sliced and diced." He shoved his glasses up his nose with the back of his thumb.

"And?" Jack pressed.

"You must be used to so much worse working with the FBI," the coroner said.

"Back to the evidence, please." Jack's tone carried impatience. "What about the urine? Was the killer's sex determined? Was a full panel run on it looking for drugs, DNA?"

"DNA?" Grafton shifted his stance and put his hands in his pockets. "That's not typically in urine."

Geppetto raised a hand, his index finger pointing up. "If there are any epithelial cells in the urine, it indicates poor health."

Jack stared at the coroner. "So were the tests run?" It was a full-time job just keeping this guy on track.

"Not for DNA, but they can be."

Jack nodded. "Have it done."

The coroner nodded. "Now, the victim was bound with handcuffs." He lifted one wrist, then the other, noting the bruising. "The presence of the contusions show that he was alive and fighting."

"Was he drugged at all?"

"The tox panel is still in progress. As you know, they take a bit of time. Well, maybe not for the FBI." Geppetto paused in some sort of reverent admiration.

Jack pointed to the body. "What else?"

"Lipstick marks were found on his face, around his mouth. It matches the tube that was found on scene. No DNA to pull, though."

Of course there isn't...

Geppetto walked a few steps. "There was irritation to the victim's face. No blood, but hairs were pulled with good force. A residue was left behind, and it's tested positive for duct tape adhesive."

Just like Malone...

Sex of the killer aside, Malone's and Hall's murders had too many similarities to not be connected. They were killed within a twenty-minute driving distance of each other. They were each found with a Rohypnol pill on their abdomen, and both men were bound and duct-taped, urinated on, mutilated, and left to bleed out.

"Did Ferris Hall have HIV?" Jack asked. The three men looked at him with a mixture of curiosity and confusion.

Grafton cocked his head to the side. "Why?"

"Please just answer the question," Jack said to Geppetto.

"A blood test wasn't done to confirm that, but again, we can do one."

"Why?" Grafton repeated.

"I'll let you in on something," Jack said. "I don't think you're looking at an isolated incident here."

"Then what exactly are we looking at, Mr. FBI?" Grafton taunted.

Jack disregarded the obvious disrespect. "We have reason to believe that whoever killed Hall has killed before."

"A serial killer?"

"Based on the MO and the level of violence, I'd say yes." He wasn't going to mention that they didn't have a third body yet.

Grafton smirked knowingly, as if he'd read Jack's mind. "But you don't know for sure."

Jack let things remain quiet, then added in a calm voice, "Are you willing to take the chance that one is roaming your jurisdiction?"

Grafton let out a deep breath. "If I agree to release her—"

"I'll vouch for her." Jack stepped toward the coroner and handed him Nadia's card. "Forward a copy of the final autopsy results and all the forensic evidence to this woman." Then Jack strode toward the door, addressing Grafton over his shoulder. "You coming? You need to release Paige and let my team into Hall's house."

CHAPTER EIGHTEEN

While Jack was at the autopsy, Zach, Sam, and I were headed to talk to Tyler Abbott, one of Malone's friends. Jack figured it was best that we find out as much about Malone's lifestyle as possible. We also needed to strengthen the connection between his murder and Hall's. Conveniently for us, Abbott lived in Valencia and we had called ahead to make sure he was home and expecting us.

Zach was driving. I was riding shotgun, and Sam was in the back behind Zach. I wasn't even sure why Jack had allowed him to tag along. Sam wasn't FBI. But I supposed he was another set of trained eyes and ears. That would have to be enough. Not that it mattered whether I accepted the reason or not. I was stuck with him regardless.

"How do you think he's making out?" Sam seemed nervous, almost jumpy. I knew that by *he*, Sam meant Jack and the autopsy.

"I'm sure he's getting some answers," I said.

"That would be a welcome thing."

I looked back at him. "We're doing everything we can."

His jaw clenched, and he looked out the window.

I got the distinct impression his mood had nothing to do with us and what we were or were not doing, but rather that Paige was mixed up in this mess to start with. The fact that she left him two nights ago had to be bothering him, too. I know that it would me.

Zach pulled into the lot for the five-story apartment listed as Abbott's address.

Sam followed me and Zach into the building, and he struck me more as a useless appendage that needed to be cut off. He was here in body, but his mind seemed distant.

"Just remember, be quiet in there," I said to Sam as I knocked.

"Yep, sure. Quiet as a mouse."

Abbott opened his apartment door without a word, stepped aside, and gestured for us to enter. He had long, wavy hair and full facial hair and resembled many depictions of Jesus.

"I'm Agent Miles with the FBI, and this is"—Zach gestured to me—"Agent Fisher."

"Yes, I know who you are." Abbott's eyes drifted to Sam. He must not have been made aware that three people would be coming to see him.

"Detective Barber," Sam offered, obviously catching the question enclosed in Abbott's gaze.

So much for the man keeping quiet.

"You wanted to talk about Kyle?" Abbott asked, his eyes on me.

"We do. Do you have someplace we can sit?" I took the time now to look around his apartment. It was compact but tidy and organized. The way the surfaces shone, I would guess the place would pass a white-glove test. There were glass jars, incense, and a large golden Buddha in the one corner of the main sitting room.

"Sure. This way." Abbott talked so slowly it was as if he was in no rush at all, and he seemed to float across the floor. He took us closer to the Buddha, where there was a sofa and a couple of chairs. There was no television in the room.

"TV is a distraction for the mind, from one's true self. I prefer to read or meditate." Abbott must have picked up on the way I was taking in the room, but with the chills racing down my spine, I wondered if he'd actually read my mind. He smiled and gestured to a chair. "Please, sit."

I sat where he'd suggested, and Zach and Sam sat down, as well, but on the couch. Abbott remained standing.

"What is it you would like to know about my friend?" His phrasing almost seemed to indicate he believed Malone was still alive.

Zach looked at me to lead the questioning, and Abbott looked from Zach to me, following Zach's gaze.

"We'd like to know a little more about what he was like," I started.

"Is the FBI looking into his death?"

"You could say that." I watched him, wondering what would make him say that when it seemed obvious by our visit here.

"He met with a violent end." Abbott's voice was still calm, but he was shaking his head now. "But what one puts out does come back to them."

"So you believe he was *violently* murdered because of karma?"

"I believe that our actions have consequences," he corrected.

"Interesting standpoint coming from a friend." I assessed his eyes, but it was like peering into glass: nothing to see but a reflection.

"Please don't misunderstand me. I was lost for some time after his passing. But I have come to a new way of thinking. I have become awakened, you could say."

"Well, in your *awakened* state, what did he do to deserve such severe *consequences*?" I wasn't buying into the becoming-awakened thing, but the guy was certainly different from most people.

Abbott's eyes seemed to return to normal, and again the shivers shot through my back. It was almost as if the man who had been with us up until now was someone else entirely. Possessed? Creepy, regardless, and I couldn't wait to get out of this guy's apartment.

Abbott took a seat in the chair next to the Buddha and steepled his hands in his lap, the tips of his fingers pointing toward the middle of the room. "Kyle did things I was never proud of. He took liberties with people he shouldn't have."

"If you didn't agree with the way he lived, why were you his friend?" Sam asked.

I turned to face him. What part of being quiet didn't he understand?

Abbott looked at me, as if he wondered if he should respond to Sam, but I nodded for him to do so. It was going to be my next question anyhow.

"He was a lost soul. He'd always liked men, no matter what his parents wanted."

So Malone was homosexual. But Hall, from what we knew, was heterosexual. So what connected them? What about them attracted the same killer? It was a glaring—and irritating—question that needed an answer. And one we had to get sooner rather than later.

Zach and I made brief eye contact.

"They were religious?" I asked Abbott, making an assumption.

"Not really, but they cared about other people's opinions way too much. I think it was because of them that Kyle went above and beyond."

"How did he do that?"

"His lavish lifestyle, his many lovers. His parents had money, and Kyle was used to that. When they cut him off, he did whatever it took to make money, including prostituting himself."

Abbott's words sank in my gut. This opened up a lot of potential motives for his murder. Maybe someone didn't want to pay for services rendered, and the situation got violent. Maybe the killer wasn't so much retaliating for rape but rather perpetrating a hate crime.

I nodded to make him think he'd given us info we already had. "We know he had HIV."

"Yeah." Abbott answered. "The way he lived caught up to him in a big way. First, the disease. Then, his murder."

"Did you tell all this to the police when they talked to you the first time?" There wasn't anything in the record mentioning that Malone was gay, that he slept around, or that he prostituted himself. If there had been, we wouldn't even have needed to come here.

"I didn't." Abbott shied away from my gaze.

"And why not? It could have led to his killer."

"I was in a different place then. Usually, I was high as hell. When I found out about Kyle, I didn't sleep for days from being strung out. I didn't want to accept that he was gone."

"Why not come forward once you became *awakened*?" I didn't mean to mock him, but it had just slipped out.

He narrowed his gaze at me. "I thought about it, but after all these years? I mean, who was going to believe me? Besides, I really don't think any of his customers did this to him."

"How would you know?"

"Oh, I don't *know*, but with everything that was done to him..." Abbott paused, emotion showing in his eyes for the first time since we'd been here. "And he didn't have a pimp or anything. Kyle managed himself."

"Why do you think it wasn't a customer?" We needed more, as based on the information presented, I had no reason to conclude a customer wasn't involved.

"I think it was someone he took liberties with. You remember me saying he took liberties? Well, I meant with people's space." Abbott opened his arms to encircle himself. "With their bodies."

"So he raped people?"

"I don't like to speak ill of my friend." Abbott fell quiet and looked around the room. "He might even be here now." Abbott closed his eyes and took a deep breath in through his nose, out through his mouth. "Yes, yes, I feel him." His eyes shot open, and he was grinning as though he had won the lottery.

Yep... Get me out of this place now!

"Did he rape anyone that you know of?" I repeated and added, "Did he use date-rape drugs?"

"I'm pretty sure he did rape people. I don't know about the drugs." Abbott's eyes glazed over the way they had been when we'd first arrived here. "Yes, he did rape people, but he's sorry for that."

"Does he know who killed him?" Sam spat out.

Seriously? He was buying this? I shot him a glare that I was surprised didn't light the couch on fire.

Abbott looked at Sam and shook his head. "It doesn't work like that."

That's because *it*—whatever *it* is—doesn't work. Talking to the dead? Really? It's not like I've never heard tell of it. You could just say I wasn't a believer.

I slapped my hands against my thighs and stood up. "All right, I think we have all we need for now."

Abbott looked pulled out of his thoughts, his expression contorted, his eyes muddled with various emotions all at once.

"Thank you for your help." I headed for the door at regular walking speed but would have happily run the hell out of there.

Zach and Sam followed me, and we met up in the hall. But there was no way I was hanging outside this man's apartment. For one, it still wasn't far enough away from him. And two, Abbott or anyone else didn't need to overhear our conversation.

In the car, I buckled my seat belt, and as I was reaching over, I met Sam's eyes. "What happened to keeping quiet?"

Sam shrugged.

His not caring about crossing the line bothered me more than the fact that he'd done it. The rage started burning in my chest.

"This case is the FBI's, not that of the Grand Forks PD," I spat.

"Technically, it's not the FBI's, either, is it?"

"Excuse me?"

"Am I wrong? I know that the three of you came all the way here to help Paige get out of jail." Sam paused for a second and continued. "You told me last night that you believe there's another murder connected to Ferris Hall's. I give it to you that there are strong similarities, but there are also differences. Not to mention the time between the murders."

"It could only mean that we don't know about other victims," I said. "The unsub could have also been unable to kill over the past six years. He could've been incarcerated, even."

"All right, but you're missing my point." Sam smiled smugly. "I think that Jack exaggerated things to his boss."

"You're implying that Jack lied to the director of the FBI?" My question lost bite partway through—I had wondered the same thing on the plane—but there was no way I'd admit that to Sam.

"He got all three of you here, including himself, obviously."

I shot him a glare. "Obviously."

"And how? By telling him that Paige was facing murder charges? Nope, had to be more. He had to tell him, or her, something."

"Him. Myron Hamilton," I said.

Sam scoffed. "Whatever. Jack had to tell the guy that there was more to Hall's murder. Like a serial killer."

Anger bubbled up from inside me. "Are you questioning Jack's ethics?"

Sam held up his hands. "Not at all. In fact, it tells me the man would do anything for his team. But how far within the shades of gray is he willing to operate?"

I couldn't believe that Zach hadn't said a word through all this. But with Sam's last statement, Zach was clenching his teeth.

"Jack is a man of integrity," I said. "And if he says that Hall was killed by a serial killer then I believe him."

"So you follow him blindly?"

I was going to punch this guy if he didn't shut his mouth...

"The level of planning and violence indicates we're looking for someone who has killed before and gotten away with it. And you'd think you'd be a little more respectful. He's trying to get your girlfriend out of jail as we speak."

"Respect has to be earned."

"What is all this *really* about?"

Sam opened his mouth, closed it, and shook his head.

"No, what is this about?" I pushed. "You didn't seem to have a problem with Jack last night when he let you in on our discussions or this morning when he said you could tag along. What is your issue?"

"It doesn't matter."

"It sure as hell seems like it does." I turned around now, my breath labored from aggravation. Maybe if I focused on Malone and Abbott, I could calm down. "What did you make of that guy?" I asked Zach.

"He's changed from the time when he was friends with Malone, that much is obvious," Zach started, sounding grateful for the topic change. "He really doesn't know who killed his friend, and he doesn't seem to accept that he is gone."

"You caught that, too?" I said, referring more to Abbott's belief in the afterlife.

Zach laughed and looked over at me in the passenger seat. "Oh, you didn't want to know my opinion of him in regards to the case? You mean his feeling the presence of the dead?"

"Do you think he's reliable?" I wasn't going to admit that he'd freaked me out, at least not out loud.

"Just because he lives life in his own way doesn't mean he's not reliable," Zach pointed out.

"You did see his eyes? How they were all glazed over and distant-looking? It was like he was possessed."

Zach shrugged. "It's all about a person's background and perspective. I found Abbott to be credible, Brandon."

"Me too," Sam spoke up from the backseat.

Somehow, I must have managed to go out of body, because I hadn't yet hit the man.

CHAPTER NINETEEN

Jack's call came through when we were still in the lot at Abbott's building. He'd called Zach's phone, and Zach put him on speaker.

"We'll catch up on the specifics later, but I wanted to let you know that Paige is being released into my custody."

Zach and I smiled at each other. I glanced at Sam, and he was leaning forward.

"They're finally seeing that she didn't kill him?" Sam's question was directed to Jack.

There were a few seconds of silence before Jack responded. "One step at a time. But given what the coroner confirmed, there are too many similarities between Malone's and Hall's murders to be a coincidence. We'll need to keep digging, but in the meantime, how did you make out with Abbott?"

"Abbott said that Malone was a homosexual and that he did rape people," I summarized.

"And Abbott prostituted himself," Sam added.

"That opens up a field of suspects," Jack said, sounding hopeful.

"Except for the fact that Abbott toasted his brain cells and has no idea who could have done this to his friend," I said.

"I'm going to get Paige now, but then we'll be going to watch the camera footage at the hotel. After that we'll go into Hall's house to have a look around ourselves. I want you guys to head over to the Budget Motel. Find out anything you can. Maybe something will shake loose."

"We'll go right now," Zach said.

Jack disconnected without saying good-bye, and Zach punched the Budget Motel into his GPS app and set his phone on the console.

Sam sat back again. I couldn't understand what his problem was. He should be celebrating the fact that Paige was being released.

"I thought you'd be happier," I said as I shifted and looked at Sam in the backseat.

"Call me reserved."

"So you think she's guilty? Because that's the only way she's not free for good."

His eyes were steely. "Of course not. But I also find it hard to believe Grafton's letting her go so easily."

I wasn't about to admit that I had just thought the same thing. "All he had was circumstantial."

"You don't think I know that?"

"You're just worried this might not all work out," Zach intercepted.

"Exactly." Sam held eye contact with me a bit longer and then turned to look out his window, but not before I saw the pain in his eyes. He genuinely cared about Paige. Maybe their relationship wasn't as casual as I wanted to believe.

"I wish that I had the faith you guys seem to have," Sam said. "But the DNA evidence points to Malone's killer being male. Obviously, with Ferris, they have reason to believe it was a woman."

Neither Zach nor I said anything, but Sam's eyes took on heat. Anger? I wasn't sure why.

"I have a question for you, Brandon," Sam said.

"Shoot."

"Did Paige use her one call on you?"

His question caught me off guard. I coughed, choking on saliva.

"Did she?" Sam repeated.

I straightened, looking back out the windshield, but caught Zach widening his eyes.

"It doesn't mean anything that she—"

"So she did?" Sam was shaking his head. "I thought so. Unbelievable."

"I'm her coworker," I explained.

"Oh, you're more than that."

"Excuse me?" The hairs were rising on the back of my neck. If he kept pushing my buttons, I couldn't be held accountable for my behavior. But I wasn't going to allow myself to get sucked into this little drama he was trying to create. "She knew I could help her. Maybe she didn't want you involved." The latter came out of its own volition.

Sam was quiet for a few seconds. "It's too late for that."

Zach pulled into the lot for the Budget Motel. To call the establishment a sleazy dive gave it more credit than it was worth. A hole in the lobby window had been patched with plastic sheeting and sealed with tape. The lettering on the roof was simply MOTEL, as if the full name would have cost too much.

I got out of the car before it even came to a full stop in the parking spot and took off toward the lobby. I needed to get away from Sam and his attitude.

Two doors slammed shut and I heard Zach's and Sam's footsteps on the pavement behind me, but I kept on moving.

Bells chimed when I opened the lobby door. No doubt it was to wake the clerk when things were slow—and I had a feeling it was slow a lot. Its busiest hours were probably lunch for cheap and cheating spouses of the working crowd, and late at night for elicit shenanigans that would be found repulsive in the light of day.

A tall, slender man came out of a back room. Midforties. Half-mast bloodshot eyes. Dark circles beneath them. Drug addict.

"Can I help you?" he asked.

I flashed my FBI credentials. "We'd like to speak to Brett," I responded.

Brett was the eyewitness from the night of Hall's murder, the one who had seen the woman Hall had been with.

"I'm him," the guy said slowly.

"All right, Brett." I pulled out my phone and brought up a crime scene photo of Ferris Hall from his neck up. "Tell us anything you can about this man."

"Yeah, I knew the guy. He was murdered here two nights ago."

A spark of hope lit inside me. "You knew him?"

"That's what I said." An odd-sounding snicker. His face fell quickly when I glared in response. Brett continued. "He came here— Hey, who are you guys?"

I pulled my badge and cred pack out. Again. "We're with the FBI." I'd included Sam by default, though I wished I had corrected the oversight the moment the words came out.

"The FBI are on this?" Brett's eyes were actually showing some life to them now. I wouldn't go so far as to say intelligence, but more like a state of fandom.

"Just tell us more about this guy. He came here a lot or just from time to time? Once a week, twice a month?" I prompted verbally and accompanied it with a roll of my hand.

"Every week mostly. He'd always pay in cash, and he always checked in late at night. Say, anywhere between ten to twelve."

"Was he usually with someone?"

"He was always with a woman. Different women."

"And the one he was with the night he was murdered? What did she look like?" I knew the answer, according to the file, but wanted to hear what Brett said.

Brett held up his hands. "Wow, I still can't believe this happened, ya know. I mean it's not like every day a guy's found—" Based on the squeamish expression on his face, he was trying to tamp down a mouthful of bile.

I turned around to gather the patience to continue—plus, I couldn't stand the thought of witnessing this guy puke—and I found myself looking straight into Sam's eyes. I faced the clerk again. At least it seemed he had composed himself.

"The woman, Brett?" I asked again.

Brett shrugged. "She had curly hair and waited in the guy's car."

I remembered the report saying that Hall's car was found here and confiscated and was being scoured for evidence, but I didn't recall any mention of her being in the vehicle.

"She was in his car?" I asked, indicating my phone and implicating Hall.

"Yeah." Brett bobbed his head and looked at me like *I* was the crazy one.

"Were you able to get a good look at her?" I asked.

"Yeah, I guess so."

He guesses so?

"It was nighttime, but you could see her clearly in the car?" I pressed.

"Ah, yeah."

I was having a hard time accepting how "clearly" he seemed to remember. I played along anyway. "Hair color?"

"Dark."

I glanced at Zach. "Dark?"

"Are you sure that it was dark?" Zach asked.

"Yeah," Brett said.

"One more question. What time was it when you saw them?" I asked.

"I can't help you there."

I pointed to the cash register. "You don't have a receipt or something you could look up?"

Brett shook his head. "Like I said, he paid cash. That means it's off the books."

I slapped my card on the counter. "If you think of anything else that might help us, call me."

Out in the parking lot, Zach looked at me. "The file just said the woman had long curly hair."

"It looks like something shook loose," Sam interjected.

Now he's on Jack's side...

"I don't remember any record of the woman being in his car, either," I added. "We're going to have to call Jack and let him know."

CHAPTER TWENTY

Paige shared a cell with a drunk and a crackhead. The former had snored all night, and the latter had thought he might have a chance with her, but she'd handled her fair share of his type in the past and she'd gotten him to back off without inflicting bodily harm. She'd even made him think leaving her alone was his idea.

Since she hadn't been able to sleep, she'd had a lot of time to think. Even though she knew she was innocent, everything was just stacking against her—her motive, her change in travel plans, the GPS in the rental car, the nosy neighbor. She sure as hell hoped the team was making progress connecting Ferris's murder to the other one Jack had mentioned or it could take even longer to get her out of here.

Her mind skipped to her parents. They never needed to know about the stint she'd done behind bars in California. It was bad enough she'd disappointed Jack and that he'd carted the entire team out here.

Then there was Sam. Whatever she had going with him was probably over now. She'd write it off as another failed relationship, but she'd never been good at holding on to men. Catching them was easy, but somewhere between the bedroom and her waking life, romances tended to fall apart on her. And she'd admit that most of the time it was her fault. It wouldn't be any different this time.

Sam devoted his life to upholding the law, and she had unlawfully entered a man's home. And she should have used her one call on him, but as long as she was reconsidering past choices, she wouldn't even have set foot in California, let alone ask him to come with her. It had been impulsive, driven by the need to right what had happened to Natasha. Of course, all this thinking was futile. The past couldn't be altered any more than the future could be predicted.

God, this was really happening. She kept wishing that she was in some sort of a nightmare, but the sour smell of puke and perspiration reaffirmed this was definitely reality.

She glanced at the clock on the wall across from the cell. *10:30.*

Footsteps coming down the hall toward her drew her attention. She recognized the sound of the soles and the gait—Jack.

He rounded the corner with Detective Grafton, who had a scowl on his face. That alone was enough to give her hope, but it was the slight bob of Jack's head that brought her joy. She was free to go.

Grafton snapped his fingers at the guard and had him unlock the cell. She wanted to hug Jack but maintained her professional distance.

"You are released into Agent Harper's custody…for now." Grafton stared her in the eye, but she managed to muster the strength to rein in her emotions. "But don't think you're off the hook yet. I will find out the truth."

"About that," Jack said, "why don't you come with us back to the Hyatt. I have an appointment with management there at eleven."

"About?" Grafton asked.

Paige turned to Jack, also curious.

"They have a little video for us to watch," he said.

Grafton rolled his eyes. "Oh, should I bring popcorn?"

CHAPTER TWENTY-ONE

The outside never looked as good to Paige as it did right now. Actually, she never would have even counted freedom as simply being *outside* before. Personal liberty was apparently something she had taken for granted up until the past twenty-four hours.

She'd collected her items from the property clerk's office, and it felt good to have her holster back on her hip and the weight of her Glock inside it. Jack was driving a rental he must have picked up. The Toyota she'd rented had been returned to the rental company, and to her knowledge, Grafton was working to secure a warrant to access the tracking device on the car. Seeing as she was here with Jack, maybe that had fallen through.

But even though she had been released, there was a niggling in her soul that made it hard to accept. She knew she wasn't guilty, but she also knew how tenacious Grafton had been in pursuing her so far, and he wasn't going to fully let her go until he had proof that she didn't do it. So much for this being a case of innocent until proven guilty. Grafton had condemned her.

Still, Jack managed to work things out enough to get her released to his custody. She looked over at him as he drove them to the Hyatt before she pulled down the visor to look at herself in the mirror. Awful. Her eyeshadow was smeared and her mascara had bled out around her eyes, making her look like she was going to a Halloween party. She pulled a tissue from a box in the console and worked at dabbing her face into at least some submission.

"How did you do it?" she asked, looking over at him.

He glanced at her briefly. "Do what?"

"Get Grafton to let me go."

"There are too many similarities between Hall's murder and that of a man named Kyle Malone."

"But I thought you said a man killed the other victim."

"The DNA left behind confirms that much, but everything else seems too coincidental. Malone's mouth was duct-taped, so was Hall's. Then you have the mutilation, which was slightly different."

"How's that?"

"Malone's penis was shoved up his anus."

Paige's stomach churned, and she saw the disgust on her face when she turned from Jack back to the mirror. Her makeup was still smudged, but it was a little neater than it had been before. She finger-brushed her hair, and as she did, she caught the image of the necklace around her neck—Natasha's necklace.

"Yes, this is quite the case you've got us involved in," Jack said.

"What about the Rohypnol? Was a dose left behind on Malone's abdomen, as well?"

"Yes, and since it's still locked up in evidence, they will be analyzing its chemical makeup to see if it matches the one left with Hall. It could be a stretch, though, as there are six years between the murders."

"Six years?" She shifted her body to face Jack. "So what was the killer doing all that time? Has Nadia found any other similar cases?"

"None."

"So the unsub wasn't able to kill for some reason," she began. "That, or his victims weren't found."

"Both are possibilities."

"Where did you say Malone's body was discovered?"

"I didn't." A tiny smile tugged at Jack's lips. "But at his apartment."

"So missing victims doesn't fit."

Jack looked over at her. "What are you thinking?"

"Well, there's Malone, who was killed in his apartment, and Ferris, who was killed at a motel. The killer clearly wasn't worried about the discovery of the bodies. And the way the unsub poses them, they are making a statement."

"Zach and Brandon just visited a friend of Malone's, and apparently Malone had assaulted a number of people when he was alive."

Her heart was thumping. Maybe that was the positive side of this whole mess: she'd stumbled across a sicko who needed to be stopped. "Maybe we're looking at someone who was raped by these men or who was defending someone they love *from* these men. It could also just be a vigilante seeking retaliation on rapists in general."

"We need a little more information at this point to make a conclusion," Jack said, "but both are valid hypotheses."

"All right, so if we have a similar MO in two murder cases, why are we still catering to Grafton?" She jacked a thumb behind them toward the detective who was following them in a police sedan.

"Because he's not going away. He's far too persistent for my liking. At least when he's got his sights on one of my own."

Jack's comment made her insides soft and warm. He wasn't going to hold all this against her? She was very lucky to have him on her side.

"Until we have all the forensics back on Hall's murder scene," Jack continued, "we need to dance."

"To dance." Paige smiled at his terminology. "Yes, and we know how much you love cooperating with local law enforcement."

He just shrugged. "Sometimes, I have no choice. And if we want to stop this killer, we can't have Grafton interfering all the time."

"True."

Jack pulled into the hotel parking lot and slipped the vehicle into a spot. He was out of the car first, but Paige wasn't far behind him. She deeply breathed in the fresh air, letting it fill her lungs, and then exhaled slowly.

Grafton parked a few spots away from them, cut his engine, and met up with them behind his sedan. He looked at Paige, the hunter still obviously alive within the detective. Jack was right, the man wasn't going to let her go easily.

Inside the Hyatt, the clerk directed them to a conference room where a television was mounted on the wall at the end of a long, sleek table. A pitcher of water was in the middle of the table with six glasses set upside down around it. A remote was next to the grouping.

Paige went right for the water. She hadn't realized how parched she was until now. She'd been given a meager food portion and water in jail, but not anywhere near the amount she'd needed.

She swallowed the cold liquid in eager gulps. It somehow tasted sweeter on the outside, too.

"Special Agent Harper?" A woman in a fitted skirt suit came into the conference room, her long fingers tapping those of her other hand. She more or less sashayed toward Jack.

How she determined that Harper was Jack and not Grafton wasn't difficult to figure out based on wardrobe, for one, and on the fact that Jack had a presence about him that told people he was in charge.

The woman held out one of those delicate hands toward Jack for a handshake. "And who are these people?" She regarded Grafton with a quick eye, but was more critical when her gaze came to rest on Paige.

Self-consciously, Paige fluffed her hair with a hand. It didn't really matter what this woman thought of her, but Paige would have been more comfortable if she'd had time to shower and change before this meeting.

"This is Special Agent Dawson." Jack gestured toward Paige.

The woman bobbed her head in acknowledgment.

"And that's Detective—"

"Detective Grafton with Santa Clarita Sheriff's Department." His cheeks were flushed red, and his gaze seemed fixed on the woman.

"Nice to meet all of you. I'm Leah Hunt, manager of this fine hotel." She stepped toward the table and lifted the pitcher. "Would any of you like some water?" Her gaze went to Paige's hands and the near-empty glass. "A refill, perhaps?"

Paige smiled at her. "Sure." She extended her glass and, after Leah filled it, thanked her.

"Uh-huh," Leah said as she poured herself a drink and took a seat in one of the leather chairs along the side of the table. She crossed her legs in one swift motion, which told Paige it was her preferred way to sit. She wore three-inch heels. Paige hoped for the woman's sake a management position here kept her mostly confined to an office. At least Paige wouldn't want to put much foot traffic in with those. "Now you wanted to see video footage from two nights ago, correct? Monday between ten thirty and ten forty?"

"That's right," Jack replied.

"I have it ready for you." Leah picked up the remote and turned on the television.

Jack and Paige took seats next to each other, opposite Leah. Grafton sat beside her.

The video played out onscreen with a time stamp in the bottom corner. They watched strangers arriving and departing, they watched moments of very little activity, and it was in one of those that Paige entered the lobby from outside.

"Pause it, please," Jack said to Leah.

Jack turned to Grafton, pointing to the time stamp on the television. "That right there proves Paige Dawson was back to the Hyatt at ten forty-two."

Grafton's pulse tapped in his cheeks, and he pulled down on his shirt. "Could you excuse us, ma'am?" he asked the manager.

With a quick glance to Jack, she got up and said, "Certainly."

Once she closed the door behind her, Grafton shot to his feet. "This is not proof that your girl is innocent." He talked as if addressing Jack, but his eyes were on Paige. "All this proves is that she came back here at that time."

"We can continue watching if you'd like, and you'll see I never left again until this morning," Paige said.

"You could have slipped out the back door."

"The employees' entrance? You get access to the tracking device on the rental and you'll know I didn't."

"You could have taken public transportation."

Paige's adrenaline had her skin almost pulsating. She shot to her feet and leaned across the table, pointing a finger in Grafton's face. "You are full of shit!"

"And you..." Grafton turned to Jack. "You are protecting a killer. You're just blind to it."

"You have nothing on her or we wouldn't be here right now." Jack's voice was calm, helping Paige cool down. She dropped her arm but didn't return to her chair.

Jack stood now and came within a foot of Grafton. "You have nothing."

Paige sensed the detective's rage and frustration from the other side of the table. His cheeks were now a brilliant red.

"I'm going to get the warrant for the tracking device on the rental car."

"As you keep threatening. But until then, the FBI will be taking over this case."

Paige was certain her mouth gaped open. Sure, there were similarities between Malone's murder and Ferris's, but what about the differences? Wasn't he acting prematurely? But she couldn't find her voice. She knew she didn't kill Ferris, and Jack and her teammates were the best chance to find out who did.

Grafton crossed his arms. "And working it with—" He nudged his head in her direction.

"She's part of the team."

"She's a murder suspect."

"We need access to Ferris's house," Jack said.

"And what do you expect to find? The only evidence there pointed to her, too."

Jack slid a glance her way. "She's explained why she was inside. The fact that she was isn't some secret. Now are you going to let us stop a killer? Or do you want another death on your hands? And before you answer that question, we spoke to someone at the Budget Motel. The woman seen with Hall had *dark* hair. You can plainly see that Paige is a redhead."

"It was late. It could have just as easily—" Grafton stopped talking, presumably realizing it wasn't in his best interest to continue.

"You see my issue, then," Jack said. "No cameras captured Paige at the motel, and the employee who worked there didn't get a clear view."

Grafton remained silent.

"The rest of my team will be coming with us to Hall's house now."

CHAPTER TWENTY-TWO

I still hadn't seen Paige, and it was killing me. I don't know why I was getting so worked up about it, but I was definitely eager to lay my eyes on her. Jack had requested that we head straight to Hall's, and Grafton was to meet us there. Paige would be coming with Jack a bit after us, as Paige had insisted on taking a shower and changing after her night in jail. I couldn't blame her.

Zach was driving, I rode shotgun, and Sam was in the backseat like before. He was fidgeting with his hands a lot and looking from his window to the windshield. He reminded me of a puppy who had to pee. You'd think Paige were going to be waiting at the house for us instead of catching up with us a bit later.

"You excited to see her?" I asked him, extending the olive branch, but not exactly sure why I was bothering to.

"Sure." He sounded casual, almost disinterested.

I glanced at Zach, and the look he gave me told me to leave it alone. But that wasn't going to happen.

"She's free," I said. "She's going to meet us at Hall's. This is good news."

Sam pulled his attention from looking out his window and met my gaze. "Super."

I sighed. "What is your problem?"

"I've told you before, I don't have one. I'm just reserving my excitement for now."

"Right, you're reserved." Maybe his body language wasn't telling me he was eager to see her but rather that he was apprehensive. Was I that messed up when it came to Paige that I couldn't separate my own feelings for her from what I saw in others?

Zach parked on the street in front of what must've been Hall's house. It was just a modest townhouse in family suburbia but surrounded by police tape.

There was already a vehicle in Hall's driveway, and I assumed it must belong to Detective Grafton. I hadn't had the "pleasure" of meeting him yet. A day of firsts, it seemed.

The three of us got to the door and didn't even need to knock. A man with graying hair opened it. His expression was as sour as his breath, which reeked of stale coffee and possibly an onion bagel.

"Come in." He stepped back, not even bothering with an introduction, and I knew this must have been the right guy.

Zach entered the house first, Sam behind him.

Grafton put a hand to Sam's shoulder, stopping him midstep. "What are you doing here?"

Sam shrugged the man off and resumed walking without responding.

His gaze skeptically trailed over me. "And who are you?"

"Special Agent Fisher." I didn't extend a hand. I didn't require that he confirm his name. With all I'd already heard about the detective on Paige's case, the hardheaded attitude coming from the man fit his reputation.

"Holy crap," I heard Sam say.

I stepped past the detective and quickly understood Sam's reaction. Inside the house, it was clear that Paige had done a great job tearing apart the place. It looked like the aftermath of a hurricane or the execution of an intrusive search warrant. I was surprised the stuffing was still inside the sofa pillows.

"As you can see, your girlfriend went to town." Grafton closed the door and stood next to Sam.

Zach started to walk farther into the house, and Grafton held out his arm. "Don't touch anything."

Zach spun around and looked at the detective. That's all he needed to do. No words. His eyes said it all. We were with the FBI, and we were taking over the case. We were free to touch whatever we wished. Of course, it would be while wearing gloves.

The three of us dispersed throughout the house. I think Grafton remained at the front door. That came as a surprise, actually, because I half expected him to take turns following each of us around. I wondered where his little buddy was— the other detective that Paige had mentioned, Mendez.

I headed toward the living room at the back of the house and took note of the sliding patio door off to the left behind a dining table. That's where it had all started...or at least where this week had started and where everything had gone downhill for Paige.

The front door opened, and my legs took me there before I even gave it conscious thought. Paige was stepping inside, Jack following her.

Her eyes met mine instantly, and our gazes locked. Her mouth twitched as if she was debating whether she should smile or not. The legs that had swept me to the door now grounded me to the floor. She was prettier than I'd remembered. Crazy, I know. And why did my mind even go there? We were friends and colleagues, nothing more.

"Hey, Brandon." Her voice was soft, bordering on sultry. Of course, I probably wanted to hear it that way. She didn't warrant any double takes from Grafton or Jack.

"Hey." I was like a bumbling teenage boy, and I couldn't keep my hands still. I was rubbing my thighs, then my ribs. I forced myself to stop and put on a smile, which I could only imagine came across as a tad insane. "How are you?"

Paige's eyes darted to Grafton, back to me. "Super."

Forget professional decorum. I hugged her tightly. She fell into the embrace, and it felt so good to have her chest pressed against mine. I inhaled her familiar scent of honeysuckle, feminine and sweet. It would have been all too easy to lose myself in this moment and overlook the fact that we had company, that we had ended things, that—

"Paige?"

—that Sam was now her boyfriend.

The sound of his voice had me backing away from Paige. "Great to have you back," I said to her.

"Thanks, Brandon." She looked past me to Sam, and there was hesitancy on her facial features, a mix of excitement and apprehension. "Sam? What are you doing here?"

"What am I— Hmm." He rubbed his jaw. "Can we talk outside for a minute?"

Paige glimpsed at me briefly, then at Jack.

"That's fine," Jack said.

Paige nodded to Sam, and the two of them went outside.

To some degree, I wished I could have followed. But that was ridiculous. I had to let her go.

Her heart was beating fast. First, the hug from Brandon… What the hell was that? It must have just been her imagination—and her heart—longing again for what wasn't there and for what she couldn't have. Second, having Sam catch her in the embrace with Brandon. He was the last person who needed to see that. He knew about her history with Brandon, and she didn't need him thinking there was more to the hug than there was.

Sam put his hands on her shoulders and pulled her to him. He stepped back quickly and tapped a kiss to her lips.

She smiled softly at him.

"Some vacation," he said.

"I know how to have a good time." She laughed, probably more because of the awkward tension that filled the air between them than because of her response. "I didn't want to get you pulled into all this. I'm sorry about ruining everything."

"Things happen." Sadness, disappointment, and even a touch of anger were embedded in his voice.

She nodded her head toward the house. "What you saw just now—"

Sam held up a hand and shrugged his shoulders. "You're just coworkers. He was happy to see you."

"That's right." She pressed her lips together. She wanted to tell him why she didn't call him, but now wasn't the time. The rest of the team was in the house, and they needed her to run them through the condition she'd found it in. "I should probably get back inside."

"I know."

She took a step, but Sam didn't move. "You're not coming?"

He shook his head slowly. "Why did you go inside his house, Paige?"

"I really don't think now's the time to talk about—"

"And some witness said that you were with Ferris the night he—"

The tangled web we weave...

Paige crossed her arms. "I lied to her."

"Why?" Sam's brow furrowed. "You know what, never mind. I'm going to head back to the hotel."

"Okay." She'd be lying if she'd said she wasn't disappointed, but she also understood...somewhat.

"You sure you're all right with that?"

"Yes, of course." She smiled at him and hoped it didn't come across as forced. "Maybe you can get that mani-pedi."

"Yeah, maybe." His tone was flat—no amusement, no emotion whatsoever. He kissed her lips again and tapped a peck to her cheek and headed toward the sidewalk, where he lifted his phone to an ear. She stayed there long enough to know he was calling for a cab, and the pain in her chest made her wonder if she'd lost him.

I had returned to the living room area, not really looking for anything in particular, but trusting that if something should stand out, it would. The seal broke on the front door, and I heard Paige say something to Grafton, but I couldn't quite make out what.

"Paige!" Zach called from upstairs.

Walking toward the base of the stairs, I met with Paige. There was no sign of Sam, and based on the downward curve to Paige's lips, I didn't need to ask if he'd left.

"Paige?" Zach repeated.

"Coming." She wound around the banister and jogged up the stairs. I followed. Grafton was close behind me.

"We're in the office," Zach said.

He and Jack both looked at us when we cleared the doorway.

"Besides that"—Zach gestured to the opened desk drawers, the mess on the floor, which I assumed had at one time been inside the drawers, and the clothes spewing from between the open bifold doors of a closet—"did you do anything else in this room?"

"No," Paige answered.

"You weren't on his computer?"

"I was looking for date-rape drugs at this point. I'd have no reason to." She hitched her shoulders.

"Well the computer is on," Jack said. "You're sure?"

"Yes, Jack."

Grafton wedged himself between me and Paige to get closer to Jack and Zach. "What do you think you've found?"

"Nothing yet, but…" Zach swung the office chair around, dropped into it, and flicked on the monitor. The rest of us gathered behind him.

Zach spoke over a shoulder to Grafton. "Besides the mess, nothing else in the house seems out of place to you?"

"No."

Zach went back to the computer and clicked some keys, then brought up various windows. "The last activity on this computer was online banking." He brought up the Internet browser, and the website for Hall's banking institution came up onscreen. "We need to log in."

"Why? What are you thinking?" Grafton asked.

"This might be a stretch, but I think our unsub may have stolen money from Hall's account online."

"Well, why not just take his debit card? Credit cards? All those things were left at the crime scene," Grafton said.

"The killer wanted more time, and cards are easily tracked," Zach said, punching at more keys.

"I still don't understand," Grafton began. "They'd just take the debit card to an ATM, take out the money, and flee."

"And they'd risk getting caught on camera," I spoke up. It got me a sour expression from the detective.

Zach kept his eyes on the monitor as he spoke to us. "What people often make the mistake of doing is allowing Google or their search engine of choice to remember their passwords. Hall didn't do this."

"How are you going to get in, then?" Grafton asked, seeming more agitated than curious.

"I have my ways."

"You'll have his records pulled," Grafton said sternly.

Zach shrugged. "There are other things we can try first. People often use programs to store passwords."

"I use one of those. They say they're secure." A faint hint of panic sounded in Grafton's voice.

"Nothing online is secure."

Grafton audibly swallowed. I knew what he'd be doing the second he left here.

"I'm opening Hall's e-mail program." Zach provided a narrative to what he was doing.

"And what's that going to tell you?"

Jack, Paige, and I just remained quiet and let Zach take the reins on this.

Zach didn't respond to Grafton right away. The program opened, and he went to the contacts tab. "People sometimes keep their passwords in this section," he explained. He smiled. "And there it is. SecureIt. The name of a password collection service is right here." Zach opened the window, and sure enough, just as he had predicted, there was a username and password.

"I'll be damned," Grafton moaned.

I smiled at Jack, who didn't return the expression. Paige had one of her own tucked away but didn't make eye contact with me.

Zach entered the information for SecureIt, and in seconds, he had the ability to access all Hall's online accounts, including his banking. He went back to the log-in screen and had access to Hall's accounts in less than five seconds. The balances on the three accounts were minimal, but there was a sizable 401(k) showing for sixty thousand dollars. A credit card showed a balance of $575.43.

Zach worked through the accounts and struck a find on the third. He pressed a finger to the transaction. "A transfer of five thousand was made as of yesterday's date."

"I still don't understand. Why not take the cash from an ATM and run?" Grafton was one stubborn son of a bitch.

Zach turned to look at him now. "He'd never have gotten that amount from the machine. Hall's ATM limit was a thousand." He maneuvered to another screen and pointed out this fact.

"So two questions… Why did our killer take—or need—so much money, and was it part of the killer's motive?" I asked.

"Add a third, Brandon," Paige said. "How did they know Hall had any money to take in the first place?"

"Was it motive for the murder?" Grafton asked, seeming lost.

"Given the other aspects of the case, no," Jack stamped out. "It was an added bonus."

"Payment for his troubles," Grafton mumbled.

"Yeah, something like that," I said.

"Well, wouldn't the bank flag a sizable transfer like that?" Grafton was like a dog with a bone.

"Not necessarily," Zach began. "And if they did, it would likely take a few days." He glanced at me, then Paige, then Jack, and back to Grafton. "And if that's the case, our unsub planned ahead."

CHAPTER TWENTY-THREE

We left Hall's house and returned to the Hyatt where the four of us gathered in Jack's room. We were able to ditch Grafton, and there was no sign of Sam. Jack had his cell phone to his ear.

"Nadia, dig further. You found Malone, and I'm guessing there's more. Expand the search to the entire United States." He paced a few steps and continued. "The forensic evidence pulled from Hall's crime scene is being forwarded to Quantico, if it's not there already. I need you to follow it through, and let us know if the results trigger anything in the system. This case is ours now." Then he paused, listening. "Yes, Paige was released to my custody. But we're going to still need to prove her innocence." Another pause on Jack's end. Based on his grimace and the way his eyes darted around the room, not settling on any of us in particular, Nadia was saying something that wasn't making him too happy. After a few more seconds, he said, "Don't worry about it. It doesn't matter now."

I sensed that *it* did matter. And it probably had something to do with Paige. My guess? Nadia had helped Paige find Ferris Hall.

"I also need you to track the money transfer made from Hall's bank account as of yesterday's date for five thousand. See if you can find out if Malone had money taken from his account at his time of death, too."

Jack put his phone away. "All right. Let's talk."

"I've been thinking about why the killer took the money, and I don't think it was the motive," Paige said.

Zach nodded. "There's nothing to indicate our unsub is using money as part of their criteria to choose their victims."

Paige looked at me. "I agree with Zach, and I definitely think the unsub is primarily targeting rapists. The victims' histories and the Rohypnol are just too obvious."

"We need to get concrete proof that Malone's and Hall's murders are connected," Jack began. "Until forensic findings come back on Hall, we'll all focus on Malone. Let's see if maybe we can find a connection in their lives, too, aside from the way they were killed."

"What do you suggest, Jack?" Paige asked.

"Kyle Malone was found in his apartment by the building manager. You and Zach go talk to him."

"We could talk to some of Malone's neighbors from back then, too," Paige suggested.

"Sounds good," Jack said.

Zach nodded. "We're on it. All of it."

"While you're doing that, Brandon and I will talk to Malone's supervisor from his last recorded job."

CHAPTER TWENTY-FOUR

Zach was driving, as he usually did, and Paige was in the passenger seat wishing she had something to say. But as much as she didn't love the silence, she didn't much feel like talking. Nadia had called and told them three tenants from Malone's time still lived in the building. They'd go find them after they spoke to the building manager.

In the quiet, her thoughts were on Brandon. She couldn't get over how fast he had made his way to her at Ferris's, how he pulled her into his arms, and then how tightly he had held her. Being so close to him was so comforting given what she had been through. It felt natural… Why couldn't her feelings for him just go away? She had Sam now. But she hated the way Brandon kept looking at her as if she were some fragile glass vase. She didn't need his pity or his support. And Sam…he seemed more angry than empathetic. Brandon must have told Sam that she'd used her one call on him. Had he just spouted it out in some argument just to hurt Sam? Brandon did have a temper and an ego… Or did it come out unintentionally? If Sam pushed him, Brandon probably wouldn't hesitate to bring up the phone call. When she had a chance, she'd have to ask Brandon about it. It was the only way she'd be able to figure out how to tackle the situation with Sam.

God, she hated this. But what she disliked the most about the last twenty-four hours—and surprisingly it wasn't her time behind bars or that the FBI director knew she'd been suspected of murder—was how she had disappointed Jack.

And while Jack was showing his normal drive to find a killer, she worried he might be seeing something that wasn't there this time. It was quite possible that the person who had killed Ferris was not the same one who had killed Malone. Jack might have been reaching to link the two cases. And their team normally investigated *only* when there was no question of serial killer involvement or if murders crossed state lines. So far, neither of those criteria had been established. But she would put everything she could into getting the answers. If they could prove Malone and Ferris were the victims of one killer, then she'd feel a little relief, as if this whole nightmare had been for some greater purpose. She didn't think she'd ever fully forgive herself for placing Jack and the rest of the team in the position of proving her innocence, though. Whatever happened to the evidence doing that?

She glanced over at Zach.

He took his attention from the road briefly and smiled at her. "How are you doing?"

"That's the question of the week, isn't it?" She laughed, even though her heart wasn't in it.

"Yeah, I guess it would be. I'm—"

She held up her hand. "No need to apologize. I still think I'll wake up and it will have all been a very bad dream."

"I bet." He looked at her over the rim of his sunglasses.

He didn't need to say any more. Anyone who had been in her position would have wished for it to be the result of an overactive imagination. She knew that she should shake off the entire experience and move on, but she was finding that hard to do. Maybe because of the way Jack would look at her periodically, as if he'd lost some of his admiration for her and she'd have to earn it back. The only way to do that was over time and with hard work. Jack's respect wasn't given easily. It was this fact that hurt her more than anything. Their relationship went back so many years. Everyone else in her life—Zach, Brandon, Sam—were new acquaintances in comparison to Jack. She had met him back when she was working in New York, before she taught at the training academy. She'd just have to sink herself into this case and prove herself to Jack again.

With that, images from Ferris's and Malone's murders flooded her mind. She had a feeling she'd remember them until her last breath.

"The coroner said that Malone's mutilation took place while he was alive, right?" she asked Zach.

He nodded. "Just like Hall's."

A wave of nausea crashed over her, and bile rose in her throat. She clamped her mouth shut and swallowed, willing the sensation to pass.

Zach turned into the lot for Malone's apartment building, and she was glad when the car came to a standstill in a parking spot and Zach cut the engine.

"The building manager's name is Roy Nichols, and he's been in the role for ten years," Zach said, refreshing her on the details.

"So four of those years were before Malone was murdered."

"That would be the math," he teased and opened his door. He must have noticed she hadn't moved. He looked back over a shoulder. "Are you sure you're up for this?"

"Yeah, I'm fine." Heck, if Zach could work this case being a *man*, with all that mutilation, who was she to play faint of heart? She opened her car door. "Let's do this."

The manager's apartment had been easy to find, and Roy Nichols, an older man with a dusting of gray hair, had answered the door on the first knock.

"Kyle Malone? Wow, I haven't heard that name in a long time," he said, pushing his oval-shaped glasses up his nose. "Not that I'll ever forget it."

Roy invited them into his apartment and led them to a living room. While he fit the image of a grandfather, his dwelling was sparsely decorated with only a couple of framed photographs on an end table. Both pictures were of the same woman. Paige guessed it was a late wife. In the corner of the small living room was a compact piano, and a brass crucifix hung on the wall above it.

"Are you a religious person?" she asked, bobbing her head toward the cross.

His gaze followed to where she had indicated. "Yes, you could say that. Darla was more so than me, but yes, I believe in God and the Devil. And *that* Malone…"

"*That* Malone?" Zach prompted.

"He brought the Devil to this building." Roy made the sign of the cross on his chest. The deeply etched ridges in his brow compressed, creating distinct rows.

Based on his age and traditional religious background, he was likely prejudiced against Malone's lifestyle. "Is that because he was homosexual?" Paige pressed him.

"I know in this day and age the proper thing to say would be, *So what? Let everyone live his life without judgment.* But maybe some of what Darla used to say stuck. I believe God made man and woman, not man and man, for a reason." His cheeks were becoming bright red.

Roy apparently clung to religion more than he realized. Paige was keeping a close eye on the man's body language, and based on the hardness of his eyes and the way he kept swallowing, he was both angry and uncomfortable with their presence and the topic of discussion. Was Roy involved with Malone's murder somehow? Or was it simply guilt for not feeling remorse over the loss of life? She wondered what kept the old man in the building. As Roy had said, Malone had "brought the Devil."

"Mr. Nichols, why did you stay here after Mr. Malone's murder?" Paige asked. "Why not move?"

Roy looked back and forth between her and Zach. "Why should I have moved? I'd done nothing wrong. It was the sinner."

It? Sinner? Ouch.

Sadly, Paige felt that Roy likely had viewed Malone as less than human for his lifestyle choices.

Roy waved a finger at Paige. "I see how you feel about my beliefs. It's all over your face, but it doesn't matter. You may also think I'm living in the past, but I tell you—" Roy let out a whistle "—he opened my eyes. And then finding him… I'll never forget that day. Still have nightmares." Roy was gnawing on the inside of his cheek. "That was the most disgusting thing I've ever seen in my sixty-eight years." He paused. "Well, I was sixty-two at the time, but you know what I mean. Nothing before and nothing since compares to that." He signed another cross and then, as if he'd finally become aware of what he was doing, dropped his hands.

"We'd like you to tell us more about when you found him," Paige said.

"You want me to relive that again? It would all be on record. Detectives interviewed me at great length."

Zach nodded. "We're aware of that."

"Good. Then read the record."

"Mr. Nichols, if you could just humor us. His murder has never been solved," Paige entreated him.

"I figured as much. And they brought the FBI in? What's so important about one faggot reaping the results of his lifestyle?"

Whoa! Paige's vision instantly flared red with rage. Roy did well hiding behind the glasses and the sweet-grandfather look, but on the inside, he was rotten from his prejudice. She wanted to lash out with *He was a human being*, but what would be the point? A man of Roy's distorted views would never be able to comprehend that every person's life was just as valuable as the next.

She clasped her hands instead and angled her head. "You think he deserved to be tortured and murdered?" It took all her willpower to water down the contempt she was feeling.

"I think that everyone reaps what they sow," Roy said, his voice cold and hard.

Paige took a deep breath—in through her nose, out through her mouth. She wasn't naive enough to think that discrimination against those who chose an alternative lifestyle would ever completely go away. Unfortunately, judging others was woven into the fabric of society. But like rust, it ate away at society, tearing apart families and friends. All because a person chose to be true to who they were. What a sad state.

"And what exactly did he 'reap'?" she asked, not able to let it go.

Zach cleared his throat. "I think what Agent Dawson means by that is, who or what caught up with Mr. Malone?"

"Who or what? The answer's clear. The man was murdered," Roy ground out. "It was because of his lifestyle. He liked men, isn't that enough?"

"No," Paige responded coolly.

"I'm sorry if you're offended, but it's God's law that—"

"Do you know anyone who would have hated him this much?" Paige was in no mood—and never would be—to discuss the stand of a biased, self-righteous man.

Roy seemed taken aback by Paige's interruption. He shook his head, but not in response so much as apparent dislike. "Read the record."

"Mr. Nichols, we have read the *reports*," she snapped. "We're here because we want to hear it straight from you."

"You want to hear it straight from me? That *faggot*"—he glanced at Paige, seemingly for the sole purpose of provoking her—"got what was coming to him. Now, whether you want to believe that or not is up to you. But when he'd go out clubbing, which was most nights of the week, and bring different people home, what do you expect is going to eventually happen? Something bad. And if you"—he pointed a finger at Paige now—"think otherwise, then you're blind."

"You said he went out clubbing?" Zach intercepted.

"I don't know if it was clubbing, but he went out at all hours. Liked the bars."

"And how do you know this? It doesn't seem like you two were close," Paige said.

Roy glared at her. "People talk."

"Any specific bar or club?" Zach asked, breaking the growing tension between Paige and Roy.

Roy looked back at Zach. "Wild Horse."

"And that's a gay bar?"

"No, I don't think so. Clancy's, out in LA, was, but it's long gone. Wild Horse is a honky-tonk out in Canyon Country. It's still there, I believe."

Paige stood. They had enough to move on now, and if she didn't leave this man's apartment soon, she'd lose more than just her professionalism. Maybe it was the time she had spent behind bars, wrongly accused, but she was angry right down to her core. Proper upbringing taught people to respect their elders, but Roy Nichols was one man who didn't deserve anyone's respect.

CHAPTER TWENTY-FIVE

Bart Kelman had been Malone's supervisor at Synergies where he worked in customer service. After Jack and I had explained who we were and why we were at his house, he stepped to the side of the door.

"You can come in, but I don't know what I could say that would be any different from what I said six years ago."

Kelman's house was a modest, beige brick bungalow with white metal shutters screwed in place next to the front windows. The picture window also had a gold-and-white metal awning. Inside, as expected based on the outside, was aged. The linoleum in the entry was made up of shades of brown and laid out in a tiled pattern.

"Here, this way." Kelman was in his early fifties and mostly bald, except for some greasy strands he combed over, clearly indicating he was in denial of his hair loss. The result only made his baldness stand out more. He gestured to the left, behind a half wall and spindles that separated the entry from the living room. Two oversized sofas filled the room, along with a coffee table old enough that Kelman may have grown up with it.

I sat at the end of one couch and Jack joined me. Kelman sat on the other sofa.

"Kyle Malone," he said. "I still can't believe something like that happened to someone I know—knew."

"You still have a hard time thinking of him as being gone?" I asked.

"Not sure it's so much that. It was just so sudden." He met my gaze. "Here one day, gone the next."

I dipped my head in acknowledgment. "We know he reported to you at Synergies."

"Happy to be finished with that place, I tell ya."

"You no longer work there?"

"You betcha I don't. I didn't leave soon enough, though. I don't even care that I'm currently unemployed. Time's too precious to waste, and I've wasted enough already. Not sure how much you know about Synergies, but it's a call center for Fortune 500 companies. The one here is the customer service hub for five states."

"Sounds like that could be a lot of pressure." I was exaggerating this, of course, to establish rapport.

"You can say that again. They have policies for policies." Kelman rolled his eyes. "Management is made up of a bunch of bumbling idiots."

"Tell us about Kyle Malone," Jack said.

"Well, he came down from Duluth—that's the one in Minnesota—when he was twenty-one. But you probably know all this. He was a terrific employee. Always on time and never in a hurry to punch the clock and leave. He'd often sacrifice personal time without asking for compensation. Good thing, too, because they are not good about overtime. They really are a bunch of dicks." Kelman eyed Jack as he leaned forward, set his elbows on his knees, and clasped his hands between his legs. "They demand too much from their employees, and I got sick of the way they treated me."

"And you'd rather be unemployed?" Jack's tone was confrontational.

"I'd rather be happy," Kelman countered.

Jack shrugged. "It's hard to be happy when you don't have money for food."

"I've never lacked."

"It's only been, what?"

"Two months," Kelman told him.

"Give it time," Jack said. "You made a decision based on emotion, and it will bite you in the ass."

I glanced at Jack. This little sideshow wasn't about Bart Kelman. This was about Paige.

"Spoken like a man who's lived it."

"Ahem." I cleared my throat and both men faced me. "Mr. Kelman, please tell us more about Kyle. Did he have any problems with anyone at work?" There was no mention of any issues in the police reports, but the case was also cold as far as the locals were concerned, so every avenue needed to be explored—or in this case, revisited.

Kelman shook his head. "Not that I was aware of, as I told the police back when he was murdered. It still seems so odd to know someone who was murdered."

Kelman seemed awfully caught up in that fact...

"So Mr. Malone got along fine with *all* his fellow employees?" I asked.

Kelman bobbed his head from side to side. "I'd say so."

"Why do you say it like that?" Jack imitated Kelman's head bob.

"As I said, Synergies puts a lot of pressure on its employees. There are quality reports and conversion reports. There are reports for the reports. And every one of them is reviewed with a fine-toothed comb after each shift. Of course, this is done by upper management, and they have no real hands-on experience handling customers. They might listen to some of the calls. You know the drill: 'Your call may be recorded for quality assurance'?"

I nodded and wondered where Kelman was headed with all this.

"But they still didn't really understand what it was like to be on the line," Kelman continued. "People don't call in because they are happy with the product they purchased."

I had originally been thinking of it from the standpoint of the killer being someone in Malone's daily life—a coworker, a friend—but what if it wasn't as obvious as that?

"Did any of these callers get out of line with Mr. Malone?" I asked.

Kelman snorted a laugh. "All the time, but Kyle wasn't special in that regard. Everyone was shit on—a lot. I mean, some of the products we represented sold for thousands of dollars, and many times we had to tell customers that there was nothing we could do. Calls were escalated to management all the time."

"And these were recorded?"

He nodded. "Yes."

There might not have been a strong basis for it, but my gut told me we had to get ahold of the company's records and see if anyone spoke with Malone multiple times. For now, I'd stab at things from another direction. "You said he got along well with people. So no one had a problem with his sexuality? I only ask because this can still elicit reactions in certain people." I knew that we weren't leaning toward this being a hate crime, but it was best to cover all the bases.

"You're alluding to the fact that he was gay?" Kelman shook his head. "Nope. Well, not that I'm aware of anyway."

"And you're sure that no one had an issue?" Jack asked.

Kelman perched on the edge of the sofa cushion. "You're saying people *should* have an issue?"

"I'm saying that people are not as open-minded as they might like others to believe," Jack said.

The two men held eye contact for a few seconds until Kelman broke the gaze. "No one had an issue with his sexual preference. Now, if that will be all, I have things to do." He hopped off the couch and crossed his arms.

Jack wasn't far behind and was to the door before I stood up. Kelman was still standing in front of where he had been sitting. I walked over to him and shook his hand.

"Thanks for your help," I said.

"Sure. But I'm not sure how much help I was." Kelman slid his gaze toward where Jack had been standing, but he'd already stepped outside.

I pressed my lips together and went to catch up to Jack. I wasn't used to him practically running from a house.

He was in the car by the time I got outside and climbed into the passenger seat. He pulled out a cigarette, put the window down, and lit up. After a deep drag and exhale, he said, "That was a waste of time."

"I disagree."

He slowly turned to face me. "How do you figure?" Another puff on the cigarette.

I put my window down, too, hoping to stave off lung cancer from secondhand smoke for at least a couple more years.

"At first, I was thinking maybe one of Malone's coworkers killed him, but police really did exhaust their efforts in that regard. Now I have a new theory."

Another inhale. Exhale. No response to what I had said.

I went on anyway. "When people called in to Synergies, they were already angry, upset over their products. What if someone had spoken to Malone repeatedly, getting more unhappy—"

"To the level of violence we're talking about? So…what? The product is out of warranty? Let's rape a guy, chop his penis off, and—"

I held up my hand and looked out the window. We were still sitting in Kelman's driveway, and I wished we would leave. But it was apparent Jack needed his fix before that would happen.

"As I said, it's a theory. But hear me out. And before you say it, yes, I know it's an extreme stretch to think someone would go that far."

"You know how much I love wild notions," Jack said dryly.

"Maybe it wasn't even someone who called in a lot. Maybe it was someone who already had a connection to Malone. They could have had a past beef with him, figured out where he was working, where he lived."

Jack tapped the ash from his cigarette and took another drag.

"I think it's quite possible our unsub might have latched on to Malone through the call center. Maybe it's a leap, but it's a possibility I feel we should explore. And if we feel the connection to Malone was a personal one for the unsub, we still have to figure out how Hall fits in." I paused, thinking about the stark difference between the two killers.

"So this theory assumes the killer lost track of Malone in the first place?" Jack took another drag.

"Yes."

"Hmm."

"Is that a good hmm or a bad hmm?"

He said nothing.

I clenched my hands into fists, frustrated and impatient. "Come on, speak."

Jack faced me, his jaw rigid, his eyes sharp.

"Sorry, I shouldn't have…told you what to do." I had a temper and was prone to speaking without thinking. But I don't remember ever being so demanding with Jack before.

He ignored my apology and kept postulating. "You could be onto something, but you might not be."

I straightened. "So can I have Nadia look into Malone's callers who were escalated to management?"

Jack nodded and flicked the cigarette butt out the window. "Have her do it, but only after she's looked into everything else."

I dialed Nadia and made the request, but I picked up on the fact that she wasn't her regular happy self. Now I had an even stronger feeling she'd been involved in Paige finding Ferris Hall. As far as I could guess, she had and was deeply regretting her contribution. I didn't blame her. If she had helped lead Paige to California, her professionalism was called into question. My take on it, of course, would be different from Jack's. What I saw was loyalty and friendship. Likely what Jack saw was a foolish act motivated by emotion. Either way, we were all in this together now, and we had no choice but to see it through.

CHAPTER TWENTY-SIX

"I can't get over that man," Paige said about Roy Nichols. She and Zach were down the hallway from his apartment. "I mean, it's one thing to have an opinion, but it's another when that way of thinking lets him believe Malone reaped what he sowed."

Zach's phone rang, and he looked at the screen. "It's Jack." He motioned for her to follow him to the stairwell. Once they were tucked away there, he answered. "You're on speaker, Jack."

"First, what have you got?"

Zach filled him in on the bar Malone had supposedly frequented, and Jack told them about Brandon's suspicions that the killer could be someone who called into Synergies and spoke to Malone.

"Where are you guys?" Jack asked.

"We're still at Malone's building. We were going to talk to a few more people who lived here at the time of Malone's murder," Zach responded.

"Sounds good. Brandon and I will go to that bar. What was it called again?"

"Wild Horse," Zach said. "It's a honky-tonk."

"Oh Lord." With that, Jack hung up.

Paige chuckled. "He sounds thrilled." Her mind went back to the building manager. "We didn't tell Mr. Nichols we'd be speaking to his tenants."

"He doesn't own the place. Besides, it's not his business what we do."

"Oh, I'm sure he'd have a different opinion."

Zach smiled at her. "Isn't that too bad." A few seconds later, he added, "We'll start with Betty Holt, apartment three-oh-two."

"Malone was apartment three-oh-three, right?"

Zach nodded. "She was living across from Malone at the time."

"I don't know if I could stay."

"I hear ya."

"And we've seen some pretty nasty shit." With her statement, the crime scene photos from Malone's and Ferris's murders flashed in her mind again. Too clearly. And while she had made the brave claim about seeing nasty shit, it was quite possible that severed penises topped the list. What kind of animal would do something like that, especially while the men were alive?

Her phone rang and she checked the caller ID: SAM. Maybe she should have talked to him before she left the hotel, but there was a lot to do.

Zach pointed to her cell. "Are you going to get that?"

"Not right now." She swiped the call to voice mail and muted the ringer. Now wasn't the time for the conversation they needed to have.

Based on the way Zach's gaze fell to her phone and then back to her eyes, she gathered he knew it was Sam. But he said nothing as he turned and headed up the stairs.

She followed, thankful that he didn't comment. She'd learned a lot about Zach in the last couple of months, and she liked what she saw. He respected her personal space, even after learning about her relationship with Brandon.

"It makes me wonder how Wild Horse was overlooked the first time," she said, eager to get back into the investigation.

"Maybe Nichols didn't think of it. He had just witnessed something awful. I didn't see Malone's crime scene in the flesh and even I'll never forget it."

They reached the third level and entered the hallway.

"Well, you never forget anything, Zach."

"True."

Paige smiled at him, and they stopped outside of Holt's apartment.

Zach knocked.

Footsteps approached and on just the other side of the door, the floorboards creaked. "Who is it?" a female voice called out.

"FBI. We need to—" Zach paused as the chain was slid across.

The door opened to a trim, yet shapely, brunette in her late thirties with the face of a cosmetics model. She was wearing yoga pants and a tank top. She gripped her ankle and stretched her leg up behind her. "What do you want?"

"Are you Betty Holt?" Paige asked.

"Yeah."

"We'd like to talk to you about Kyle Malone."

She switched legs. "Kyle? Wow, he was killed a long time ago."

"Six years," Paige specified. "Can we come in?"

She let out a deep breath and lowered her leg. "Sure, why not…"

Her apartment was furnished with the brush of IKEA— simple and affordable. The space was open concept and led directly into the living room. A small closet next to the door and floor mat was all that served as the foyer. The couch was only ten feet from the door. Betty didn't offer them a place to sit.

"What can you tell us about Kyle?" Paige asked.

Betty's eyes drifted over Paige but returned to Zach. "He was murdered."

Paige tried not to roll her eyes. "We know that much, but do you know if anyone had an issue with him?"

Betty's face screwed up in seeming confusion. "I gave my statement to the detectives when this first happened. I'm not sure I can tell you anything new."

Zach stepped closer to the woman. "Ms. Holt, the case—"

Betty fluttered her lashes at Zach. "You can call me Betty."

"All right, *Betty*," Zach began. "Mr. Malone's murder now has the interest of the FBI, and we're revisiting witness accounts."

"Witness?" Betty crossed her arms. "I'm hardly a witness. I never saw anything. I only heard things."

Heard things? Was Betty alluding to word of mouth about what had happened to Malone, or had she had heard yelling, a struggle?

"Heard? Can you clarify that?" Paige asked.

Betty wrested her eyes from Zach. "Heard? That means *to hear...*"

"Was it just gossip, or did you hear something during the time of the actual murder?"

"Oh, no. I never heard anything during— God, no. I would have said something."

Zach was watching her and resumed the lead. "Malone was apparently quite popular."

"Yeah, with men mostly."

"Mostly?" Zach pressed.

"I'd guess so, but sometimes it was really hard to tell. Kyle dressed in drag occasionally, but he was definitely the guy in his relationships. Whether that meant front door or back... I'm not even sure it mattered to Kyle."

Zach gave Paige a quick glance. She wondered if he was thinking what she was. What if the curly-haired woman who had been seen with Ferris at the motel had actually been a man in drag?

Betty wagged her finger. "Actually, now that I'm thinking about this again... There was one man who really looked like a woman. She...he... I never know what to call them. Anyway, we'll say *they* had a trim figure, long legs. They looked better in a short skirt than I do. But that one was definitely a man." Betty rubbed her throat. "Adam's apple."

"What about her hair?" Zach asked.

"If I remember right, it was long and curly."

Paige's heart bumped off-rhythm. "Had you seen her before?"

"No, but that doesn't mean anything. I rarely saw repeats. I don't think Kyle liked doing the same guy twice."

Paige's stomach churned. Kyle Malone had HIV. Did he let his lovers know about his disease, or did he gamble with their lives?

"Was he always this way?" she asked.

Betty nodded. "As long as I lived here. Right up until he was murdered."

Maybe Malone's killer was someone who had contracted HIV from him. If that was the case, and they were looking at a serial killer here, the disease would show up in the DNA findings at Ferris's murder scene.

"Do you remember anyone who had a problem with the one-time arrangement? Did any jealous lovers show up? Any angry visitors?" Paige asked the stream of questions, and Zach looked at her.

"Not that I saw or recall. Roy, the building super, hated Kyle, but I can't see him being behind his murder."

"When did you see the person who looked better in a skirt than you?" Paige asked.

Betty narrowed her eyes into a glare. "I think it was around the time of Malone's murder. Not sure. Sorry, it was a long time ago."

"You never mentioned this in your statement to the police," Zach stated.

"I did say I saw someone. If they didn't record that she had curly locks, that's not my fault."

"All right, well, if there's anything else you think of after we leave," Zach said, going for a card from his pocket and handing it to Betty.

"I will call." She nudged her chin forward and smiled.

Paige fought rolling her eyes. Zach seemed to have this Casanova effect on some women.

"Okay, thank you for your help," he said.

"You're welcome." Betty was still smiling as she let them out and closed the door behind them.

In the hall, Zach and Paige faced each other. "Oh Lord, Zach."

"What?"

Paige laughed. "We're not out here looking for dates."

Zach held up his hands. "Hey, she came on to me, not the other way around."

"And you enjoyed every minute of it."

"I'm just a guy."

"Uh-huh."

Zach tilted his head side to side. "What if the woman in Ferris's car wasn't a woman, but rather a man in drag?" he asked, changing the subject. "But he could also be a cross-dresser or be transgender or transexual."

"For fear of sounding like ignorant Mr. Nichols, what is the difference?"

"A cross-dresser literally dresses as the opposite sex, and a transgender person wants to be seen and treated as a member of the opposite sex. The term *transsexual* is a subset of being a transgender person, where he or she actually undergoes, or plans to undergo, gender reassignment surgery."

"Thank God, I have a walking encyclopedia with me." Her thoughts turned darker. "It's been brought up that Malone might have assaulted his killer, but what if that wasn't all that pushed our unsub over the edge. What if they contracted HIV from Malone?"

Zach didn't say anything for a while, obviously reasoning on what she had proposed. "It could explain the need for money. If the killer's trace indicates HIV, medication for the disease isn't cheap. From there, we'll need to prove that our cases are without a doubt connected."

CHAPTER TWENTY-SEVEN

Sam hung up after his fifth attempt to reach Paige. He knew she was working on a murder investigation, but still. He could tell by the way he was immediately dumped into voice mail that she was ignoring his calls. Maybe he deserved it for leaving her at Ferris's house, although, he had followed her all the way to California in the first place.

Not that his intentions were entirely pure. He'd wanted to change her mind about seeing Ferris. If he were a good boyfriend, he wouldn't have tried to manipulate her. He knew that the evidence in this relationship made him out to be the bad guy, but it was still hard to accept. Maybe he just sucked at romance. All he was absolutely certain of was that he was hurting like hell.

He'd hit the hotel bar after he'd left Ferris's and was still there trying to drown his pain in shots of whiskey. He was starting to wonder, though, if the drinking was only making things worse. He stared into the near-empty rocks glass, knowing the waitress would be back soon. He'd told her to return with a fresh drink every hour—a request he made after he'd knocked back a few shots in rapid succession.

He just couldn't stop replaying things over in his mind. Paige's obsession with Ferris Hall and the fact that she'd used her one call on Brandon. She hadn't even been straightforward enough to admit that. And what would be her defense? That Brandon was on her team and was somehow better equipped to help her? He was a detective and just as capable of getting her solid legal representation. No, her reason had to go beyond that. He saw the way she'd closed her eyes when she and Brandon had hugged. She still cared for him, and he for her.

Sam drained the last of the whiskey. He no longer felt the burn as the amber liquid slid down his throat. He had gone numb, numb all over. It was ridiculous how he'd let himself get caught up in this affair. And surely that's all it was. They'd slept together quickly, and no commitments were spoken. For all intents and purposes, he should have walked away after that first time. But his heart hadn't let him. It was also responsible for making him believe he'd be able to distract her once they got out here and that she'd forget all about Ferris Hall. Again, he should have known better. She was a respected FBI agent because she was hardheaded and focused. Ironically, the fact that she was career-minded and independent had been one of the very things that drew him to her in the first place. So why was he trying to change that about her?

And around in a circle I go...

He truly was a conflicted mess.

His feelings of sadness morphed into anger. Who would blame him if he walked away from this relationship? She had her FBI friends. She had Brandon. She was covered, taken care of. Why did she need him?

He paused with that question, considering it. The truth was, as long as she had Brandon, she didn't need him.

He lowered his drink to the table. The rocks glass hit with a thud, and a couple of patrons looked his way. He shot them a glare to mind their own damned business. They heeded his request and went back to their conversation.

Maybe he should just go home.

He saw his waitress and gestured for the check.

She acknowledged his request with a bob of her head.

Now, what was he just thinking?

His mind was beyond hazy from the alcohol. Then he remembered. He was going to leave, as there was no reason for him to stay. Paige had Brandon.

And while Brandon might have been out of Paige's life—or so she said—there was still obviously something between them. He felt the heat standing six feet away from them. And the fact that their jobs had been responsible for ending their relationship said more to Sam than anything. Remove the BAU from the equation and they'd probably run back into each other's arms. At least Sam had enough logic left to realize that people didn't stay in the same job forever.

The waitress returned and dropped off his check.

Sam touched her arm for her to wait and pulled out a credit card.

"I'll be back in one moment."

One moment. That's all it would take. He'd settle things up here and arrange to be on the next flight home.

CHAPTER TWENTY-EIGHT

Jack and Brandon were on the way to the bar—a honky-tonk, no less. Jack would have sent Paige and Zach if they weren't already speaking with Malone's former neighbors. High up on his list of dislikes was the twang of a country singer. And don't even get him started on the fiddle.

He tried to focus on something else. He had heard back from Nadia on Grafton's background not long ago, and the man had an interesting past. Grafton's older brother was arrested by federal agents at the age of twenty-one and sent to prison. He had been involved with a gang most of his life and managed to keep it a secret until he had gotten in too deep and wound up in the wrong place at the wrong time. The FBI had swept in one night and brought down the leader, as well as members of the gang, including Grafton's brother.

Grafton had been fifteen at the time. Not long afterward, his parents had separated. His father had faced multiple drunk-and-disorderly charges, and his mother had spiraled into a deep depression and committed suicide less than a year after her son was arrested.

Jack surmised that Grafton blamed everything on the FBI and had some kind of need to prove himself superior. If it hadn't been for them, then he'd have his brother back and his parents might still be together and alive.

The detective was no different from anyone else, really. His life experience had formed his beliefs and opinions. In his case, it had tainted his opinion of the FBI, and the feds had become the enemy.

What Jack found interesting was why Grafton became a detective at all. Why not a lawyer? If Grafton had that training, he could have used it to reduce his brother's sentence somehow.

There were things about every person that remained a mystery, even sometimes from themselves. The world was always painted by our perceptions, and for Grafton, finding an FBI agent in Hall's house made it too easy to run with his prejudice. What if the same principle made it so Jack couldn't see these cases clearly?

Jack tapped a cigarette out of his pack and lit up as he drove. He took a drag on it and savored the nicotine.

"Really?" Brandon said. "You have to do that in a closed car?"

Jack lowered his window as he looked over at Brandon and bobbed his head toward his door panel. "You know, you have a button that does the same thing on your side."

"Fine, it's only my health at risk here." Brandon put his window down, and Jack suppressed his smirk by taking another drag. "What are you thinking about anyhow? You haven't said a word."

"You say that like it's a bad thing."

"We could be talking about the case."

"Fine, what do you have to say?" Jack glanced at him long enough to catch the glint in Brandon's eyes, almost as if he thought this was a test. He'd seen that look on the kid before.

"I think we have to remove the killer's sex from the equation. The evidence points both ways."

"I agree."

"You agree with me?"

"That's what I said, isn't it?"

"Huh."

Jack laughed and glanced at Brandon, who was just staring at him.

Brandon likely realized that Jack held onto a slightly prejudiced view of homosexuals. Though, he probably wasn't very good at hiding how he felt in that regard. But it came down to life experience, and he'd been brought up by a religious mother who had told him that God created man and woman and that any other union was unnatural. She'd also tried to put the fear of Hell into him. But it wasn't until Jack's time in the military that he even believed Hell existed. Instead of a place of burning torment guarded by the Devil with a pitchfork, though, it was here on Earth. He had seen the most brutal side of humankind in those days—the lustful, hateful drive that made one country's citizens think they were better than those living under a different flag.

"Do you want to share what you're thinking?" Brandon asked impatiently.

Jack took another puff and flicked the cigarette out the window. "When we go in there, we have to keep an open mind."

"Regarding?"

"The gender and sexuality of our un—" Jack looked over his shoulder and caught the sign for the Budget Motel. "That was the motel where Hall was found."

"Yes." Brandon straightened his posture. "Wait, the motel where Hall was murdered is this close to the bar Malone frequented?"

"Looks like it," Jack said as he pulled into the parking lot for Wild Horse.

The similarities between the two cases were growing, but had I heard Jack right when he'd suggested to keep an open mind? Our case involved gender confusion—not to the individual, but to those of us on the outside who didn't fully understand—and usually Jack was more old school in this regard.

"Open-minded," he repeated.

I thought he was saying it more for himself at that point. And no matter how much he spoke of being open-minded, he was probably happy that Wild Horse wasn't a gay bar.

I stepped in front of Jack to get the bar's front door for him, but he stopped beside me. "Let's start by asking about Hall." His eyes were fueled with determination.

I nodded.

Inside, country music was playing at a low volume. It was late afternoon, and the place had no patrons, just a lone bartender drying out the inside of a glass. He could have been a hippie at Woodstock or an eighties rock star with his long, straight hair and half-baked expression. He was looking straight at us.

"What will it be? You"—the bartender tilted the glass toward Jack—"look like a bourbon-on-the-rocks man."

He couldn't be further from the truth. Jack preferred vodka martinis.

Jack didn't answer, just pulled out his cred pack.

"The FBI? What's this about?" The bartender set the glass on the counter and tossed the towel over his shoulder.

"Would the owner be in?" Jack asked.

"You're speaking to him. I'm Clive Simpson."

"Special Agents Harper and Fisher."

"Are you here about that guy who died?" Simpson plucked the towel from his shoulder and picked up another glass.

"That guy?" Jack asked, prying for specifics.

"Yeah, it was all over the news. Ferris something? I only remembered his name because of that movie."

I glanced at Jack, but his gaze remained on Simpson.

There was something odd about the way he phrased it, as if his knowing Ferris's name didn't have to do with the news. Otherwise, why would he have to remember the name?

"Did you *know* Ferris?" I asked.

"*Know* might be a little strong, but he'd come in here." Simpson set the glass down and wiped the towel across the bar.

He was keeping his hands busy, essentially fidgeting. People fidgeted when they were uncomfortable, impatient, or had something to hide. In Simpson's case, I would've gone with the latter. He knew more than he was telling us, but I had a feeling he might clam up if we pressed him about Ferris. It was interesting, however, that the two victims we knew about had both come to this bar.

"When was the last time Ferris was here?" I asked.

"Monday night."

"Time?"

"Just after eleven."

"You sound pretty certain about that."

"I remember, and there ain't no crime in that." Simpson let go of the towel and wiped his hands on his jeans.

"Was he here alone?" I followed up.

"Yes and no."

I cocked my head to the left. "How does that work exactly?"

"He came in alone, but he made a friend at the bar."

"A man or a woman?" Jack asked.

"A lady. And oh yeah, she was a looker."

"Describe her," I said.

"Long, dark, curly hair."

"Do you remember anything else about her?"

"Nice legs, short skirt, a silk scarf around her neck. Oh." Simpson seemed to have lost his footing or balance and stumbled backward a bit.

"What is it?" Jack asked.

"I've seen her before." He swallowed audibly. "Ah, guy's name was Kyle. Kyle Malone." Simpson was braced against the bar now, sweat beading on his forehead. "Do you know what happened to him?"

"We were actually going to bring him up," Jack stated calmly.

"Wait here. One minute."

Simpson disappeared into the back and returned holding a black ledger. He slapped the book on the bar and thumbed through the pages. He stopped and pressed an index finger to a mess of handwriting.

"What is this?" I asked.

Simpson was reading, his lips moving, nothing being said out loud. "Aha." He looked up at Jack and me. "After I heard about his murder, I thought I'd write down my memories. You know, just in case the fuzz came by."

The fuzz? *Put something in a movie and it never dies.*

"I noted who he spoke to and left with," Simpson continued. "But I also made a note of something else." He spun the book to face me, and I did my best to read his barely legible handwriting. Even leaning in close, I couldn't discern it for the life of me.

"Here." Simpson wriggled his fingers to get the book back. "It's my writing, isn't it? I probably should have been a doctor." He looked at us. "That was a joke."

I'd laugh if I found it funny.

"I wrote down, *Dude who looked like a lady.* Long, curly hair. But I remember her eyes. Very dark and mysterious." Simpson paused for a few seconds and then went on. "She was drinking with Malone the night of his murder. I can't remember if they left together, though. She seemed nice, not dangerous or violent. I wasn't going to the police with this. They'd have laughed in my face."

"Yet you found her noteworthy enough to add to your little book there?" Jack pointed to it.

"I guess." Simpson's hands were shaking. "She killed Kyle and Ferris?"

"It's too early to say," Jack said. "Do you have security cameras?"

"No."

"None inside or in the parking lot?"

Simpson shook his head.

I wasn't sure what Jack was thinking, but I was wondering where the lines intersected to attract the same killer—assuming it was the same killer. Had our unsub used their looks to lull in Ferris? Was this all about rapists who used date-rape drugs? Regardless of the answer, we needed to figure it out if we were going to catch this killer.

CHAPTER TWENTY-NINE

By the time Zach pulled the rental car into the parking lot of the Hyatt, it was already evening. He and Paige had spoken to the other two tenants who had been living there at the time of Malone's murder but didn't get anything useful from them.

Paige had shuffled Sam to voice mail five times before he'd stopped calling. The last time he'd tried to reach her was at least an hour ago. But the conversation they needed to have would take longer than a couple of minutes so she wasn't about to answer his calls on the road. Right now, she and Zach were supposed to meet up with Brandon and Jack to discuss the investigation so far, but she couldn't avoid Sam forever.

"Tell Jack I'll be up in a bit," she said. "I'm going to check on Sam."

Zach nodded. "Probably a good idea."

She bit her bottom lip and hurried toward the elevator bank. One was showing on the fifth floor and the other on the fourth. She should probably take the stairs, as it would give her more time to decide how to approach things. But she opted to take the elevator, hoping she'd come up with some miraculous compilation of words that would manage to smooth everything over. She didn't really want to come clean about calling Brandon first. What if Sam didn't know? Then she'd be opening that discussion up for no reason. Whether she felt she had a good reason or not, Sam wouldn't like it.

Zach loaded onto the car with her and remained silent until it stopped at the third floor. He was headed to Jack's room on the fifth.

"See you up there," he said.

"Yep." She tossed a halfhearted wave to him as she got off the elevator.

She approached a framed mirror mounted above a table across from the elevators, tugged down on her blouse, and studied her appearance. She touched fingertips to her sagging brows. She looked as tired as she felt.

She stopped outside their door. *Their* door…to *their* room. She really had jumped into this relationship quickly. And what had she even expected? A happily-ever-after?

Should she knock or just let herself in? She was stuck in a moment of awkwardness. He was going to be mad at her. He'd surely know she'd ignored his calls. Maybe she could just tell him she was busy with the case. That much was true.

She knocked and waited. There was no sound coming from inside. She was surprised by the ache in her chest, the pinpricks spiking her heart, at him not responding.

She knocked again and still nothing from inside. She fished out her key, and the second she opened the door, her eyes went right to the bed and Sam's bags on top of it. She walked toward them, letting the door close on its own behind her.

A sob heaved in her chest and bubbled up her throat. Why was she upset when logic told her what their relationship was and wasn't?

Then she heard a keycard being inserted outside the room. Someone was at the door.

She wiped away the stray tear that had fallen, and then swiped her palm on her pants.

Keep it together, Paige. You'll move on. You'll be fine.

She suddenly felt faint. She took a deep breath, closing her eyes briefly to gather the strength to get through this. Every romance ended. It was only a matter of when. At least that's how she used to think. With Sam, she had hoped to break the streak of failed relationships.

She turned around when the door opened, and Sam sauntered into the room, barely giving her a glance.

"I hadn't expected to see you," he said.

"This is our room."

"It's yours now." His voice was cold, unfeeling.

"I'm sorry I didn't take your calls. I was in the middle of things, and—"

His chilly gaze stalled her words. "No need to apologize."

"I should have answered when you—"

"It's fine." He stuffed something into the outside pocket of one of his bags.

"It's obviously not fine." She briefly covered her mouth, willing herself to stay strong. "You're leaving?"

He flung the strap of the bag over his shoulder. "I am."

"Were you even going to tell me, or were you just going to leave?" Hurt was quickly being replaced by anger.

"I was going to write you a note, actually, but seeing as you're here..."

"You were going to write me *a note*?" She raised her voice. "After what we had, you were—"

He set his bag back on the bed. "What did we have, Paige? I mean, exactly."

Her chest became heavy. She didn't know how to answer. She just knew they had enjoyed each other's company, and they seemed to think the same way about a lot of things. She didn't know what to tell him.

"See?" He gestured toward her. "You don't even know what the hell we had."

She picked up the smell of whiskey. "You're drunk."

"Yep, but it's not your problem."

"So you're leaving me? We're over?"

He stared into her eyes. "I'm not sure what's so hard to understand, Paige."

They stayed there, gazes locked. His eyes grew darker by the second.

"I've gotta go. My flight leaves at nine."

She couldn't believe this. "You're leaving because I couldn't answer your calls?"

"Couldn't or didn't?" he growled.

"If this is about that woman and what I said to—"

"It's not. I get that you lied to her now."

"What's this really about, then?" He had to know she'd used her call on Brandon, but she wasn't going to be the first to say it.

"I don't think this is a good idea." He took a step toward the door.

She stood in front of him to stop him. "You don't think it's a good idea to talk, but you're leaving me because I wouldn't talk?"

His jaw clenched, and his eyes seemed to look right through her. "Do you really want to know?"

"Ah, yeah." She ground her fists into her hips.

"I saw you hugging Brandon."

Her brow furrowed. "Even you said that he's a coworker."

"Let's just say it bothered me more than I originally let on. Do you normally close your eyes when you hug a *coworker*?"

She couldn't breathe, let alone talk.

"Nothing to say to that? I figured as much," he said. "I'm leaving because you still love Brandon."

She felt her lungs expand in the deepest breath she'd taken since she came into the room. "I love Brandon? I'm with you."

"Just because you're *with* me doesn't mean you don't *love* him. And I see the way he looks at you." His eyes flickered, glazing over, but then, just as quickly, they took on a hard edge. "And you're *with me*? I could have helped you out of this mess. Do you trust me so little that you had to call *him*? He was all the way across the country! I was right here."

Her heart was breaking. So he did know... "Did Brandon tell you?"

He scoffed. "I can figure some things out on my own." He shuffled past her, resuming his path to the door. She didn't say a word.

"Just as I thought." Sam said, and he left, the door closing behind him.

She wanted to cry out, to beg him to stay, to deny all that he'd said...but she couldn't.

CHAPTER THIRTY

Paige was taking her sweet time meeting us in Jack's room. Jack didn't want to get started on things until she joined us, and it had been at least forty-five minutes. A *long* forty-five minutes, if anyone asked me.

"Maybe one of us should call and—"

A knock on the door interrupted me.

I opened it to find Paige.

"Sorry I was so long," she said, entering the room.

"Uh-huh," Jack replied.

I had assumed that the lovers were going to kiss and make up, but with the energy coming from Paige, I had a feeling that things went the opposite direction. "Are you all right?"

"I'm fine." She came farther into the room and clapped her hands. "Let's get started, then."

Jack gestured toward her. "Seeing as we were waiting on you, you go ahead."

My attention was on her but not so much to glean what she was going to share about the investigation. I was trying to read between the lines. Something had her really upset. Her eyes were red and her cheeks were flushed. And it was from more than exhaustion. She had been crying.

I noticed how none of us asked where Sam was and Paige wasn't volunteering the information. All these factors were enough for me to conclude Sam was heading back to North Dakota. And if that was the case, she deserved someone better, a man who would actually stick around during the hard times.

"Assuming that the same person killed both men, and that Malone was the first, his mutilation was very violent," Paige said. "The killer was definitely motivated and driven. They could be getting revenge for being raped by Malone, but it's unlikely it was the same thing that triggered them to kill Ferris."

"Now, Clive Simpson—that's the owner of Wild Horse," I began. "He told us a woman was with Malone the night he was murdered. He described her as having long, dark, curly hair."

"A woman matching that description has come up at least three times now between the motel, the bar, and Malone's neighbor," Zach pointed out.

Jack nodded. "There are too many coincidences piling up here to be ignored."

"Here's something that's been sitting off with me," I said. "Malone was clearly into men, but Hall was into women. What about them attracted the same killer? Does it have something to do with the fact they were both rapists?"

"It's clear that sexual orientation isn't the basis for the unsub's targeting." Zach grabbed a soda from the mini bar and sat on the edge of the bed.

"We need to focus on the similarities in these two cases until we hear back from Nadia on the forensics. Besides this woman, what do we have?" Jack prompted his team.

"The Rohypnol," Paige said.

Next, Zach. "The mutilation of the genitalia."

Everyone turned to me.

"Both men were urinated on."

"All right. So this is a good start. We can also add that the men lived within a twenty-minute drive of each other and both went to Wild Horse," Jack summarized.

"We know that Malone had HIV, too. Maybe our unsub contracted it from him and retaliated," I suggested, revisiting a point that had been brought up before.

"It's still rather extreme to cut off a man's penis…" Paige let her words trail off.

"Really? I don't agree. HIV is basically a death sentence," I responded. "And if the unsub contracted it from Malone, it would make them very angry."

"I suppose," Paige conceded.

Zach cracked the tab on his soda can and took a drink. "We know the murders were planned and orchestrated. They must have been. The unsub brought the drugs, the duct tape, the cuffs."

And a full bladder...

"Let's revisit the fact that Malone was a homosexual and Ferris wasn't. It's unlikely that both men raped their killer, as I said earlier, so they aren't targeting those who have raped *them*, but rather those who rape *period*." Paige lifted her chin, obviously pleased with her conclusion.

Jack's phone rang. He glanced at the screen and swiped a finger to answer. "You're on speaker. Talk to us, Nadia."

"The forensics are back now. The DNA in the urine matched in the two cases, but it showed male in the urine left at Malone's scene and female at Hall's."

My reaction was instantaneous. "What? How is that even poss—"

"Our unsub is a hermaphrodite," Zach said simply. "Or the more politically correct term these days is to say they have an intersex condition." He went silent, staring at the can in his hands, brooding for a few seconds. "Basically, he was born with parts belonging to both sexes. Usually, when the child is young, parents make the decision—"

"They choose their child's gender," Paige interrupted, crossing her arms. "I know about it, not that I agree with it."

"I never said it was right, Paige." Zach met her gaze. "I'm just explaining what the situation is."

I took a few steps and stopped when the revelation struck. "This wasn't about personal revenge with Hall at all. The killer severed Hall's penis because they were speaking out about their own sexual frustration. What if the parents chose to make them male, but they resonated more with the female side?"

"That could have created a serious issue for them. They would have felt like an outcast. To top it off, the parents would also have had to put the child on testosterone injections," Paige said. "Of course, they could have hidden this from him as a youth, added it to drinks, for example. Then as they get older, they find out the reason they never fit in was because of the sex their parents had chosen for them. That's the recipe for a bad start in life."

"And we all know how formative our younger years are," Zach added.

I considered what was being said. Our unsub likely had a rough and confusing childhood. They probably spent a lot of time alone. Many killers were born from isolation. I paced a few steps. "So let me make sure I understand. Our unsub, who obviously identifies with the female side, assuming the long-haired woman is the killer—"

"They likely have a penis," Paige finished my sentence and continued on with the topic she'd started. "I can only imagine how lost they would feel, especially if the parents withheld the fact they were born intersex. They'd have gone through life wondering why they were different. If they found out—and I believe we can assume our unsub did—it would be devastating. They'd feel betrayed."

"It might have been enough to prompt him or her to kill." I wasn't even sure what gender to use when referring to our unsub. "That's without being raped or contracting HIV."

"We'll consider our killer female from now on," Jack said, seemingly reading my mind. "Nadia, what else do you have?"

"In Malone's case, HIV wasn't present in the urine, but in Hall's it was," Nadia answered.

"It can take up to three months for HIV to show in blood tests," Zach began, "but it can show in as little as two weeks. Seeing as there were six years between the murders... Well, that's plenty of time."

"Obviously she was already ill when she exacted revenge on Malone," I concluded based on the fact that epithelial cells were in the urine at his crime scene. "Was Hall drugged?"

"He wasn't," Nadia responded.

Hall might have been a rapist, but for some reason I felt a little empathy for him right then.

"Hall wasn't HIV-positive," Nadia continued, "and nothing useful came back from his car."

"Have you found any similar cases?" Jack asked.

"Nothing. And that's taking the DNA and running it through all the databases. However, the chemical makeup of the Rohypnol at Malone's crime scene is a match to the pill left at Hall's."

"She held onto those for a long time," Paige muttered.

Thoughts were swirling in my mind, coming close but swooping out of my grasp. When we'd spoken to Bart Kelman from Synergies, he had said that Malone had moved to California from Minnesota when he was twenty-one. Why did he come all the way out here? It couldn't have been to work at a call center.

"Nadia, how are you making out on those calls to Synergies?" I asked.

"The warrant was issued and I have the list, but I haven't had a chance to get to them yet."

"All right, I'm just wondering why Malone came to California in the first place. If there is a caller who had been trying to track him down, why was that the case? Was Malone in California just because his parents didn't approve of his lifestyle, or did he just need a change, or was he running away or hiding from someone?"

"Are you thinking that maybe he raped someone and fled to California?" Paige asked.

I nodded. That was exactly what I was thinking, but I still wasn't sure how Hall fit in.

"Once I get to look at what I received from Synergies, I'll pull callers' backgrounds and see if any of them tie back to Duluth, Minnesota," Nadia said.

"It could be a shot in the dark," Jack opined.

I figured it best not to point out that his suspicion that Hall was the victim of someone who had killed before was initially more of a gut feeling. But if Jack's intuition turned out to be right, it might prove that shots in the dark do sometimes pay off.

"Jack, do you want me to conduct the search?" Nadia asked.

Jack spoke with his eyes on me. "Before you do that, how are you making out with tracking down the recipient of the money transfer from Hall's account?"

"That's still in progress. I'll let you know once I have anything to share."

"The *second* you have anything, Nadia."

"Of course, Jack. So do you want me to dig into the backgrounds of the callers to Synergies?"

He nodded, even though she couldn't see it. "Go ahead."

With that, Jack ended the call, his gaze landing on me. In fact, Zach's and Paige's eyes were on me, as well.

Maybe I was getting ahead of myself asking Nadia to look into the callers. There was more there, though, if I could just— My jaw dropped slightly. "That's it!" I took my eyes from Jack, looked to Paige, then turned to Zach. "None of you picked up on it?"

Paige angled her head. "Brandon, it's one thing to have an idea, it's another to rub it—"

"We tossed around the idea that the unsub was getting even for being given HIV," I said. "We even mentioned rape being a possibility."

"Yeah…?" Paige dragged out the single word.

"Well, Nadia just confirmed that Malone's killer didn't show as HIV-positive. Even though she obviously wasn't well if she left epithelial cells in her urine," I added.

"Speed this up, kid." Jack was tapping his breast pocket— craving a cigarette no doubt.

"Okay, so if forensics didn't see the disease, how would our unsub have known she had it? So she couldn't have been getting even for being infected."

"She was getting even for being raped," Paige said.

"And if that was the case and Malone's murder was for personal retribution, we have to figure out how it was personal with Hall."

CHAPTER THIRTY-ONE

Paige stared at the ceiling as she stretched her hand along to the mattress beside her. There was an ache in her heart when her hand met with nothing. The emptiness made it hard to breathe as tears slid down her cheeks.

She was alone. Again.

Hours before, she had excused herself when the team had headed for dinner. Even now, she wasn't hungry. She'd chosen, instead, to wallow in her loneliness, condemning herself for even considering that a long-term relationship was possible for her. After all, she was in her forties and hadn't yet found the right person. Even though she had loved Brandon, he wasn't an option. It was pretty obvious that reciprocated love wasn't going to happen in her lifetime. But maybe that was okay. She'd built a career she was proud of.

And one she had damaged.

The thought crashed over her. Jack seemed to be handling all the recent events rather admirably, but he would be well within his rights to add a citation to her file. She had used government resources for personal reasons.

She rolled over, having lost count of how many times she'd switched sides since she'd lain down.

The clock on the nightstand read 11:30.

She kept hearing Sam say, *I see the way he looks at you.*

Brandon had no right to look at her in any other way than as a colleague. He had no claim to her. Was it his feelings for her that made him tell Sam that she'd used her one call on him? Sam had said he'd figured it out on his own, but she needed to know if he'd been nudged toward that conclusion.

She got up and threw on jeans and a T-shirt. She scooped her tousled hair back into a ponytail—something she rarely did, but her curls were out of control. She put on a light coat of foundation, smeared on lipstick, and left her room.

Brandon was staying in room 510. She took the elevator up the two floors, all the while trying to talk herself out of doing this, but she had to know.

In front of his door, she held her hand braced to knock, but common sense finally made its case. She turned to leave, but Brandon was coming toward her wearing a pair of workout shorts and a T-shirt, a towel hanging over a shoulder. He must have been returning from the hotel's gym.

His brow furrowed as he approached. "Paige? What are you doing here? Are you all right?"

She wanted to say yes, she'd even settle for nodding, but she couldn't bring herself to do either. Instead, she shook her head and said, "No. Can we talk?"

There seemed to be confusion in his eyes almost immediately, maybe even a little panic.

"It's about Sam," she added quickly. She didn't want Brandon to think this was about him or their former relationship. She wasn't here to get back together with him, but she needed some clarification. What exactly had he said to Sam? Had he even said anything?

Brandon's gaze traced her face. After what seemed like minutes of silence, he pointed toward his room. "Do you mind waiting while I take a quick shower?"

"Yeah, sure." Just his brief mention of a shower had the past washing over her, the times when they had taken showers together, when their two bodies had become one. There was no way she could wait in his room. She didn't trust herself that much.

"I'll meet you in the lobby?" Her voice was small, and she swore it cracked. If Brandon gave her any encouragement at all, she'd join him. Her weakness was despicable, but all she could think about was the temporary surrender to the familiar and easing her broken heart. She had to accept that what she had with Sam—whatever it had been—was over. The hurt and fire in Sam's eyes, the rage... He wasn't coming back. And a part of her couldn't blame him, especially given the flood of emotion she was starting to feel in this moment. How easily she would slip back into Brandon's bed...or shower.

He inserted his keycard into the door and turned to her. "I'll be down in ten minutes."

It took all my power not to ask Paige to join me in the shower. No matter how much I wished the memories away, they'd come at the most inconvenient times. It was just the pain in her eyes, the heartbreak screaming off her that made me want to pull her into my arms and soothe her hurt. But I was the least qualified, and I knew it. I had been responsible for so much of her pain already. I had no right to toy with her emotions. There shouldn't even be a draw or a pull to act on anything.

Paige and I had gone over it many times. For one, I wasn't ready for a committed relationship. Even with Becky it was casual, a coupling built on convenience, not love. I hadn't even thought about her since I got to California. And secondly, if either Paige or I wanted to stay on the BAU team, we had to forfeit any feelings we had for each other.

Yes, whatever I felt for Paige, I had to refuse acting on it. I'd continue to bury them in denial, between the legs of another woman—whatever it took. Otherwise, the disservice to both myself and Paige would be monumental.

I tossed my dirty clothes aside and got into the shower. Alone. But in my mind, I still wished that Paige were with me.

CHAPTER THIRTY-TWO

Paige sat in the lobby, watching the few people who were coming and going at this time of night. Her mind was churning with thoughts of two men now. Really, how could speaking to Brandon about another man she cared about have any kind of positive outcome? To make matters worse, Sam had seen what she had failed to: she was still in love with Brandon, even if on some buried level. And she sensed Brandon felt the same way…

If only feelings could be willed away and dismissed as if they didn't exist. She had managed to compartmentalize her heart and her body with other men, but for some reason it was different with Brandon.

She closed her eyes and took a deep breath. When she opened them, she realized the bar was still open, but despite her inclination to bury herself in a drink, she'd resist. It would weaken her defenses. And giving into what was familiar wasn't the answer. Again, that was making the assumption that Brandon would even let her. Not to mention that it would go against the reason she was here, which was figuring out how to right things with Sam.

She thought back to Tuesday morning, before everything had fallen apart, before she had gone to Ferris's house. How she and Sam had made love. And no matter how much she wished to discount the act as less, there was no other label that could be assigned. It was more than simply sex with him. She and Sam had connected on a deeper level.

"Paige?"

She turned to see Brandon slip into the tub chair to her left and sink into it. In his eyes, she saw hope, but she was probably imagining it there because she wished it to be so. She hated herself for the thought. Would she ever fully move on?

"Sam left," she said softly.

"I think I figured that out. I'm sorry."

She met his eyes. "Are you?"

Irritation licked his eyes briefly.

"I'm sorry," she said. "I shouldn't have said that… Listen, I need to ask you a question."

He nodded. "Shoot."

With the way he sat there, so nonchalant, she may have only seen what she'd wanted to see earlier. He wasn't thinking about getting back together. He was keeping his distance.

"I probably shouldn't have bothered you, and I wouldn't have unless—"

"Go ahead. It's all right." He leaned forward, putting his elbows on his knees.

"I care about him, Brandon." She watched that sink into his eyes, and eventually, he nodded.

"I figured that, too."

"I've never been good at love. God, look at me. I'm forty-three. Single. An ex-con."

Brandon laughed. "Technically, you'd have to be sentenced and spend time in prison to be an—"

She narrowed her eyes at him. "Close enough. But I was always happy being free and unattached. It's how I wanted things. Then there was you."

"We've been through—"

She held up a hand to stop him. "I know, Brandon. What I was going to say is that starting with you, I began thinking about having more than just causal relationships."

"And Sam was going to be the guy?"

Was there a tremble in his voice, or am I imagining that, too?

She locked eyes with him. "He was."

"Why did he leave?"

A few seconds of silence passed between them. Should she come out with what Sam had accused Brandon and her of, or stick to the phone call?

In the public space of the lobby, she felt confident in her ability to talk about all of it.

She took a deep breath and licked her lips. "Sam said that you're still in love with me."

Brandon remained quiet and sat back in the chair again.

"I know that's crazy," she continued. "I mean, you never loved me in the first place." The latter statement had him breaking eye contact and shifting in his chair. "And we can never be more than friends."

"No, we can't."

Why did that fact still hurt after hearing it and saying it so many times?

"Listen, I know you've moved on. And I have tried." She stopped, panicked by her last words. She needed to rein them back in. "With Sam, I mean. I tried to move on *with him*. And you and me, well, we've exhausted this conversation so many times there's nothing left to say. I want to discuss Sam."

"Okay," Brandon said, dragging out the word.

"Did you tell him that you loved me?" The question was out without thought, and it wasn't even the one she had intended to ask.

Brandon shook his head. "He told me I did."

"Oh? So *he* just keeps saying you do..." She stopped talking and pondered this. Brandon was one of the more confusing men she'd been involved with. Maybe it was the enigma, the mystery about him, that made her want to investigate him, get the answers, and solve the man. "What happened between you and Sam? Please, Brandon, be honest with me. I know something happened for him to leave." She couldn't add *me*. Simply saying as much as she had was stabbing her in the heart enough.

"He accused me of still loving you." His eyes met hers again.

"And what did you say?"

"I didn't say anything, Paige."

She briefly closed her eyes. "Was anything else said?"

Brandon went quiet, and there seemed to be a wall building up around him.

"Brandon? What happened? Did you tell him that I used my one call on you?"

He sighed. "It might have come up."

"*It might have come up?*" She raised her voice. "Why? Why would you do that?"

The fire was back in Brandon's eyes. "You're implying that I did it on purpose to cause trouble between the two of you."

"Did you?"

Brandon's gaze softened, peering into hers. "Why did you use that phone call on me anyway?"

She'd thought she had known why—the motivation was clear, the logic sound. At the time. But being faced with the direct question from Brandon left her speechless.

"Tell me," he prompted.

"I called you because I trusted you. There was nothing more to it."

"So you don't trust Sam? Because if you don't, I'm having a hard time understanding why you'd want to be with him."

"You're talking to me about trust? You cheated on your wife."

"With *you*. And only you. What does this have to—"

"I don't want to stir it all up again."

"Then why did you?"

Suddenly, she felt so exposed. "You know me better than anyone. I knew you'd believe I was innocent."

"And you didn't think Sam would?" He shook his head. "Wow, what a winner, Paige." He widened his eyes and mouthed *winner*.

"Stop it, Brandon."

"Listen, you wanted to talk, we talked." Brandon stood. "Now I'm calling it a night."

"Brandon, don't—"

"Good night, Paige."

With that, he was gone, his back to her, his long strides eating up more and more of the lobby as he walked toward the elevators.

Despite not wanting to dredge through their past, it had been exactly what they'd done. Their history had churned up anyhow, like seaweed in a stormy sea. That was a good analogy for what things were like between her and Brandon. Stormy. Choppy. She should have known that simply being friends wouldn't work. Too many feelings had been laid bare, raw from exposure and lack of reciprocation, poor timing, and even poorer discretion. But what stuck with Paige with even more strength as she watched Brandon get onto the elevator was something else: *did* she trust Sam?

CHAPTER THIRTY-THREE

I didn't sleep well at all, but it was kind of hard to after the conversation—*confrontation?*—I'd had with Paige. I was struggling enough with why she had contacted me instead of Sam without her bringing up the subject. But we had a job to do, and I was going to see it through.

I focused on last night's group discussion. It had led to the conclusion that the killer's motivation started with a rough childhood full of sexual confusion, only amplified by rape and a sexually transmitted disease.

I was about to head down to the lobby when there was a knock on my door. I opened it to find Jack and glanced to the clock.

5:30.

I was really ahead of schedule today. We weren't supposed to meet in the lobby until six thirty. So why was he here?

He eyed my outfit and met my gaze, seemingly surprised to find me already dressed for the day. "There's been another murder."

Another murder? Just the way he'd said it, this wasn't a case Nadia had found in a search. This was a fresh homicide.

"Well, don't just stand there," he said. "The victim is Clive Simpson."

"Simpson?" I hadn't seen that coming. Was the unsub feeling threatened by us? Simpson's murder could be confirmation that we were getting too close for her comfort.

I stepped into the hall and closed my door. "How did you find—"

"Detective Grafton called me about thirty minutes ago."

"Why did he call you?"

Jack made eye contact with me. "He knew we were talking to Simpson yesterday."

"How did he— He was following us?"

"He was, but he's aware of the DNA match between Hall's and Malone's cases now," Jack said.

"Then he knows Paige didn't kill Hall," I stated the obvious as we loaded onto the elevator.

"The crime scene is still being processed," Jack went on. "Simpson's body hasn't even been removed yet."

"Where was he found?" I asked.

"His house."

Like Malone.

I swallowed a mouthful of pasty saliva. "Was his—"

"Yep."

I was going to be sick. It was one thing seeing the photographs, but it would be another to witness the mutilation literally in the flesh. I'd have to pare it down to a black-and-white focus on the facts. "Who found him? The sun's just come up."

"It was called in at about four thirty this morning, and—"

The car dinged its arrival to the lobby.

Paige and Zach were facing the elevators and standing only about ten feet back from the doors. Paige's gaze darted around, looking at everything but me.

"Let's go." Jack pointed toward the hotel exit and headed toward it. We stepped in line with him.

As we walked, I realized I still didn't know who found Simpson. I'd have to ask again on the way there. I also didn't want to point out what Jack had likely already realized: Grafton waited a half hour before calling in Simpson's murder to Jack.

Jack had us take both rental cars because, as he had said, "Who knows where this day is going?"

That statement could pretty much sum up my existence since I'd joined the FBI.

Simpson's house wasn't far from his bar, but it was still a drive. It was likely our unsub had transportation of her own to be able to follow him to his house. Of course, it was possible she'd looked up Simpson's address and took public transit there.

Jack had filled me in on the details of the murder as he drove. Clive Simpson was found by his girlfriend, a woman in her late forties. According to her, it wasn't unusual for her to show up in the wee hours for a booty call before her shift at Walmart. Apparently age had no bearing on the use of that terminology, which I thought better suited twentysomethings.

Police cruisers cordoned off the street, and people were turned away if they tried to enter unless they were residents. Jack and I were cleared to continue by a young officer who looked like he was barely old enough to shave. Crime scene tape had been tied to stakes along the front of the property and was fanning in a breeze. A forensics van was parked at the curb, along with one for the coroner.

We showed our credentials to an officer stationed at the edge of Simpson's property, and he permitted us access. We had just stepped past the tape when Grafton opened the front door.

"I've got people over at the bar, too, so we'll see if that can provide any leads," Grafton said, getting right down to business.

"This case is the FBI's," Jack stated.

"Uh, yeah, I know, but—"

"That means we're in charge."

Grafton's cheeks went red, and he nodded. "Just tryin' to help."

Paige and Zach pulled up then and parked behind our rental.

Grafton's gaze slid behind me, and I assumed he was looking at Paige. There even seemed to be something apologetic in his eyes.

"What are your initial thoughts?" I asked Grafton, trying to take his focus off Paige.

"Where is he?" Jack demanded, sidestepping my question. He took the lead through the front door.

"His bedroom. It's up the stairs and to the right." Grafton followed directly behind Jack; Zach, Paige, and I took up the rear.

What we gathered about our unsub so far was that she contemplated her actions before carrying them out. As a result, I'd wager that our unsub was already in the house when Simpson got home.

"Were there signs of a break in?" I asked Grafton.

He nodded. "The back door. But whoever did this knew what they were doing. There was only a faint indication—a little paint scraped from the doorframe and small scratches on the brass lock."

"Make sure to swab for trace. Have you talked to the neighbors yet?"

Why am I the only one asking questions?

"Officers are canvassing now. Simpson's closest neighbors were asleep at the time and don't recall hearing anything suspicious."

I would ask if Simpson had been drugged, but it was too soon to tell. Besides, if the killer had adhered to her regular MO, Simpson would have been conscious when she'd attacked him. "Is the back entrance secluded?"

"Yeah. Simpson has a six-foot privacy fence around the backyard."

I nodded, stepping onto the upstairs landing. The smell of death washed over me now. Simpson hadn't had much time to decompose, but he would've lost control of his bowels when he died. In addition to the stench of shit was the metallic smell of blood. I mentally prepared myself as I stepped through the doorway into Simpson's bedroom.

The coroner—a gray-haired man with round glasses—was working over the body and paused to acknowledge Jack with a bob of his head. The investigators around him were snapping shots of the scene. But my attention wasn't really on them. It was on Simpson.

He was naked on the bed. Excrement stained the sheets. Blood was everywhere. Like Malone and Hall, his genitals were mutilated and his penis severed. A pill sat on his abdomen alongside the word GUILTY, which had been written in blood. Also unlike the previous two cases, Simpson's femoral artery was slit.

Bile hurtled up my throat. It took all my willpower not to expel it. The smell was overwhelming, but there was no way I could leave. Paige and Zach were behind me and Jack was right there, too. It was bad enough that I had vomited at a crime scene in the past. The last thing I needed was to be responsible for contaminating this crime scene.

I briefly closed my eyes before taking in Simpson. Again, a wave of nausea swept over me.

"Was Simpson urinated on?" Jack asked Grafton.

"No."

Jack tapped the pocket that held his cigarettes. "Did you look at Simpson's background?"

"Yeah, no record."

I swallowed and tried to center myself.

Focus on the facts...

I turned away from the body. "We should speak to the girlfriend and see what she has to say about Simpson. Malone didn't have any assaults on his record, either, but apparently that didn't mean anything."

Zach nodded. "Our unsub knows more about her victims' lives than any database."

"We were able to talk to the girlfriend a bit before she was hauled off in an ambulance." Grafton paused, looking around at us. "When we first arrived on scene, she was passed out in the hallway. It turns out she can't stand the sight of blood," he explained. "She swears Simpson was an upstanding guy and said she can't think of any reason why someone would do this. As for Simpson's records, all I really got was that he owned and operated Wild Horse for the past six years. There wasn't even a mark on the company's records. He operates in the black, and his personal credit is clean."

"Time of death?" Jack asked.

The coroner, who hadn't really paid us much attention so far, turned to us now. "Based on liver temp, I'm placing death between two and four this morning."

"So he wasn't dead long before his girlfriend found him," I said, stating the obvious. "He would have just closed up the bar and come home. The unsub likely was already inside the house waiting for him."

Grafton turned toward the four of us, gesturing us to the hallway. "What are you guys thinking?"

"You're aware that Hall and Malone were connected," Jack said. "But you might not know that it's Simpson who connects them."

CHAPTER THIRTY-FOUR

Grafton angled his head at what Jack had said about Simpson connecting Malone and Hall. "How's that?" he asked.

Jack told him both Malone and Hall were customers of Simpson's and that he saw a woman with long, dark, curly hair around both men. I was surprised by how much Jack was sharing, as he usually withheld more.

"So you're thinking it was a woman?" Grafton slipped a glance to Paige. "But that doesn't fit with—"

"The unsub we're looking for has an intersex condition," Zach explained. "Physically, this person is both male and female but identifies more with the female gender. She has the full-developed parts of a man, but inside, she feels like a woman. So for all intents and purposes, our unsub is female."

Grafton's mouth was slightly agape.

"We think that she was raped," Zach said.

"You believe that Malone was his...er, *her* first murder?" Grafton asked while facing Zach.

"It seems likely."

Grafton's phone rang, and he stepped down the hall to take the call.

"Assuming this is the same killer—" Zach began.

"Assuming?" I interrupted. "It seems quite clear."

The team turned to me, and I had to explain myself. While there were clear differences, it had to be the same killer. "Well, it seems obvious, doesn't it? The mutilation of his genitalia, the pill on the abdomen, the severed penis. Then there's the woman who keeps popping up. It's possible our unsub knew that we spoke to Simpson." I turned to Jack. "I didn't see anyone following us, though, and the bar was empty when we were there."

Yet, we didn't see Grafton, either…

"Simpson was on her hit list regardless of our involvement," Jack said.

"There wasn't much time between the body being found and the time of death. I believe she sliced his artery to speed up his bleeding," Zach theorized, leading us down another avenue to explore.

"So she was aware that Grafton's girlfriend would show up at four thirty." Paige rubbed her arms.

Grafton was still talking on the phone, standing down the hallway, his back to us.

"Why Simpson, though?" I asked. "We figure that Malone and Hall were rapists and targeted for that reason. Was Simpson one, as well? He did manage to keep a girlfriend…"

"It wouldn't be a first for a rapist to have a girlfriend or wife," Paige said coolly. "And obviously, he was guilty of something given what the killer put on his chest."

I had to give her that…

Jack patted his shirt pocket for the second time in the past ten minutes. He was definitely craving another cigarette.

Grafton cleared his throat as he slipped his cell phone into his pocket and approached us. "CSU found ledgers at the bar going back sixteen years."

I instantly remembered the notes Simpson had shown us the day before. He'd said they were to keep track of his memories after Malone's murder, but maybe it was more than that.

"What kind of ledgers?" Jack asked.

"It looks like Simpson extended tabs to several men."

"Only men?"

Grafton nodded.

Taking another stab in the dark, I said, "Let me guess. Ferris Hall was on that list."

"How did you—"

"And Kyle Malone?"

Grafton appeared dumbfounded. "Uh, yeah."

Was it a coincidence that two people from that list and the person who had managed it had been murdered? I didn't think so. As an agent, I wasn't taught to believe in or accept coincidences. I sensed the rest of the team was thinking the same thing as we shared glances. The eye contact with Paige was brief but communicative regardless. Assuming our unsub was aware of the ledger's existence, we both knew it was a hit list.

"Have your people scan and send the ledgers to Nadia Webber." Jack pulled a card from his pocket and extended it to Grafton. "All her information is there."

"All right." Grafton sounded disappointed to have lost this case to us.

"We'll also need to find out where Simpson was before Wild Horse," Jack said, looking from me, to Zach, to Paige. "I'll have Nadia handle that. We have sufficient evidence to conclude the three murders are connected, and I have a feeling there will be more. It's possible there already are. I think our killer might know about that ledger and be using it as her hit list," Jack said.

Apparently, it wasn't just Paige and me thinking that way.

Grafton blanched. "And the motive?"

"All that seems absolutely certain is that the victims being chosen are guilty of or somehow connected to rape."

"As I said, though," the detective responded, "Simpson's record is spotless. Not even an accusation that he raped anyone."

"Simpson has the word *guilty* on his chest in blood. I'd guess he was involved somehow with the rapes that happened or rapes that were occurring," I said, expanding on my internal brainstorming.

Grafton nodded. "He extended credit for booze knowing what his patrons were doing with the drinks."

"That's a large assumption." I turned to Jack. "Simpson didn't mention anything questionable about Malone or Hall when we spoke with him." The revelation hit me like a smack to the side of the head. "But then again, why would he if he were somehow involved with what they were doing?"

"What are you thinking, Brandon?" Zach asked.

"Our killer labeled Simpson guilty, and we have this ledger. I don't believe it was just for supplying alcohol. All bartenders do that. What if Simpson supplied the date-rape drugs?"

Paige nodded. "So Simpson would spike the drinks…"

"And the women wouldn't have had a clue," I finished.

"Except one obviously did," Paige ground out.

"We need to search Simpson's bar and house top to bottom for drugs," Jack said to Grafton, who picked up his phone and called his people at the bar again.

"Now what about the money that was transferred? We know funds were taken from Hall but we need to see Simpson's computer." Zach set out down the corridor, and we followed him to a second bedroom that had a desk and a laptop.

Zach took a seat behind the computer and quickly accessed it. There was no password to log on to the laptop itself, and Zach got to work, repeating the same process he'd used on Hall's computer.

"Simpson had a SecureIt account, too." Zach proceeded to enter the password information from SecureIt, and in seconds, he had access to Simpson's banking.

A look at the account history showed a transfer *today* for three thousand dollars.

"Just like with Hall," Zach said.

Grafton entered the room. "What was like Hall?"

"Another money transfer." Jack pointed to the transaction on the screen, and Grafton followed the direction of Jack's finger.

"Then we hunt them down, right? We find their name and address just like with Hall. Speaking of, did that lead anywhere?"

"It's in progress," Jack said, pulling out his cell phone. A few seconds later, he spoke into his phone. "How are you making out with tracking the money transfer from Hall's bank?" Jack's eyes skimmed over the four of us as he listened to Nadia's response. Then he directed her to look at the transfer from Simpson's account and check out his employment history.

About a minute later, he hung up. "A few things," Jack began, looking at his team. "Nadia confirmed that no money was stolen from Malone's bank accounts, and she had an update regarding the funds transferred from Hall's account. She has the receiving bank's information, as well as the account holder's name and address. Name is Leslie Shaw. Both her and Golden State Bank and Trust are in Los Angeles."

Grafton led the way out of the room. "Then let's go."

CHAPTER THIRTY-FIVE

A background on the name Leslie Shaw was unsuccessful, but it figured that our unsub would choose a unisex name.

The address on file with Golden State Bank and Trust was about an hour and a half from Simpson's house and outside of Grafton's jurisdiction. Jack and I were on the way there now with Grafton following behind us. I was surprised Jack let him tag along, even if the man was in his own car. This case belonged to the FBI, but Grafton was determined to help. Maybe he was feeling bad about what he had put Paige through, or it could have been as simple as just wanting to find the killer.

We left Zach and Paige at Simpson's to analyze his computer, see if they could get anything else. They'd also be on hand if anything turned up that needed a quick response back in Canyon Country.

I couldn't help thinking, though, that the targets our unsub chose might not have anything to do with Simpson's ledger. It could just be a fluke or even meant to throw us off. And really, until we had more to go on, I couldn't see Jack sending officers or agents from the local field office to check on each of the men on the list. Not to mention, with it dating back so many years, there would be far too many people to track down.

Jack pulled the car to the curb in front of a vacant patch of land surrounded by a chain-link fence.

"This is it?" I asked.

We should have checked the address on our phones first, looked at the location from Google Street View. But we had been so happy to have a lead that we'd run with it. Of course, I wasn't going to mention any of this out loud. The oversight would become my fault if I did, or at least that's where the blame would land.

Jack lowered his window and lit up a cigarette.

Grafton parked behind us, got out, and walked over to Jack's side of the car.

"Dead end here," Grafton said. He coughed, likely due to a plume of smoke from Jack's cigarette hitting him in the face. "But I got a call on the way here. My people found a stash of date-rape drugs at Simpson's bar. What do you suggest we do now?"

Jack had yet to say a word since he'd parked. He kept up a stream of exhaled smoke, however.

Grafton leaned down to look across at me in the passenger seat. I wasn't going to say anything.

One more drag on the cig and an exhale, then Jack spoke. "We go to the branch and see if they have footage of our unsub from the day and time the account was opened. They'll also have a record of the name of the teller who opened the account, so we'll know what wicket to watch." Another calm puff on his cigarette. Jack didn't seem fazed in the least that we'd driven an hour and a half and, as of yet, had nothing to show for our trouble. That wasn't like Jack. He must have planned to hit the bank in the first place.

"All right, and while you're doing that?" Grafton prompted Jack for direction.

"You just make sure a copy of those ledgers gets to Nadia Webber."

"That was the other part of the message. The list has already been sent to your girl."

Jack pressed his lips together. "Hmm."

I'd worked by Jack's side for the better part of two years, and I sensed impatience in his hum. He was probably wondering why we hadn't heard from Nadia yet.

"There have to be a lot of names in that ledger," I said, offering justification to any seeming delay Jack may have seen on Nadia's part.

Grafton looked from me to Jack. "What's the deal with the ledgers we found anyway? You mentioned they could be a hit list for the killer. How? We found them at the bar intact."

Jack raised his brows. "She could have taken a picture of the list with her phone."

A flush touched the detective's cheeks.

"If she did that she likely wouldn't have gotten all sixteen years that were recorded, as that would have taken far too long. And we don't even know that she had access to the ledgers," I said, my doubts rising to the surface. "She might just be aware of who Simpson serviced from watching him over the years."

"Nope." Jack shook his head. "If that were the case, Simpson would have mentioned she was there often."

One step forward, two steps back.

CHAPTER THIRTY-SIX

Paige stood behind zach while he remained in front of Simpson's computer. The coroner had taken off with Simpson's body, leaving behind a slew of investigators working over the house in microscopic intensity.

Zach had found an account with an online payment system called Money Buddy that made it possible to keep money in a virtual wallet, but the funds there remained untouched.

"Why transfer three thousand from a bank account and none from this account?" Paige asked.

Zach closed out the browser window he was working in and turned to face her. "Money Buddy offers secure money transfer and management. They make it easier to trace and reverse disputed transactions."

"All right, makes sense why she left it alone, then." All Hall's and Simpson's credit cards were left behind along with their identification, too. The killer clearly didn't want it to look like robbery. But with the amount of money that had left the men's accounts—eight thousand total—it was factoring in as at least a side benefit. "Was the killer selectively targeting only those she knew had some money, as well? But why not take the same amount from each?"

"I don't think the amount mattered. She took what she could from both men. But I don't think it would be a bad idea for Nadia to filter out people who have some savings once she gets the list from Grafton's investigators," Zach said.

Paige nodded. "Or at least those who have reliable jobs." Paige shared their insights with Nadia and hung up. "Nadia's got the list and is already working on it." Paige paused. "I was just thinking, though… In Malone's case, money wasn't stolen. So why start now? Was it just to help with HIV meds?"

"Hard to say." Zach faced the laptop again, and as her gaze followed his movement, her eyes went to the screen. The wastebasket icon showed paper inside.

She pointed to it. "Look."

Zach double-clicked the icon and opened it to review the contents. The filename was "Cheers."

"Open it, Zach." She knew she didn't need to tell him the next step but verbalized the directive anyhow.

A spreadsheet opened with each tab labeled by year. On each sheet was a list of names, dates, and amounts owed and settled.

"I guess we just confirmed that our unsub knows about Simpson's list. She even tried to get rid of the evidence."

"I'll call Jack."

Jack had just hung up from talking to Paige when his phone rang again. He answered it on speaker. "Harper, here."

"It's Nadia. I looked into Clive, and he worked for a company called CL Corporation, but I'm having a hard time finding out more. I'm going to requisition his previous IRS filings and get an address for the company from his W-2. As for the ledger, Paige recommended that I search for people who had secure jobs or were well-off. I did that first and narrowed things down to those who had criminal records or complaints on file."

"I want you to see if either Hall or Malone are in the ledger sixteen years ago," Jack began. "I also want to know if any other names from back then show up in the last year."

"On it."

"Conduct thorough backgrounds on them, too."

I wanted to ask how she was making out with the Synergies callers, but it wasn't the appropriate time. Jack was on a roll here.

"We also need warrants for Leslie Shaw's bank that covers account particulars and camera footage. Send them through to my phone the minute they arrive. And find out the history on the address that Leslie Shaw provided to the bank." Jack hung up and dialed someone else without saying a word to me. Obviously something had struck him while on the phone with Nadia.

This time the phone wasn't on speaker. "Paige? I need you to do something for me. Was my business card there among Simpson's things?" There was a pregnant pause, followed by Jack clenching his jaw. "I need you to check his garbage cans."

More time passed. He flicked his cigarette butt out the window, barely missing Grafton. A few seconds later, "Son of a bitch."

Jack hung up and looked at Grafton. "Have your people look for my business card at the bar. I need to know right away if it's there or not." The detective stepped back from the car and made the phone call.

Grafton hung up from his conversation and put his smartphone back in his shirt pocket and hunched over, his elbows propped on the driver's-side window ledge. "No sign of your card. Simpson could have gotten rid of it somewhere else, though. It doesn't mean—"

"She knows we're in town," Jack interrupted.

"Do you think you're in danger?" Grafton asked.

"I'm not sure." Jack paused, turned to Grafton, and immediately drew his head back. Obviously Grafton was too far inside the vehicle. Grafton stood up straight, my line of sight now directly at crotch level. I faced forward.

"Go back to Canyon Country," Jack directed Grafton.

"But the bank? It's here in town."

"We've got it under control. I need you back by the crime scene and the bar. I need you on call if Agents Dawson and Miles require backup."

"All right." Grafton skulked off toward his department-issued sedan and pulled away.

He was gone, but my mind was stuck on the fact that our unsub likely knew about us. Whenever killers caught a whiff of the FBI, things got worse before they got better. I tried to think positively, though.

"Okay, now that she knows we're involved, shouldn't she be trying harder to cover her tracks?" I asked.

"Either that or she'll lure us in. It might become more of a game to her."

"Do you think our lives are in danger?"

Jack stared me straight in the eye. "We took that risk the second we donned a badge."

CHAPTER THIRTY-SEVEN

This particular branch of Golden State Bank and Trust was large and located on the corner of a bustling intersection. Jack and I entered the bank and went straight to the manager's office. The blinds were closed in the window next to his door but there was an etching in the glass: Artem Kozak, Manager. The door was shut, but that didn't stop Jack from knocking and then entering right afterward.

The man behind the desk shot to his feet and gestured to a couple sitting across from him. "Excuse me, but I am with clients." His voice got louder with each word, and he was coming toward us.

Jack held up his cred pack. I followed suit.

"FBI Special Agents Jack Harper and Brandon Fisher. We have a few questions for you."

I glanced at his customers. I'd guess they were a married couple, even though I couldn't see their wedding bands. They held hands, dressed similarly, and had the same hair and eye color. Even their skin tones were a perfect match. Experts would say they were "meant to be." To me, though, too much of the same equaled boring and predictable.

The woman's mouth gaped open. The man wrapped his arm around her, and they both stood.

"We'll make another appointment, Artem," the man said.

"No, please, this shouldn't take long," Artem beseeched his customers while keeping eye contact with Jack.

"We're here about a serial murder investigation," Jack said, his voice hard.

The woman gasped, and the couple cleared the doorway and were quickly heading for the bank's exit.

Artem watched after the couple and then turned to Jack. "You better have a really good reason for what you just did."

Jack held out his phone. "Ferris Hall." On the screen was his DMV picture.

"What about him?" the manager asked. "I've never seen him in my life."

"He was murdered."

"Well, I didn't do it."

"We never said you did. Money was sent from an account he held to one at your branch."

"Any help you can provide us would be appreciated, Mr. Kozak," I pitched in, taming Jack's abrupt approach.

"We need to know about the account holder."

Artem sighed and looked at me and Jack. A few seconds later, he consented with a bowed head and gestured for us to take a seat.

I sat, but Jack remained standing. Artem shut his door again—this time he locked it—and walked behind his desk. "If you want account-holder information, I assume you have a warrant."

"It will be coming through soon," Jack said.

"I'm sorry, but I can't help you until that happens."

Jack's phone chimed that he had a message. He consulted the screen. "It looks like I spoke too soon." He flashed his screen at Artem. "It's here." He handed his phone to me, and I referred to one of the business cards in a holder on the manager's desk and forwarded the warrant to his e-mail. No one spoke.

I gave Jack his phone back and said to Artem, "You should have an electronic copy of the warrant in your inbox now."

Artem made no effort to confirm that he did and crossed his arms. "What do you want, exactly?"

Jack gave him the account number, and Artem scribbled it on a pad of paper.

"I want you to confirm the name of the account holder and his or her address," Jack said.

"Also the date it was opened," I added.

"Fine, then." Artem stared blankly at Jack and me before pulling out his keyboard tray. He angled the monitor so we could see what he was typing and the results. Artem still read them off to us. "The account was opened a month ago by a Leslie Shaw." Artem paused and looked at us as if he was assessing our reactions.

He didn't get any and continued to provide us the same address Nadia had given us.

"Do you take ID to open accounts?" I asked, figuring it was standard protocol.

"ID would have been checked, yes."

"Well the address on that account isn't a legitimate one. We've already been there, and it's an empty lot."

Artem blanched. "Well, I don't know what to say. We don't drive out to verify customers' addresses." The last statement was said in defense, not apology.

"We'll need access to your camera feed for the date and time the account was opened," Jack said.

"Why do you need the camera feed?"

"We want to *see* Leslie Shaw."

"Don't you have a database for something like that?"

Artem's question grew stagnant until he obviously realized the stupidity of the question. A fake address was provided, and it was likely the same for the name.

"She killed someone..." Artem stated this dryly, and incredulously, as if the purpose for our being here was just starting to sink in for him.

"The investigation is open at this time and we cannot comment," I said.

Artem swallowed visibly and nodded.

"The camera feed," Jack prompted. "And a copy of the ID if you have it."

"Yes, certainly." Artem got up and tugged down on his jacket. He didn't quite reach the door when he spun around. "Actually..." He walked back behind his desk and checked something on the computer. "This isn't regarding the camera feed, but the teller who opened this account is very thorough. A lot of times she'll even photocopy a customer's ID. One second." Artem left the room and returned a few minutes later.

The hope he had built up in his absence came crashing down the second I saw his face. Artem shook his head.

"No such luck this time," he began. "The teller was told that it was unnecessary to make a copy of the ID and stopped doing so a few months back."

"Who told her it was unnecessary?" Jack asked.

Artem diverted his eyes. "I did."

"But you just assured us you always take ID," I said.

"I said it would have been checked, not copied," Artem defended himself.

"The camera feed?" Jack pressed again.

"Ah, yes. Here's the thing with the cameras: the feed goes live to a security company who monitors it."

"Let me guess, they are not on-site," Jack said.

Artem shook his head, still avoiding eye contact with us. "They are located about ten minutes from here."

"What else is there?" I asked.

"The account..." Artem's voice sounded dry and pasty. "The teller told me that she also closed the account just about an hour ago."

"Closed?" Jack rushed to his feet. "And you're just telling us this now? You didn't see it in your computer a moment ago?"

The manager shook his head. "The system updates overnight."

CHAPTER THIRTY-EIGHT

She watched them leave the bank. Risky. Stupid. Careless. Maybe a combination of all three, but she had to find out more about this Jack Harper. Up until she'd found out about his existence, last night had been going according to plan. It had even turned out to be financially advantageous. But what excited her the most was that she had made the big time.

She'd found the business card on Clive's dresser after she'd killed him: SUPERVISORY SPECIAL AGENT JACK HARPER.

Her work had the attention of the FBI, not just local law enforcement. *Federal.* She had to start covering her tracks even more carefully now, and that was why she'd gone to Los Angeles and been ready the second the bank had opened its doors. And she was still in the parking lot, back far enough that she shouldn't be spotted, but she could see the bank's entrance.

She knew she should have left, but she was drawn to wait and see if Harper had found the money transfer. And the gamble paid off. She watched them go into the bank. Whether it was Ferris's account or Clive's that had led them here, it didn't matter. Two men in suits, obviously armed and reeking of being federal agents, studied their surroundings on the way into the institution. Based on her sixth sense, the redhead seemed to have something to prove. She pegged Harper as the older of the two, and he appeared to be the type most would strive to impress. His ramrod-straight back indicated he was someone who lived and breathed the job.

She eased into the front seat of her car, a smile finding its way to her lips. She was worthy of *his* attention? Impressive. And she hadn't even tried to make him take notice. She had simply been following her urges, killing those who deserved it.

At least she had beat them here. She was still a step ahead. The cash was secured in her purse on the passenger seat, and she put her hand over the bag. On the way here, she had worried about what would happen if she had lost her nest egg. All that money, gone. Now she had the funds to feed the greedy pharmaceutical companies. At least a little while longer.

There was no way she was going to let the FBI interfere with her plans. Everyone needed to make a living, and at one time, she had tried doing so the conventional way. Not that everyone would consider her career choices conventional. She had wanted to be an actress and light up the screen. But it wasn't meant to be.

And she'd had such huge dreams. She had planned to be a movie star, a diva who would warrant a trailer and entourage as she traveled the world starring in box-office hits.

Then the diagnosis of the disease had come, and she'd learned that Hollywood wasn't as open-minded as they liked to claim to the masses. But she'd found one true way to bury her sorrow…

She wondered just how much the FBI knew and, with a satisfied smile, concluded they probably didn't know the half of it.

But there was something else she had netted from last night besides the money—the list from Clive's computer. She hadn't known what it was until she'd seen Ferris Hall's name, but then she'd quickly realized it was an accounting ledger. She had forwarded the list to herself, and as she had waited for the agents, she examined the e-mail attachment.

She keyed in *Kyle Malone*. And the document returned a finding that had her seeing blood red. Not that she had ever experienced remorse over her kills, but she had been in the right to kill Clive. Labeling him *guilty* as she had was an apt finish for a man responsible for so much pain, let alone his contribution to her own rape. After all these years, the experience from that night was still fresh in her mind. The loud music, the cramped quarters, the urinals, the grunting pig behind her…

She closed her eyes and took a few deep breaths. The only time she experienced any sort of peace was while torturing and killing those scumbags. Then her mind calmed and went quiet, soothed by the pain and discomfort of another. She needed to do it more often.

But she didn't consider herself an evil person, which was the way the world likely viewed her. That and a freak of nature, even in this "accepting" society where people were able to live as they saw fit, to do whatever it was that made them happy. *Live your bliss* was a statement preached by those too afraid to follow their own. It was something most hid behind, a shield to protect themselves from judgment. But she was no longer going to hide, not in a proverbial closet, nor was she going to hold back from what made her happy…even if it meant dying behind bars.

She clicked on the sheet for the current year and was about to select the name Guy Owen at the top of the list, but her gut churned.

"No!" she cried out as she realized her own stupidity. Her gaze was now back on Harper's card.

The FBI had found the money transfers. Did they also find the ledger? Now she was doubting herself. Had she deleted the file from Clive's recycling bin on his desktop?

She clenched her hand into a fist. Her options were limited and growing smaller.

Take down another violator, or go out with a bang…

She picked up the card. Maybe covering her tracks was no longer an option.

CHAPTER THIRTY-NINE

Roar Securities was situated in a strip mall, and they boasted the nicest front of all the businesses there. Their signage was embossed brass lettering, and I was certain that, at night, lights would shine from behind to showcase the business name. Their windows were tinted and weren't covered in advertisements like their neighbors' were.

The door chimed when we entered, and a cute blonde was seated at the front desk. She wore a headset clipped over one ear, and when she smiled, she was even more attractive. And that was saying a lot. Her wardrobe was conservative— white blouse paired with a black jacket. Whether she wore them with a skirt or slacks, I didn't know. The desk was in the way. Her hair fell in loose curls over her shoulders, and her eyes were clear, alert, and the color of a stormy sky.

"Good day. How can I help you?" she asked, her gaze sliding over me.

"We're agents with the FBI," Jack answered. He pulled out his cred pack and told her we'd like to see the footage for the bank and for what days and times.

"Oh." She blinked rapidly, almost as if she had something in her eye. "Sure, let me get Joni for you."

"Who is Joni?" Jack asked.

"Joni Pounder is the manager." The blonde tapped the counter. "One second and I'll be back."

Pretty much true to her word, the blonde returned quickly, a woman who was tight in all respects by her side. Not only was she in great physical shape but her face had hardened edges, carved as if by the hand of a skilled sculptor. Her hair was pulled back into a bun so tight it probably tugged on her scalp. It almost gave me a headache just looking at it.

She reached a slender arm toward Jack. "My name is Joni Pounder. I'm the manager of Roar Securities. I understand you have a warrant to view some camera footage." She shook Jack's hand, then mine.

"We have a warrant to *obtain* it, actually," Jack said, "but we'd like to watch it immediately."

"May I see this warrant?"

Jack let her view it on his cell phone screen.

"We'll e-mail you an electronic version," I said.

Joni lifted her gaze from the phone. "I will need you to wait for about twenty minutes. Stuart—he's our best tech guy—will need to set things up for you. I assume you have a date and time of interest."

"It's *dates* and *times*, plural." Jack provided the data from when the account was opened and this morning when it was closed. By comparing the two images, we'd hopefully learn something useful.

"All right, then. Please take a seat. Stuart will be out for you shortly." With that, Joni slipped away.

The blonde met my eyes and smiled at me. "Would either of you like coffee while you wait?"

I smiled back. "I—"

"No, thank you," Jack intercepted.

The blonde faced me, the question written in her eyes. I nodded for her to get me a cup, and she walked away.

Jack and I sat quietly until the blonde came back with a black coffee, two creamers, two sugar packets, and a stir stick.

"Is that good?" she asked as she handed everything to me.

I nodded. "Perfect."

She smiled and returned to her desk.

I really needed to figure out how to keep this woman smiling. She was breathtaking when she showed the expression, and it seemed she shared it rather easily.

I took a sip of the coffee, and it was good and fresh.

Soon a stereotypical computer nerd—complete with wide-rimmed glasses, acne, and a gangly frame—came into the waiting area and approached me and Jack. He pushed up his glasses and sniffled. "You're the agents?"

I glanced around the room. We were the only ones here.

His smile showed yellow teeth. "I'm Stuart Watkins. I have the first video up for you now, if you want to come back."

Both Jack and I were on our feet quickly, and it seemed our speed must have surprised Stuart because he jumped back a bit. "This way," he said once he collected himself.

Being closer to him now, I could smell his stale coffee breath. I put more distance between us, both to get away from his mouth and to save him from mine.

Stuart led us to a small conference room, sparse with furnishings. A long table took up a good portion of the floor space, and six chairs were positioned around it. At the far end of the room was a television on a cart, like the kind they'd wheeled into classrooms when I was a kid. The forty-inch flat screen seemed out of place when I was used to seeing a crappy tube TV on those dollies.

The video on the screen was grainy but focused on a teller wicket. A customer's back was to the camera, but the person's hair was dark and long.

Jack sat in a chair at the table, and I took one across from him. Stuart dropped into an end chair.

"Here we go," Stuart said.

The video started, and we watched Leslie interact with the teller. With movement, it was easier to distinguish that her hair was also curly. She wore a short skirt, and from the back, which was our viewpoint, it would've been easy to conclude that she was biologically a woman.

After about fifteen minutes with the teller, Leslie turned to leave. She didn't even seem to acknowledge the camera and walked nonchalantly out of the bank.

"Pause that there." Jack directed Stuart to stop it at the point when her front was in direct view.

Except for the subtle shadow of an Adam's apple, Leslie Shaw appeared to be female.

"Send a copy of that still to this e-mail." Jack gave his e-mail address to Stuart. "Then I want a copy of this footage sent to Nadia Webber, including the still shots." Jack flipped out another card and put it on the table in front of Stuart.

Stuart picked it up and glanced at it. "Sure."

My attention went back to the TV. There was the face of our killer. Still a stranger and an enigma, even though she had a face now.

Stuart backed out of the video and brought up another one. The time stamp dated it as being taken this morning.

In this one, Leslie had her hair wrapped up in a handkerchief. Her walk was fast, then slow, as if she was trying to pace herself. She lost her balance at one point, twisting her ankle slightly, but she recovered quickly.

"Are you picking up on the same thing I am?" Jack asked me.

"I think so..." When she opened the account, she hadn't paid any attention to the cameras, but this morning, she'd avoided looking directly at them and, in fact, did her best to keep from facing them altogether.

Jack locked eyes with Stuart. "Send both videos to Nadia. Right now."

CHAPTER FORTY

The four of us were back at the hotel in Jack's room. It seemed to be the best location for privacy.

"It's obvious our unsub opened that bank account for a questionable purpose," I began, "but what I don't understand is why not hide her face from the camera the day she set up the account? To do all that planning and then not worry about it? It doesn't make sense."

"It doesn't have to," Zach said, "but what it does tell us is she didn't think she'd get caught."

I took a bottle of water from the mini fridge.

"And the way she walks… She's confident in who she is— at least now," Paige said.

I turned to her. "And what makes you say that?"

"Well, it's like we discussed last night. Those with an intersex condition can be very confused, especially when parents have taken the decision from them to choose which gender they relate to," Paige explained.

"This morning she did all she could to avoid the cameras," Jack said, steering the conversation back to the video.

"She knows we're on to her," Paige stated.

"But it's not enough to stop her from coming out of hiding. She didn't want to lose the money," I reasoned.

"I think that tells us even more," Zach said. "Not only does she know we're onto her but she's no longer afraid. That can only mean one thing: she's going to kill again. And soon."

"Or she's got her money and will be making a run for it," I countered.

Jack's phone rang. "It's Nadia." He raised his phone to silence us and answered on speaker. "Lay it out for me."

"I've got a lot for you."

"Good," Jack said.

I dropped onto the edge of the bed, figuring I might as well get comfortable. I hoped her updates included the calls to Synergies.

"I'm still working to find out more about Simpson's previous employer, and unfortunately, the images from the bank footage couldn't be cleaned enough to be run through facial recognition. That's the bad news. But I tracked the money transferred from Simpson's account, and it went to the same place as Hall's money. I also pulled the backgrounds for everyone listed in Simpson's ledger from sixteen years ago, and again within the last year. I have eleven names. Seven, including Hall, have a record of rape charges. They paid their fines, served their sentences—"

"Got a slap on the hand and walked," Paige spat out.

Nadia let a few seconds pass before talking again. "None of the seven have anything great by way employment, but two have what you'd call *secure* work."

"Only two?" I asked.

"There was a third, though, who had more-than-secure work. He's got big money. Guy Owen. He's a movie director."

"A movie director?" I heard the incredulous tone to my voice. "Why would a movie director go to Canyon Country for drinks? I know I'm not from here, but even I can tell it's a dive. And Wild Horse of all places? I'm thinking he makes B movies."

"Porn," Nadia clarified.

"Oh…"

"He's had numerous complaints ranging from sexual harassment to assault and rape. None of the charges stuck. And Owen is worth just shy of a million. His address is coming to you now," Nadia said. "Brandon, I also got to the recordings from Synergies and narrowed it down to one caller from Duluth—a Sandy Hoss. A deeper look into her history showed that Hoss lived down the street from Malone when they were both teenagers. Now, the DMV shows a woman with dark, long, curly hair, age twenty-seven. More digging revealed that she was born with intersex condition in Wisconsin. Shortly after, the family moved to Minnesota, and then Sandy's parents died when she was three. She continued to live there with her aunt and uncle."

"Where she crossed paths with Malone," I surmised, my gut twisting. We might have found our killer.

"Likely. When she was eighteen, she enrolled in an acting course in Texas of all places. At twenty-one, she moved to Valencia, and that's where she's lived since."

"She moved to California probably full of dreams and was raped for her troubles," Paige said, shaking her head.

"Or Malone raped her in Minnesota, she found him through Synergies, and tracked him down here," I offered.

"Not sure how all this factors in, but Hoss never completed the classes. I called and spoke to her teacher from the time and was told that her grades were horrible and she seemed preoccupied. They actually recommended that she seek therapy," Nadia explained. "Sandy was diagnosed with HIV not long after that."

Jack rubbed his chin, thinking. "Hmm, so if Malone raped Sandy, it would have happened before she was twenty-one."

"Actually nineteen, Jack. That's when she left the acting course. The teacher remembered that Hoss took a trip to California then, too, and wasn't the same when she got back."

"So she was raped while on vacation, but returns to live here a couple years later? Sounds like she came back for a reason," Paige said.

"You're forgetting that there wasn't evidence of HIV in Malone's case," Zach said, rendering us all silent.

"Crap, you're right," Paige responded.

Nadia continued. "Now, I went ahead and obtained a warrant for Hoss's health records. If Hoss is our killer she had a good reason not to be killing for six years. She had a really rough time with the HIV and even required hospitalization."

Paige took the time to look at each of us. "That wouldn't be cheap."

"Sandy wouldn't need to worry about that, though, Paige. She was the sole benefactor when her parents died. She received one million on her twenty-first birthday. And before any of you ask, it's all gone now."

I was stuck on an entire million dollars being gone. "Our unsub comes into all this money, sees herself as a woman but has male anatomy, so why not pay for a sex change?"

"Our unsub may not have qualified for sex reassignment surgery," Zach said. "The surgery is quite involved, and the body treats the constructed vagina as a wound. Since Sandy is HIV-positive, she might have been at high risk of becoming infected or rejecting the change."

There was a sharp intake of breath on Nadia's end of the line. "During the time Hoss was in Texas, there was a murder in her town that remains unsolved. The victim's name was Leslie Shaw."

I glanced at Jack. "Now doesn't that name sound familiar…"

"Dig up all you can on Shaw and send us Hoss's address," Jack told Nadia.

"Right away. I'll get a BOLO out for Sandy's car, too."

Jack hung up and turned to Paige. "You and Zach go to Owen's, and Brandon and I will go pay Hoss a little visit."

"Be careful," Paige said, her eyes slipping from Jack to meet mine.

CHAPTER FORTY-ONE

Paige didn't envy jack or Brandon going to Sandy's and hoped that Jack had the sense to call for backup from the local field office. Normally, the four of them would approach a suspect's house together, but with the possibility that Guy Owen was in danger, an exception had to be made.

And combining the facts that Owen had sexual assault accusations on file and he made his living catering to sexual fantasies, he fit the victim profile.

Zach pulled the car into the driveway of a luxury townhouse. Not that it was ostentatious, but the property was pristine, as was the gated community in which it was located.

They parked and headed straight for the door to Owen's unit. Paige rang the doorbell, and based on the way the chime deadened, she'd guess the place was heavily furnished.

No sound came from inside.

Paige pressed the bell again, not certain anyone was home. "Maybe he's out making one of his slimy—"

The door cracked open, and a potbellied, balding man answered the door. He wasn't wearing a wifebeater or a gold chain around his neck, but he otherwise fit the image of a sleazy creep given the way his gaze lingered on Paige's body. When he brought his eyes back up from her chest to meet her gaze, it took all she had to remain civil.

She pulled out her cred pack. "We're Agents Dawson and Miles with the FBI."

He puckered his lips, bobbed his brows, and held out his wrists. "Are you here to arrest me?"

This asshole wasn't making being civil easy. "You're Guy Owen?"

A smug smile, and he dropped his arms. "Yes, I am."

"Can we come in?" Paige asked.

Owen's eyes drifted to Zach, then back to her. "You most certainly can, darling."

She narrowed her eyes at him. "My partner comes with me."

"Hmm." He eyed Zach. "I could make that work."

When he turned to retreat into the house, she was tempted to smack the back of Owen's head. But they needed to confirm he was safe and that meant going inside, even though she didn't want to.

Zach closed the door behind them, and this seemed to signal Owen to turn around.

"What's all this about?" he asked.

"Do you recognize her?" Paige extended her phone, which showed a picture of Sandy as taken from DMV records.

"You mean *him*? Yeah. I've seen him a few times. He gives me the creeps."

"*He* prefers to be called *she*," Paige corrected him.

"Well, good for him, but when *she* has a penis, I'm sorry but I still call them *he*."

"How do you know her?" Paige refused to let Owen's discriminatory mindset affect her.

"I know this will probably come as a surprise, but a bar called Wild Horse. It's a real dump, and you're probably wondering why a person like me would go there." He swiped a hand down his front.

Yes, that's exactly what I'm thinking...

"I am somewhat of a celebrity," Owen added.

"A celebrity? You make porn flicks." Paige's words dripped with disdain.

"A very lucrative business. Anyway, I can keep a low profile there."

"Do you pick up women there?"

"Ah, sometimes. Why? I ain't ever picked *him* up." Owen pointed to Paige's phone.

"We think that your life might be in danger," Zach said bluntly.

Owen laughed. "Why? Do you think he's going to kill me?"

"We think you could be the next target, yes."

"Next target? As in he's killed before?" Concern kissed his voice now.

"*She.* And yes," Paige said, unable to hide her exasperation.

Owen's gaze volleyed back and forth between them. "Why are you here and not out arresting him, then?"

"Agents are headed to her home as we speak, but it seemed probable she could be coming for you."

"That's why you're here? To make sure I'm breathing and not—" He covered his mouth as if the severity of the situation was finally sinking in.

"That's right." Paige moved farther into his house. "Have you come across anything strange lately? Doors or windows being unlocked that you swore were locked? Have you felt like anyone's been watching you?"

"No. Well, not more than usual."

"What do you mean?"

"As I said—"

"Right, you're a celebrity." She had to restrain herself from rolling her eyes.

"Listen, lady… Whatever." He opened his arms, his palms open and facing her. "I know who and what I am."

"Does that include being a rapist?" Paige asked. "You have a record of complaints against you."

He pointed a finger in Paige's face and must have thought better of it once he saw her glare. He lowered his hand. "I've never been formally charged."

She shrugged. "It doesn't mean you're not guilty."

"That's why you're here?"

"We told you why we're here, but did you ever make a move on her?"

"On him? No, never." He shook his head. "I don't roll that way."

"You're certain?"

"Yes. Listen, I make the boring type of porn. Traditional. Sexy librarian. Nympho secretary. Lusty flight attendant."

Traditional and porn… Interesting combo.

"No guy on guy or he/she's," Owen continued.

"He/she's?"

"Yeah, you know? Men who dress like women or think they're women. He/she's."

Paige gritted her teeth. He filmed people having sex for God's sake. Yet, here he was, judging the lifestyle of another person.

"I think I know why you liked Wild Horse," Paige said, bobbing her head in a know-it-all fashion.

"Why's that?"

"Well, the owner gave you a tab for one…"

"Yeah, Clive's a great—"

"And he was your drug supplier," she stated with heat.

Owen paled. "Hey, I know my rights. This is harass—"

"Clive Simpson was murdered last night."

Owen swallowed audibly and flushed. "Why didn't you say something sooner?"

Neither Paige nor Zach responded to his question.

"Was it him? The one from the picture? He did this?" Owen asked.

"*Her,*" Paige stressed again. "And, yes, we think so. Did you drug women at Wild Horse?"

He held up his hands and vigorously shook his head. "No, no, I don't do drugs."

"That wasn't her question," Zach said.

Owen's eyes slid to Zach and then back to Paige. "I'm not proud of this."

"Proud of what?" she ground out. Natasha's face flashed in her mind. Ferris had grown up to be a sniveling weasel, just like this shit. She'd never say it out loud but the world was a better place without him. And Paige couldn't help but think Sandy was doing people a favor by taking out men like Ferris.

"Yeah," he said with a sigh. "Sometimes I'd have something slipped into their drinks."

"By Clive Simpson?" Zach confirmed.

"Yeah."

"Did she—" Paige shook her phone, inferring Sandy "— ever see that happen?"

"Maybe? Yes? I don't know," Owen said, his voice soft now, a little frightened.

"Well, if she did," Paige told him, "you could definitely be her next target."

CHAPTER FORTY-TWO

Jack pulled the rental car to the curb. We had called for backup from the local field office, and the other agents were already on scene. The warrant had already come through.

Sandy's apartment building was old and redbrick. We headed up to the third floor, three agents tailing us. We were wearing Kevlar vests, not that the material would be effective against a blade, but it was best to take precautions. Just because her preferred weapon was a knife didn't mean it was the only weapon she had at her disposal.

Jack banged on Sandy's door. "FBI! Open up!"

It was quiet inside the apartment.

He smacked the door again. "Sandy Hoss! This is the FBI!"

His efforts met with silence.

We stepped to the side, and one of the agents behind us went at the door with a battering ram. We were inside Sandy's place in seconds.

The studio apartment was compact but kept neat and tidy. There was a small kitchen, a small living room, and a small bathroom. A twin-size bed was positioned in one corner.

Jack was moving things around on the counter with gloved hands. We were looking for any clue as to Sandy's possible whereabouts, as well as anything to implicate her in the murders. I stepped into the living area of the room while our backup stood in the hall, cordoning off Sandy's apartment.

Jack read off labels from prescription bottles he'd found on the counter, and I googled the drugs to find their uses. A few were for HIV.

Jack went rooting in a kitchen drawer.

"Agent Harper," one of the local field agents called out to Jack. There was another man standing beside him in blue jeans and a Budweiser T-shirt. "This is Glen Westerly. He's the building manager."

"What's going on in here?" Westerly asked.

Jack kept focused on the drawer, not even acknowledging Westerly, so I headed over to talk with the manager.

Westerly was probably about ten years older than me, but his eyes skimmed over me and the judgment there was plain to see. All he saw was my age, and he wanted to speak to the man in charge.

I squared my shoulders. "I'm Special Agent Brandon Fisher."

"What are you doing here?" Westerly moved to peer around me at Jack.

"When was the last time you saw Sandy Hoss?" I asked, countering his question with another.

"Sandy? Hmm. I don't know. A week or so ago. It doesn't mean she hasn't been here. I just have a life, ya know?" He took a step in an effort to get past me, but I stopped him with a flattened hand to his chest.

"Did you ever speak with Sandy?"

"Not really. Once in a while we'd say, 'Hi, how are you?' but we didn't stop to chat. I know that he—*she*—liked men. I wasn't into *that* and never wanted to give her any indication that I was." Westerly's eyes met mine.

"How long has Sandy lived here?"

"Six years, give or take. Why?"

"Do any of the other tenants complain about her or have any issues with her?" I asked.

Westerly seemed to give the question some thought and, after a bit, shook his head. "Not that I know of. What is this about?"

"At this time, I can't comment on that. It's an active investigation."

Westerly grimaced, and while I couldn't blame his frustration, I wasn't going come out with our suspicions about Sandy being a murderer.

I made eye contact with one of the local field agents, and he nodded.

"Come with me, Mr. Westerly," he said. "I'll take your information just in case we have any more questions for you."

Westerly scowled at me again before leaving with the agent.

Jack and I continued looking over the apartment for about twenty minutes, finding nothing. I returned to the kitchen area and looked over a shelf of books. Most were cookbooks, but one was a high school yearbook.

"Jack," I called, "come over here." I held up the find. "This is a yearbook from a school in Northern California from eleven years ago."

"None of that makes sense." Jack came over and took the book from me. He started flipping through the pages. He stopped and pressed a fingertip to a picture of a young man with delicate features. "Look familiar?"

I took a closer look, and while the images on the bank security camera were fuzzy, there was enough there to confirm that this was the younger version of the same person. I read the list of names, and one stood out—Leslie Shaw.

Jack pulled out his cell and dialed on speaker. "Nadia, I need that info on Leslie Shaw's murder *now*."

Nadia took a few seconds before responding. "Shaw was found in a motel room, wrists slit in the bathtub. Investigators thought it looked like a staged suicide because of the angles of the cuts and nothing indicated Shaw was depressed. No note, either."

"Who identified the woman as Leslie Shaw?" I asked.

"Her parents." She paused for a moment. "What are you guys thinking?"

"We're not sure yet. Keep talking," Jack directed.

"Well, the room was rented under her name, and her ID was found on scene. The deceased was wearing a pair of cubic zirconia earrings in the shape of dolphins, and Leslie's parents said she wore them everyday."

"No dental record comparisons?" Jack asked with some heat.

"No need for that, according to the reports," Nadia said. "The parents were certain it was Leslie Shaw."

"Sandy and Leslie must have looked a lot alike," I began. "And they each had an intersex condition?"

"They did," Nadia confirmed.

"Send us the picture from the murder scene," Jack said.

"Sure— Oh."

"Nadia?"

"I'm looking at a crime scene photo and comparing it to a snapshot of Leslie Shaw from the bank. Leslie and Sandy look almost identical."

"That would have made assuming Sandy's life pretty easy for Leslie," I reasoned.

"Send over the crime scene photo," Jack said.

"You got it."

"And, Nadia, dig into Leslie's past. Find anything you can."

Jack hung up, and his phone chimed with a message a second later. The face looking back at us had me losing my balance.

"Leslie Shaw *did* kill Sandy Hoss, took her identity, and staged her own death," I said.

"And collected a million dollars for her troubles," Jack growled.

I nodded, stunned. "Leslie hasn't completely let go of her true identity, though. She opened a bank account under that name. Seeing as she left her ID with Sandy's body, she must have had fake ones made." I paused a few seconds. "And they were both born with a fairly rare condition. What are the chances they'd find each other?"

"There's got to be something more to this." Jack tapped his shirt pocket at the same time Zach and Paige entered Sandy's—or really, Leslie's—apartment and beelined for us.

"No sign of Hoss at the director's house," Zach said. "We have a couple agents sitting outside his place."

"Well, we have something." I went on to share all the new info with them.

"It's quite possible. And the two of them do look surprisingly alike. But was it just for the money? Her other murders go deeper than that," Paige reasoned.

"It's too early to conclude her motivation," Jack said. "I have Nadia digging into Leslie's past to see if she can uncover anything."

Jack's phone rang, and he answered on speaker.

"Leslie's parents are still alive," Nadia began, "and they moved from Northern California to Texas after Leslie's apparent murder, and they've been living there ever since. Leslie ran away from home at sixteen. Records indicate the parents had no idea how or when Leslie even made it to Texas for that acting school."

I thought back to what Nadia had told us about the school—how Sandy's grades were so poor and how she'd seemed preoccupied. "Unbelievable," I muttered. "It seems Leslie was brazen enough to assume Sandy's life to the extent that she attended Sandy's classes after murdering her."

Paige raised her eyebrows. "*That* is what you find unbelievable?"

I disregarded her attitude, my mind going back to Leslie's parents. "So they moved to where Leslie was allegedly murdered?" I supposed everyone reacted to tragic events differently, but it seemed odd to me. "They were probably in denial that she was gone. And in this case, they'd be right.

They didn't bury their child. They buried someone else's. One question, though... If Leslie was a runaway, where did she get money to go to Texas?"

"I can answer that, too," Nadia chimed in. "The parents reported money was stolen from the family's bank account."

"Nadia you had said that Sandy came out to California for a vacation and wasn't the same when she got back?" I asked.

"Yeah." Nadia seemed hesitant.

"What if that's when Leslie and Sandy first crossed paths?" I brainstormed out loud. "Maybe something happened here that made Leslie follow Sandy back to Texas and kill her."

"Or maybe Leslie just found out about Sandy's money," Paige suggested.

"We don't believe money was Leslie's motive. Didn't you just say that?" I looked at Paige.

Paige narrowed her eyes at me and crossed her arms.

There was a brief lull in the conversation, and Nadia broke the silence.

"I finally made headway with that vacant property listed on Leslie Shaw's bank account," Nadia began, "as well as with Simpson's employment history. It seems they *are* connected."

"Talk," Jack said.

"There used to be a club called Clancy's on the property. It was—"

"A gay night club..." Paige's eyes were wide. "Malone's building manager said that Malone would go there, but that it had shut down."

"It burned down actually," Nadia said. "Ruling was arson and the owner fell under suspicion of having the fire set. The club was managed very poorly. But this is the point that's really going to make you love me. I can tie Hall and Simpson to Clancy's. And Paige just said that Malone went there."

The four of us remained silent.

"Simpson used to deal date-rape drugs out of Clancy's. We know that from the ledger. And Simpson was also the club's manager," Nadia said.

"And Hall?" I asked, curious as to how he tied into the club.

"He worked for the accounting firm that did Clancy's books. In fact, Clancy's was Hall's account. And when Sandy Hoss took that vacation to California, the club was still open."

"Then it seems that whatever happened to Leslie took place at Clancy's," I said. "And somehow Hoss got pulled into the mix."

"Does anyone else on the ledger tie back to Clancy's?" Jack asked Nadia.

"Yes. Peter Foreman. He worked there as a bouncer. His address is coming to you now."

CHAPTER FORTY-THREE

She'd find out just how good the FBI was. She was outside Pete Foreman's townhouse in Canyon Country, not too far from Wild Horse. It was seven in the evening, and so far, there was no sign of the FBI. Leslie was used to working under the cover of complete darkness, but sometimes exceptions needed to be made. Now was one of those times. She wanted to beat the FBI here, kill Pete, and then track the FBI's moves. Risky, she knew, but the thought of doing so was thrilling.

It was a two-story unit with front and back entry on the main level and no basement. A van was in his parking spot, and an upstairs light was on. She hadn't had the opportunity to do research and gather intel the way she normally did on her marks. But she doubted from what she did know that he had settled down. When she'd been better acquainted with him, he was muscled and obnoxious. More recently, when she'd run into him at the bar, any brawn he'd once had was now replaced with blubber.

He'd even gotten fresh with her the one night at the bar, and it had taken all her power not to act impulsively. She'd watched him leave with women on several occasions in the past. Most of the time they were stumbling over their own feet, intoxicated and likely drugged.

But drugging women was probably the only way the man could get laid—especially these days. He was homely—crooked teeth, a nose that was too large for his face, and he was pushing the scales at about three hundred pounds. What he lacked in heredity, he didn't bother to compensate for with good hygiene, diet, and exercise. Pete just didn't care. Even the barely conscious women he bedded weren't what anyone would consider beauties.

She knocked on Pete's door. She wasn't going to go about this all cloak-and-dagger. While Pete was a heterosexual, Leslie had fooled many men into thinking she was the genuine article. It was in her genes—without a word of a lie. All except for what lived in her underwear. But she was stuck in this form thanks to the disease-carrying violator Malone.

Pete's steps came toward the door, padding against what sounded like a wood floor. She couldn't see him wearing shoes in his home—he struck her as more of a plaid-pajamas-and-dirty-underwear kind of guy—but he had on something with a sole. Slippers, perhaps?

He opened the door. His wardrobe was exactly as she had predicted, except he wore a stained white T-shirt instead of the matching top that went with his pajama bottoms.

"Hello?" He let his eyes trace her from the toe of her stilettos to her ruby lips. Then his mouth slightly curved upward. He leaned against the doorframe. "Well, hello. What can I do for you?"

He obviously didn't remember her. Huh. She wasn't used to being forgettable. "I'm with building management, and we're performing random maintenance checks on our units."

If he bought that line, he really was an idiot.

"Certainly. Come on in." Pete backed up, his smile parting his lips now, showcasing those stained teeth.

She tried to tamp down her nausea. She wasn't looking forward to seeing him naked.

He locked the door behind her. "Can I get you anything to drink? A beer?"

"Ah, no thanks."

"Come on, it's evening. I was just having one myself."

So that's what the stink was…

"No, thank you." She met his eyes and, as she did so, was tempted to draw her knife right then and there and end his pathetic life, but she needed to be farther from the door. "You can come with me as I look around the place." She tried to smile, to lure him in.

Pete was grinning like a teenaged boy. "Sure."

To the right of the front entrance, a staircase climbed to the second level, and straight ahead was a back rec room and patio door. She wanted Pete as far away from an exit as possible.

"Let's start upstairs," she said.

"Okay. And you're sure you don't want that drink?"

Pete was making this too easy. He deserved what he had coming.

He stepped back, as though waiting for her to take the first step. He probably wanted to watch her from behind.

She tried not to shudder as she led him to the second level and waited for him to get away from the stairs before taking the knife from her purse and pointing it in his direction. "You will do as I say."

Pete's eyes widened, and he swallowed loudly against the backdrop of the silent house. A muted TV cast colored shadows in the next room.

"Who are you?" he asked.

"Take your clothes off," Leslie demanded, thrusting the tip of the knife toward him to add urgency to her directive. She didn't want to see this man's junk. In fact, the thought made her stomach roil.

A slimy smile crept onto his face. "Oh, you want to see me."

"Strip naked," she told him. "Now!"

Pete lifted his shirt over his head. Then he slowly lowered his pajama bottoms. Did he think he was performing?

Just take the damn pants off!

No matter how much she wanted to look away, to spare her eyes the vision in front of her, she had to remain focused. If she diverted her attention from him for even a second, she could find the knife inside her.

Now his pajamas were around his ankles.

Oh God! He wears tighty-whities.

They complemented no man, let alone this one.

"And the underwear," she said, trying not to cringe. "Take them off."

Pete's face was mix of confusion and arousal. "Ah, you like what you see."

She did her best to purge her mind of the conjured image of this man grunting over a drugged woman. The last thing she wanted to see was him naked, but it was necessary.

Once he was stripped completely, she kicked the discarded clothing away from him. "Sit in a kitchen chair." She had spotted the dining area the moment she got to the second floor, and the spindle-backed chairs were ideal for restraining him.

The second Pete's fat ass hit the chair, she whipped out a pair of cuffs from her purse. She snapped one end around his wrist, the other end to the chair.

"You're into role playing?" He grinned, clearly trying to be sexy but failing wildly. "I like it."

He was apparently ugly *and* dumb. She wanted to hit him in the head so hard that he wouldn't come to, but what fun would that be?

She pressed the tip of the blade into his neck. "The other hand. Now!"

Pete yelped, and she retracted the blade, realizing she might have pierced him deeper than she had intended just then. Blood was trickling down his neck.

When both his wrists were secured, she took out two more sets of cuffs to bind his ankles to the chair, but they were too big for the cuffs to fit around. She pulled out her roll of duct tape. She'd have to make do. But it was awkward to hold the blade on him with one hand while unwinding the tape with the other. At least he was too dumb—and frozen by fear—to kick her.

She resumed her full height once she was done, and looked at Pete, who had tears streaming down his cheeks now. She pressed the metal into his neck again.

"Wh-what are you going to do to me?"

Finally, we have comprehension.

She walked around in front of him and slapped a piece of duct tape over his mouth. Her answer would have him screaming and attracting good Samaritans, and she didn't need anyone ruining this party.

With a final smack to the tape across his face, she hunched over to meet him at eye level. "I'm going to kill you. But first, I'm going to torture you."

CHAPTER FORTY-FOUR

We left Shaw's apartment with a few agents watching over it. CSU was being called in to scour the apartment and collect anything that might incriminate her in the murders of Malone, Hall, Simpson, and the real Sandy Hoss.

Jack, Paige, Zach, and I set out to Peter Foreman's townhouse, along with some other agents. Even though a BOLO was in place, Jack called in Grafton to specifically check the area for the car registered under the name of Sandy Hoss.

We were in the parking lot for the complex when Grafton came hurrying toward us. "A deputy found the car two blocks east."

"So, she's here," Jack said, turning to his team. "We don't know when she showed up. Foreman could already be dead, but we act as if we have a man to save, you got it?"

The three of us nodded. I even noticed Grafton bob his head.

"And if she wasn't worried about us spotting her car…" I let my words trail off. This scenario wasn't good.

"She's calling us out," Jack concluded. "Paige, you and Zach go around the back of Foreman's unit to the patio door. Go now."

Paige and Zach jogged off and swooped around Foreman's building to the back. Jack and I stuck close to the side of the building as we made it to Foreman's front yard.

There was a minivan in the driveway, but the curtains were closed in the house.

Jack drew his gun. "Pick the lock, but don't go in until my mark."

I did as he directed, stepped back, and pulled my weapon.

"We go in on the count of three."

I nodded.

He chopped his hand in the air three times, and I went in first.

I smelled it the moment I entered—blood.

Across from the entry was a rec room and the patio door. I saw Paige and Zach standing outside it, and Jack went to let them in after directing me to cover him.

Once we were all inside, Jack pointed toward the ceiling and the four us made our way cautiously up the stairs, Jack in the lead. We all had our guns drawn. It was best to be prepared. And with the intensity of the smell, there was a lot of blood loss. She could still be here.

We reached the second level and found an unbound naked man sitting in a chair. Pete Foreman, I assumed.

Around his ankles was a patch of missing hair. She'd improvised his shackles with duct tape. Blood pooled on the floor beneath him. A trail of red had made a river down his neck. But it wasn't the main source of blood. In the pool of blood on the floor was the man's penis.

Vomit hurled up my throat so quickly that my cheeks puffed to avoid expulsion. Somehow I managed to swallow the sour bile.

Avoiding making any contact with the blood on the floor, Jack got close enough to press two fingers to Foreman's neck. "He's got a pulse."

I had my phone to my ear in less than a second. "We need an ambulance." I provided Foreman's address to the emergency dispatch.

Foreman moaned, and his eyelids fluttered. "Jack…"

My breath caught. Did I just hear him right?

"Jack?" This time the name came out as a moan.

"I'm Jack," my boss told Foreman.

I knew what I should be doing, and my eyes kept going to the dismemberment. The thought of picking it up and bagging it… The vomit was in my mouth again. I swallowed roughly.

I heard Paige opening cupboards and then the freezer in the fridge.

"Here." She handed me a plastic sandwich bag and a container filled with ice.

"Me?"

I wasn't sure I was cut out for this task. In fact, I knew I wasn't. My stomach was churning something fierce…

Paige rolled her eyes. "My God." She snatched the items back from me and had Foreman's penis bagged and on ice in seconds.

That was it. I couldn't hold it back any longer. I rushed for the kitchen sink and emptied my stomach. I smacked the edge of the counter, angry at myself for being weak. The last time I was sick over a discovery, Zach had teased me about it, but at least I had Paige on my side at that time. After last night, I couldn't exactly picture her in my corner now. I washed the chunks down the drain and splashed some cool water on my face before rejoining them in the dining area.

None of them were looking at me. Their focus was on Foreman.

"She…said you'd…" Foreman's eyes rolled back into his head.

"Stay with us," Jack cried out, slapping Foreman's face lightly.

Foreman's eyes returned to us. "Scene…crime."

Paramedics raced into the room then, and the four of us stepped aside. Paige handed Foreman's severed penis to one of them, and he took it from her as if he saw this kind of thing every day, while the other paramedics loaded Foreman onto a gurney.

"Leslie knew we'd come here. She's playing with us," Jack said.

"She's emboldened and calling you out," I added, my gaze drifting to the men working on Foreman.

"*Scene. Crime.*" Paige said. "What do you think that means? Does she want us to meet her at one of her past crime scenes?"

Jack shook his head. "I think she wants *me* to meet her at one."

My jaw dropped a little. "Just because she has your card?"

"We can't let you go alone," Paige said.

"We don't even know what crime scene she means," I insisted.

Zach took a few steps away from us, his hand to his chin. "She knew we'd come here. She's either picked another target and wants to meet there, or she's alluding to a previous one."

"And she obviously had some sort of getaway plan to slip away undetected. Her timing was ideal…for her," Paige pointed out. "And now she's calling out a federal agent?"

"It seems like she's not afraid of being caught anymore." Zach paused. "Thinking about her actions so far, she's thorough and methodical. But Foreman was a last-minute decision. She left him alive, even if barely, just to deliver the message to Jack."

Paige nodded. "If we had arrived any later, Foreman might have bled to death."

The paramedics rushed down the stairs carrying the dead weight of a man who was easily three hundred pounds. Their biceps bulged beneath their shirts. I would bet they were thankful they were in good physical shape. When my gaze left them, it met with Paige's, her green eyes like chiseled emeralds.

"We have to figure out what Leslie meant," I said to the group, trying to keep everyone focused.

"A crime scene possibly..." Zach ruminated. "It wouldn't be Simpson's house. It's still being swarmed by CSU. And Hall was murdered in that motel room. It's too public and exposed. And Malone—"

Paige's eyes widened. "Clancy's?"

Zach nodded. "Could be. She's definitely calling us out and likely knows how this will end. Clancy's could be where it all started for her, and she wants her story told."

She had grabbed one of Pete's trench coats, tucked her curls up under a man's hat, and exchanged her heels for a pair of Pete's sneakers. And despite the stench from the shoes curdling her stomach, she had no choice but to wear them. While she thought she'd have more time with Pete, instinct had told her otherwise. Either that or she'd panicked. But it turned out that her intuition had proven invaluable. She had seen the police cruisers headed toward the row of townhouses, and none of the deputies seemed to pay her any attention. How different that would have been if she had been dressed as herself. Her short skirts and heels always turned heads.

She wondered how long would it take for Supervisory Special Agent Jack Harper to find her. A smile spread across her lips. Did he get the riddle she left behind with Pete?

CHAPTER FORTY-FIVE

"But we have her car," I said. "And Los Angeles is an hour and a half from here."

"There are other methods of transportation she could've used, though—buses, taxis, rental cars." Paige's voice grew in volume and hope with each option she noted.

Jack pulled out his phone and requested that Nadia pull the financials for Sandy Hoss and Leslie Shaw, but there weren't any credit cards to flag under either name.

"Won't that make it hard to rent a car?" I asked.

"Not if she hit some dive that didn't care," Paige said. "They could have taken a cash deposit."

"Paige could be right," Zach agreed.

Jack nodded. "I'll check with the bus station, Zach and Brandon, you contact taxi companies, and Paige, start with the low-end rental companies."

A few minutes later, Jack, Zach, and I were off our phones.

"No buses are headed out tonight," Jack said.

"Of the taxi companies I contacted, none would take a fare to LA," Zach stated.

"I found one who would, but they had no requests to go to LA in the last hour. They will call me immediately if they get one," I added.

Paige hung up. "Fair Rate Rentals just rented out a Kia Rio ten minutes ago to a Sandy Hoss. I've got the color and plate."

"We'll just get a warrant for the tracking device on the car." Jack had his phone out again.

Paige shook her head. "Low-end, remember? The company told me equipping their cars with tracking devices wasn't in their budget."

Jack clenched his jaw. He paced a few feet and took a cigarette out of his pack. "I will go in one of our rental cars. The three of you will take the other," he directed. "I want you to stay back from me, though."

"Jack, you're crazy," Paige protested. "You can't walk out there on your own—"

"We have to bring her down."

I was with Paige. Jack was crazy for considering this, but I wasn't going to say anything. At least he was having us come along as backup, even if it was from a distance.

Paige, Zach, and Brandon were on the way to the lot in LA. Her stomach was swirling, and it had nothing to do with Brandon being in the backseat and their argument the night before. It was about knowing that if anything happened to Jack, it would be her fault.

If it weren't for her coming out to confront Ferris Hall, none of them would even be here. And did that mean that Simpson might still be alive and Foreman might not be fighting for his life? She knew she had to release that guilt. Paige wasn't the one wielding the blade. But she'd never forgive herself if Jack was hurt...or worse. He was her father on the road, her guardian angel, if one believed in such things. Paige wasn't sure what she thought in that regard, but she did know that Jack was always there for her. Even when she was certain he was disappointed in her and would have preferred to lash out at her.

As she thought of Jack and what the four of them might face when they arrived at the abandoned lot, she prayed to God the killer remained predictable and only wielded a knife. From a strategic viewpoint, there were four of them—

armed with guns—against one, but experience had taught her that hunting a killer was never routine. Things could take a bad turn quickly. If something went sideways, she might not ever see Sam again to smooth things over, either.

If only she had left everything alone. Not only would the bloodshed have been avoided but she'd still have Sam. But did she really want a man who didn't stick around during the rough times? Then again, it wasn't about her being a murder suspect. It wasn't even about her shuffling his calls to voice mail. It was about Brandon.

The two of them had made their peace a couple of months ago. She had moved on with Sam; he had moved on with Becky. And all that sounded good, but what if Sam had a point? Brandon had always proclaimed he cared for her, but he would never commit. Yet, what if that changed? What if their jobs changed? Even if she and Sam worked things out, would she leave him to resume a relationship with Brandon if given the opportunity? Would Brandon make life difficult for her if she tried to stay with Sam?

As she analyzed her thoughts, she didn't much care for the words that kept popping up.

If.

Try.

Lasting relationships shouldn't exist because of *trying.* They took work, sure, but it shouldn't take a concentrated effort to stay together. Was she making too much out of this? Giving Brandon too much power over her again? Sadly, she had the inclination to do just that.

CHAPTER FORTY-SIX

Jack had directed his team to hang back from his vehicle. He wore a comm to communicate with his team and was still wearing the Kevlar vest—for good reason. The vacant land was rather isolated, but there were other buildings in the area. Most of them appeared to have closed up shop years ago, but Leslie could be hiding in any one of them, making him that much more exposed. Even though her weapon of preference was a knife and she seemed to enjoy killing up close, he had to factor in the possibility that she might have a gun.

He turned the car's headlights off and then pulled to the side of the road and cut the engine. Leslie would expect him to show up in front of the lot, but he wasn't going to stick to a script.

He locked the car, despite the fact that his agents were watching his vehicle from about fifty feet back. The last thing he needed was Leslie finding a way into his backseat and holding a knife to his throat. The thought instinctively had him rubbing his neck.

He walked slowly toward the lot, keeping close to the curb on the right side of the road. Streetlights were casting a muted glow around the area, creating shadows that made it look like an abandoned military test zone. As he looked around, staying alert, he considered that this location didn't fit with the rest of her murders—she typically killed indoors. But this had to be about Leslie getting her story out. And if she was looking for understanding, it wouldn't be coming from him.

She based her actions on emotions, and that only made for poor decisions. Feelings were useful, however; they let him know intuitively when things were off. And they were off right now.

He reached the property, faced it, and looked around cautiously, taking his steps diligently. It soon became apparent that no one else was out here but him.

Jack spoke to his team. "She's not—"

A noise came from his left, and he turned toward the sound, and a rabbit jumped out from beneath a shrub.

Just a rabbit...

Jack rolled his eyes. The darkness had a way of playing with one's mind. Add in stalking a serial killer, and the worries and possibilities just became worse, even for someone like him who had a lot of experience dealing with psychopaths.

He walked around the area for a while longer. Eventually, his phone rang.

"Is this Supervisory Special Agent Harper?" a woman cooed.

Even her voice sounded like a woman's. "Leslie Shaw." He said her name for two reasons. One, to let her know he was aware of her true identity, and two, to let his team know to trace his phone.

"Would you be expecting someone else?"

"I thought you'd be here, where Clancy's used to be." He inflected a hint of disappointment into his voice.

"Ah, well, you jumped to the wrong conclusion." She sounded pleased with herself.

"Where are you?"

"Oh, if I told you that, it wouldn't be any fun. And don't bother trying to trace this call. It won't get you anywhere."

"What do you want?" he asked.

"I want you to know why I did what I did," she said, "why I killed those people. To stand where I was when—"

"When what?" He had to keep her talking, but as he kept the conversation going, he remained vigilant to his surroundings.

"At least you are there. I knew I could count on you."

Click.

Jack squeezed his hand around his cell phone. "Tell me we got something," he said to his team.

"Unfortunately not," Zach informed him.

"Son of a bitch!" He ripped the comm from his ear and stuffed it into a pocket as he hurried back to his vehicle. But he went past his to go to his team's. He tapped a cigarette out of his pack and lit up, savoring every little bit of nicotine that hit his system.

Zach put the driver's-side window down.

Jack exhaled a puff of smoke. "She's not here, and this was a fucking waste of time."

Paige leaned over the console to see him. "Do you think we interpreted the clue wrong?"

Jack shook his head. "No, she wanted us to come here. Not that it seems she had any intention of joining us here. She wants to make sure that we understand her and know what happened to her."

"And she had to drag us all the way out here to do that?" Brandon asked.

"She's trying to manipulate us, and she's done a fine good job of it." Jack took another deep drag from his cig.

Ah, almost as good as an aphrodisiac.

But it still didn't calm the frustration over having wasted the time coming here. "Let's get back to the hotel and talk this out. Who knows when she'll kill again…"

CHAPTER FORTY-SEVEN

We made it back to the Hyatt around eleven at night, but it felt like two in the morning. While we had been in California for a couple of days, my body still hadn't adjusted to the time change. I wasn't sure what else we were going to accomplish tonight, though. It seemed apparent we were letting Leslie call the shots right now, and there still hadn't been any hits on the BOLO for the rental. Trying to track the GPS in Leslie's phone also met a dead end, which meant she was smart enough to call Jack from a burner cell.

The four of us entered the lobby. Paige yawned, and Zach and I followed suit. Jack seemed immune.

"Maybe we should pick up in the morning, boss?" Zach suggested.

I liked his proposition, but I wasn't about to request any leniency on bedtime.

Jack's jaw tightened, and I wasn't sure what he was going to say to Zach but I had a feeling it might not be so nice.

"All right," Jack said on a sigh. "Five o'clock in the lobby."

Shows you what I know.

We all headed to the elevator bank. Paige was the first off the car as her room was on the third floor. The rest of us continued up to the fifth floor. I couldn't wait to sink into the pillow-top mattress and drift off to dreamland.

"Night," I said to Zach and Jack as I stopped at my door and slid in the keycard.

I wasn't sure if I had enough strength to even get undressed before dropping into bed, but I managed to walk out of my clothes as I went across the room. I set my gun and holster on the nightstand, crawled under the sheets and comforter, and I closed my eyes.

But my mind wouldn't rest. What had we missed? That clue left behind with Foreman... Two words: *crime* and *scene*. What did they mean?

I rolled onto my side, willing my mind to shut off.

It wasn't working.

I rolled onto my other side.

Seconds later, I was sitting upright, eyes wide. There were actually three words in Leslie's clue to us, only we hadn't put them together. The first word was what Foreman had said when we first got there. *Jack*. We had thought Jack was just being addressed with the message, but what if Jack was supposed to be connected to the other two words? What if she was actually threatening to kill Jack? What if she meant Jack's crime scene?

"Shit!"

I jumped up, stubbed my toe on the nightstand—how I managed that, I don't know—and let out a string of curse words. I turned on the light.

I fumbled with my clothes as I tried to get them back on. This was crazy. I could be totally wrong about this. I tried his cell phone, but it was going to voice mail. Maybe he couldn't get to it or he didn't hear it?

He could be asleep already, I reasoned.

No, that wasn't like Jack...

But I'd try calling his room before I got too worked up. If he answered and everything was fine, I'd figure out something to say.

I dialed. One ring...two...three... I let it continue until it rolled over to voice mail.

All right. I had to breathe. Maybe he was just in the shower or in the bathroom and couldn't get to the phone.

I called Paige and Zach to let them know what I was thinking, hoping that my gut feeling was wrong.

Not counting the night she had spent in jail, Paige hadn't remembered ever being this tired. But she wanted to be strong for Jack and the others. Mainly Jack. She had been so relieved when Leslie hadn't shown up at the address. And she had been just about as relieved when Zach made the suggestion to resume things in the morning. It had been a good call. What else were they going to do tonight?

But as tired as she was, her stomach still growled for food. They'd worked right through dinner, so as soon as she stepped off the elevator on her floor, she hit the vending machine for a bag of chips.

She opened the bag and stuffed a few chips into her mouth before unlocking her door. Inside, she slipped out of her shoes, dreaming of setting her weary bones on the soft mattress when she noticed a silhouette in the chair next to the window. She dropped the bag of chips and had her gun drawn and aimed.

"Put your hands up!" she shouted as she closed the distance.

The figure moved, and it looked like the person was wiping his or her eyes.

Paige flicked the light switch on the wall beside her. As her eyes adjusted and she made out her visitor, she holstered her gun. "What are you doing here?"

Sam came toward her, arms extended, hands reaching out to touch her. "Listen, I can understand if you're mad at me."

She held up her hands and backed up to where she had dropped her chips. Her appetite was gone, but she had made a mess, and she rather wanted the distraction of cleaning it up. She was bent over picking up the chips when she felt his hand on the small of her back. She stood and looked him in the eye.

"I'm sorry, Paige."

Since he'd left, she'd been thinking about reconciliation, but now that he was in front of her, she was angry. "You made me look like a fool. At the very least, feel like one."

"I know. I'm sorry." He paced a few steps. "I was hoping that we could—"

"You left *me*, Sam. I came to California to spend time with you."

He angled his head. "Be honest. You came to California to confront Ferris. It wasn't about us."

"I could have come by myself, but I didn't."

"You just wanted someone to tell you that you were doing the right thing by dredging up the past."

Her heart was pounding so hard she could hear it beating in her ears. "I *was* doing the right thing. People like Ferris—*rapists* like Ferris—need to know that their behavior isn't acceptable, that it has real-life consequences."

"And I get that, Paige, I do."

Silence fell between them.

What was she supposed to say? She had hurt him, too, let him down. But somehow, in her mind, his leaving her trumped all she had done.

"Why did you come back?" She wasn't going to ask him where he had been for the past day. She hoped wherever he had been that he'd regretted leaving her every second.

"I'm hoping that you'll forgive me." He searched her eyes, his own gaze soft and sincere. After a few seconds, he added, "But if we're going to make a relationship work, I need to know it's over between you and Brandon."

She pressed her lips together, not wanting to say anything she'd regret. "I told you it was over, but you didn't want to believe me."

"I still don't understand why you called him first."

"You want to know why? Because I knew I could trust him. I didn't want to give you a bad impression of me. Here your new girlfriend is suspected of murder, and I knew how you felt about me going to see Ferris in the first place, let alone by myself." She crossed her arms.

"What if he still loves you?"

"Brandon?" She puffed out a lungful of air. "The only person he loves at this point in his life is himself."

Sam shook his head. "I don't believe that." When she didn't respond, he went on. "Do you?"

He obviously wasn't going to let her bypass the subject. She looked him straight in the eye. "What does it matter if he loves me or not? What we had is over." She held up her hand because Sam opened his mouth as though he was going to say something. "And even if things did change—one of us got another job, Brandon decided he did love me—none of it would matter if I'm in a relationship with someone else."

"Are you in a relationship?" Sam studied her eyes. The pain in his gaze mirrored what she felt inside.

Her old self would have given him the power to decide their status, but if Brandon had taught her anything, it was that she needed to assume that power for herself. "How about we take it one day at a time?"

Sam's shoulders sagged.

She touched his arm and caressed his cheek. "Neither of us is good at the long-term thing."

"I'm willing to give it a go with you, Paige." He took her hand from his face and held onto it. "I promise I'll never run out on you again. I'll trust you."

"And I—" she took a deep breath "—will trust you." She pointed a finger at him. "But if you ever leave me again, I will give you a swift kick in the ass."

Sam laughed and scooped her into his arms. "Deal."

She let herself sink into his embrace. Whether she had another day with Sam or fifty years, she was going to enjoy the moment. Then her cell phone rang.

CHAPTER FORTY-EIGHT

Jack flicked on the light as he entered his room, closed the door, and slid the chain across. The day had seen far too much murder. First Simpson and now Foreman. He had received the text from a local agent on the way from the elevator to his room, telling him that Foreman had died on the way to the hospital. He wasn't going to bother his team with that news right now.

Let them go to sleep thinking they saved a man.

Calling it a day might have been the right move for his team, but Jack wasn't built that way. He could only rest when circumstances dictated it, and while he knew he should have been exhausted like the others, his mind whirled with thoughts about Leslie Shaw, aka Sandy Hoss.

Jack reached the nightstand and slipped out of his shoes as he set his phone down and worked to unfasten his holster. It was then that he felt the sharp point against his back. He didn't have to turn to know who it was.

"Leslie Shaw," he said looking over his shoulder, figuring she had been hiding in the bathroom.

The pressure on the blade eased slightly. It told him she didn't like being called by her real name.

"Put your gun on the nightstand," she said.

He held up his one hand and used the other to do as she directed. As he put the gun down, he noticed his cell screen light up with a message. He read the part that showed. They found the rental that Leslie had taken out under the name Sandy Hoss in a lot near the Hyatt. He let out a deep, yet controlled breath.

"Brilliant move telling me to meet you at the crime scene," Jack said.

Appeal to her narcissism, make her think she is in control.

The phone rang on the nightstand.

"If you get that, I'll kill you," she hissed.

"What is your plan, Leslie?" He kept his tone calm, controlled, submissive.

"Why must I have a plan?"

"You always do," he said, matter-of-fact. "You kill for a purpose."

"You FBI think you know everything." Her words seemed to lack conviction. She'd had no previous run-ins with the FBI on which to base her opinion.

"We don't."

"Damn right you don't." She had found a spot beneath the edge of his Kevlar vest and had the blade on an upward angle. She applied pressure. He was well aware that a thrust upward would meet perfectly with his liver.

"Why are you here?"

"You interfered. You got involved."

"Did Malone rape you?" he asked. "If so, he got what he deserved."

Say whatever is needed to get on her good side.

The pressure on the blade eased again. "Turn around and face me."

He did, slowly, realizing that if she stabbed him, he could die.

"Tell me what you think you know," she spat out, poking the tip of the knife to his abdomen.

He nodded. "Malone raped you and gave you HIV."

"Keep going."

"You found him and got even."

"Yes." A sick smile. "I did. What else?"

"The rape happened at Clancy's."

"Yes, and?" She seemed to be enjoying his telling of the assault. Most rape victims wouldn't derive pleasure from reliving the event, but her mind wasn't really on the past, it was on what she had done to rectify it. This fact sent a shiver of fear mixed with adrenaline through Jack's system.

"Why don't you tell me? I can only surmise," Jack said.

Her eyes darkened. "Malone raped me in the club's restroom, and no one helped me!"

"People saw what—"

"Yes!" she interrupted. "And I thought Sandy was a friend! She saw what was happening but just left. She did nothing to help." Her eyes softened. "At least not until I followed her back to Texas where I killed her." She peered into Jack's eyes. All he saw was an inky pool of nothing.

"And you assumed her identity and took her million dollars."

"Ah, yes," Leslie said. "She paid for her negligence. Her money, ironically, kept me alive."

"And Clive Simpson drugged your drink that night," Jack stated.

"You found his stash of drugs?"

Jack nodded.

"Good. He was guilty."

"Why Peter Foreman?" he asked.

She tsked at him. "I'm disappointed, Jack."

He remained quiet, not taking the bait that entreated him to talk.

"Pete let the violators into the club," she ground out.

Along with the anger in her eyes, Jack picked up on something else. "You burned the club down, didn't you?"

A proud smile. "Yes, that was me."

"Why confess now?"

"Those who needed to really pay for their crimes against me have done so." She shrugged. "And I suppose all good things must come to an end."

Jack's cell rang again, and it proved to be enough of a distraction for him to put sufficient space between them that he no longer felt the blade. He turned quickly, grabbed his gun, and poised to see the butt of his weapon meeting Leslie's temple, but his movements stopped short when the knife buried into his flesh. He howled in pain, his vision going to pinpricks of white and red.

Leslie twisted the blade, and it chewed his insides with a fiery intensity. And then she withdrew the knife.

Jack dropped to the ground, clutching his side with one hand. With the other, he still held onto his gun.

He heard clamoring out in the hallway and did his best to scream, but it came out as a garbled whisper.

God or no God, he wasn't going out this way.

He put all his strength and focus into lifting the gun. His hold on it wobbled, but he pulled back on the trigger.

The bullet fired wide, missing his target.

Leslie came at him again, swiping the knife at him. In this moment, with all his senses heightened, the blade made a whooshing noise as it sliced through the air next to him, barely missing his face. But he knew she'd been aiming for his throat.

He managed to kick out one of his legs, taking her down. But he hadn't thought it through. With her on the ground next to him, she became a tougher target to hit.

Pain had his mind slipping in and out of logical thought, and his vision was going blurry.

He did his best to aim the gun again, hoping he'd have enough strength to pull the trigger one more time, but he found his power lacking. He dropped the hand holding the gun to the floor. His other hand still clutched his injured side, and he shut his eyes and succumbed to the darkness.

I ran into Grafton in the hallway outside my room.

"Her car's in the area, and there's no response from Jack," he said.

Oh, this really wasn't good at all.

The elevator dinged, and Paige and Sam unloaded.

Sam? I did a double take.

"I can't reach him. Has anyone—" Paige didn't finish her sentence, and her voice was riddled with panic.

Zach came out of his room a few doors down from Jack's. He reached Jack's door before the rest of us, and we all fell silent as Zach pressed his ear to the door.

It took less than a second before he nodded and whispered, "She's in there."

"I've got a keycard for the room from the front desk," Grafton said, speaking low and holding it in front of him.

Zach, Paige, and I made eye contact briefly before I took it from Grafton and put it into the lock.

I took time to look at my fellow team members, Sam, and Grafton. We all readied our weapons, except for Sam, who wasn't carrying.

"You have to stay out here," I said to him, and he nodded.

I opened the door slowly, fully expecting the chain to be engaged. My suspicion was correct, and I threw my shoulder into the door, putting all my muscle behind it.

"FBI!" I cried out as we breached the room, the five of us filing in, all armed and ready to take down a killer.

Paige was immediately behind me because the entrance from the door into the room itself was too narrow for us to walk side by side.

Leslie turned to us, a smirk on her lips. She was braced over Jack, holding a knife dripping with blood. Jack wasn't moving beneath her, and his eyes were closed.

"No!" Paige screamed.

It was the flicker in Leslie's eyes that set me into action. I squeezed the trigger, and the bullet hit her in the left temple as she was starting to crouch down to take another stab at Jack. The force of the blast caused her to fall on top of Jack, the blade dropping from her hand and harmlessly coming to rest on the carpet.

Paige ran past me and pushed a wide-eyed Leslie off Jack.

Grafton took Leslie's pulse and shook his head. "She's gone."

I stared down at the woman who had been responsible for so much death but who had suffered so much pain.

"He's not responding, Brandon." Paige's eyes were pooling with tears as she held Jack's hand and looked up at me. "Oh my God, Brandon, we can't lose him."

"We need an ambulance…"

I was aware Sam was in the background on his phone, but it was like all movement stopped in that moment. I got down on the carpet next to Jack and so did Zach.

"Do you think our lives are in danger?"

"We took that risk the second we donned a badge."

"Come on, Jack," I said to him, "you're too damn stubborn to die. Now fight!"

CHAPTER FORTY-NINE

The team was in the waiting room at the hospital, as were Sam and Grafton, waiting for word of Jack's condition.

Grafton was talking to Paige, and while I hadn't meant to eavesdrop, I overheard their discussion.

"For what it's worth, I'm sorry," he said.

"I appreciate the apology, but it's behind us now." She squeezed Sam's hand but still spoke to Grafton. "You came through when it mattered."

Grafton nodded and smiled.

I closed my eyes and took a deep breath. The shooting back at the hotel flashed through my memory. Leslie had been my second kill in as many years with the FBI. Some officers might consider it a badge of honor, but I didn't view it that way. I'd rather these creeps face justice in court, followed by a long prison sentence. If they rotted behind bars, so be it; at least then I wouldn't have pulled the trigger and taken a life.

But I knew Leslie's death couldn't be helped. It was a good shoot, and if I hadn't fired when I did, Jack's body would have accompanied Leslie's to the morgue. As it was, he'd lost a lot of blood.

A male doctor in teal surgical scrubs came toward us. We all hurried to meet him partway.

Paige reached him first, and I stepped up beside her, as did Sam, Zach, and Grafton. My legs felt weak beneath me, and lightheadedness washed over me. I tried to read the doctor's expression, his body language, but my instincts were firing amiss.

"Tell us he's okay," I said.

Paige looked over at me and put a hand on my shoulder.

"He's lost a lot of blood, and the knife cut into his intestines."

I didn't like the pallor of the doctor's face or the way his posture had him hunching forward.

"His blood pressure went quite low a number of times during surgery," he continued, "and we thought we'd lose him, but—"

"But we haven't?" Tears streamed freely down Paige's face. "Right?"

I could only imagine what she was feeling. I knew she would be blaming herself, even if she hadn't been the one to stab Jack. If she hadn't come out here, Jack would never have been here.

The doctor's face softened, and he nodded.

All the air whooshed out of my lungs at once. Was I seeing what I wanted to see?

"He's got a long road to recovery ahead of him," the doctor added, "but he's going to be fine."

"Yes!" I hugged Zach and then turned to Paige. She had parted from an embrace with Sam, and I caught his eye past her. He nodded, and I wrapped my arms around Paige.

"We should have known better than to think anyone could knock Jack down," I proclaimed. "He's too stubborn of a bastard."

We all laughed, even Sam and Grafton.

Somehow everything had turned out all right. Paige had gotten her closure, and we had stopped a killer.

Catch the next book in the Brandon Fisher FBI series!

Sign up at the weblink listed below
to be notified when new Brandon Fisher titles are available
for pre-order:

CarolynArnold.net/BFupdates

By joining this newsletter, you will also receive exclusive
first looks at the following:

Updates pertaining to upcoming releases in the series,
such as cover reveals, book descriptions, and firm release
dates

Sneak peeks of teasers and special content

Behind-the-Tape™ insights that give you an inside look at
Carolyn's research and creative process

There is no getting around it: reviews are important and so is word of mouth.

With all the books on the market today, readers need to know what's worth their time and what's not. This is where you come into play.

If you enjoyed *Violated*, please help others find it by posting a brief, honest review on the retailer site where you purchased this book and recommend it to family and friends.

Also, Carolyn loves to hear from her readers, and you can reach her at Carolyn@CarolynArnold.net.

Upon receipt of your e-mail, you will be added to her newsletter mailing unless you express your desire otherwise.

Keep on reading for a sample of *Remnants*, book 6 in the Brandon Fisher FBI series.

PROLOGUE

The time had come to select his next victim. He had to choose carefully and perfectly—he wouldn't get a second chance. The mall was teeming with life, and that made for a lot of eyeballs, a lot of potential witnesses. But he supposed it also helped him be more inconspicuous. People were hustling through the shopping center, interested solely in their own agendas. They wouldn't be paying him—or what he was doing—much attention.

He was standing at the edge of the food court next to the hallway leading to the restrooms eating a gyro. The lidded and oversized garbage bin on wheels that was behind him would ensure that anyone who did notice him would just think he was a mall janitor on his lunch break.

The pitchy voice of a girl about eight hit his ears. "Daddy, I want ice cream."

Trailing not far behind her were a man and woman holding hands. The woman was fit and blond, but his attention was on the man beside her. He was in his twenties, easily six feet tall with a solid, athletic build. He'd be strong and put up a fight. Yes, this was the one. And talk about ideal placement—he was across from the Dairy Queen.

He wiped his palms on his coveralls and took a few deep breaths. What he was about to do wasn't because of who he was, but rather, because he had to do it.

And he had to hurry. The family was coming toward him.

"It's almost lunchtime," the woman said, letting go of the man's hand.

"Daaaaaaddyyyyy." A whiny petition.

The man looked to the woman with a smile that showcased his white teeth. "We could have ice cream for lunch?"

The little girl began to bounce. "Yeah!"

"Really, Eric?" The woman wasn't as impressed as the girl, but under the man's gaze she caved and smiled. "All right, but just today…"

"Thank you, Mommy!" The girl wrapped her arms around the woman's legs but quickly let go, prancing ahead of her parents and toward the DQ counter.

"Brianna, we wash our hands first." The woman glanced at him as she walked by and offered a reserved smile. Had she detected his interest in them?

Breathe. She thinks you work here, remember?

Smile back.

Remain calm.

Look away and act uninterested.

"Oooh," the girl moaned but returned to her mother anyway.

"We'll just be a minute," the woman said.

"Hey, doesn't Daddy have to wash his hands?" the girl asked.

Sometimes things just work out…

The woman smiled at the man. "Eric?"

"Yes, he does," he playfully answered in the third person.

Mother and daughter headed to the restroom, the man not far behind.

It was time to get to work.

He took the last bite of his sandwich, crumpled the wrapper, and tossed it into the bin. He casually moved behind it and pushed it down the hall into the men's room.

He put up a sign that said it was closed for cleaning and entered, positioning himself next to the door. From there, he could see his target at one of the urinals and another man washing his hands at the sink. Otherwise, it was quiet.

Just as if it was meant to be...

The stranger left the restroom without a passing glance. This left him alone with his target.

He twisted the lock on the door and then moved behind the man, who paid him no mind. He took the needle out of his pocket and plunged it into the man's neck.

The man snapped a hand over where he'd been poked. "Hey!"

It would take a few seconds for the drug to fully kick in. He just had to stay out of the man's way and block the exit in the meantime.

"What did you..." The man was away from the urinal now, coming toward him on unsteady legs. Both his hands went to his forehead and then it was lights-out. He collapsed on the floor.

He hurried to the bin, wheeled it over to the man's body, and lifted him just enough to dump him inside. Once the man was in there, he lowered the lid, unlocked the restroom, collected his sign, and left.

His heart was thumping in his ears as he wheeled the bin out a back service door. Some people were milling around, but they didn't seem curious about him. He went to his van and opened the back door. He put the ramp in place and simply wheeled the bin inside.

When he was finished, he closed the doors and headed for the driver's seat. He wanted to hit the gas and tear out of the lot. The adrenaline surging through his system was screaming, *You got away with it again*, but he didn't like to get too cocky.

Still, he did take some pride in the fact that he'd gotten what he'd come for—and it had been so, so easy.

CHAPTER ONE

Savannah, Georgia
Tuesday, February 14, 1:05 PM Eastern

Valentine's Day would have to wait until next year, and I couldn't say I was disappointed—or surprised. Working as an agent in the FBI's Behavioral Analysis Unit makes planning anything impossible. This time, being swept out of town for an investigation was saving me from a day that was otherwise full of expectations and pressures. And even though my relationship with Becky was casual, it had been going on for several months now and she would be expecting a romantic evening.

But all that was hundreds of miles behind me now…

When I stepped off the government jet, the warm Savannah air welcomed me and made me think of my childhood in Sarasota, Florida. No cold winters there, either, unlike Virginia, where it could dip below zero this time of year, occasionally bringing that white stuff along with it.

My boss, Supervisory Special Agent Jack Harper, walked in front of me. This was his first time heading into the field after an unsub had almost killed him this past summer. He'd barely scraped by, but he was far too stubborn of a bastard to die. Having come so close to death, though, he had to be looking at life differently. I knew when I had just *thought* I was going to die during a previous investigation, it had taken me a long time to shake it.

He had more gray hairs than I'd remembered, and the lines on his face were cut deeper. His eyes seemed darker these days, too. More contemplative. He had been cleared for field work, but I still questioned how he could have fully bounced back in six short months.

I looked over my shoulder at the other two members of our team, Zach Miles and Paige Dawson. Zach was a certifiable genius, and although he was older than my thirty-one years, he had the sense of humor and maturity level of a college student. He'd found endless amusement in calling me "Pending" for the entire two years of my probationary period. Another reason I was happy to be a full-fledged agent now.

Paige was another story. She and I had a rather complicated history, and whether I wanted to admit to it or not, I loved her. But we had to make a choice—our jobs or our relationship. Since we'd both worked far too hard to throw our careers away, the decision to remain friends was, in effect, made for us.

We silently weaved through the airport and picked up a couple of rental SUVs. Jack and I took one, as we usually did, and Paige and Zach were paired together. We were going straight to meet with Lieutenant Charlie Pike, who commanded the homicide unit of Savannah PD, and his detective Rodney Hawkins, at Blue Heron Plantation where human remains had been found in the Little Ogeechee River. According to our debriefing, an arm and a leg were found there a week ago, and yesterday, another arm showed up. Savannah PD had already run tests confirming that we were looking at three different victims, and that was why we'd been called in.

The drive went quickly, and when the plantation's iron gates swung open, I spotted a female officer guarding the entrance. She lifted her sunglasses to the top of her head as Jack rolled to a stop next to her and opened his window.

Jack pulled out his credentials. "Supervisory Special Agent Jack Harper of the FBI. I'm here with my team."

The officer's hazelnut eyes took in Jack's badge, then she looked behind us to Paige and Zach in the other SUV. She lowered her sunglasses. "Lieutenant Pike is expecting you. He's just down there." She pointed to a path that came off a parking lot and seemed to disappear amid cattails.

We parked the vehicles and wasted no time getting to where she had directed us. The echoing calls of red-winged blackbirds and the whistling cries of blue herons carried on a gentle breeze, but the presence of investigators wearing white Tyvek suits drove home our purpose here and it had nothing to do with relaxing in nature.

As we approached, a black man of about fifty was talking animatedly into a phone. He was easily six foot four, thin and fit, and he had a commanding presence, even from a distance.

A younger male officer in a navy-blue uniform stood in front of him and gestured in our direction.

The black man turned to face us, his phone still to his ear. "Gotta go." He tucked his cell into his shirt pocket and came over to us while the officer went in the opposite direction. "I take it you're the FBI."

"SSA Jack Harper, and this is my team." Jack gestured to each of us.

The lieutenant took turns shaking our hands and getting our names. He finished with me, and I was surprised by how firm his grip was.

"Brandon Fisher," I said. "Good to meet you."

There was a loud rustling in the tall grass then, followed by a splash.

"Probably just an alligator," Pike said.

Yeah, just *an alligator…*

As if on cue, twenty feet down the bank, someone began wrangling one of the reptiles, the animal's tail and head swiping through the air as it tried to regain its freedom.

No such luck, though, as its captor worked to get it away from the investigators. I took a few steps back. There was no harm in being extra cautious.

"I'm glad all of you could make it as quickly as you did. I'm Lieutenant Pike, but most people call me Charlie."

Maybe it was his age or his rank, but I knew I'd continue to think of him as Pike.

"Unfortunately," he went on, "Detective Hawkins won't be joining us today or for the remainder of the case. He's dealing with a family matter."

"I hope everything will be all right," Paige said, showing her trademark compassion.

Pike shook his head. "They were expecting and just found out that they lost the baby."

His words had my past sweeping over me. I knew exactly how that devastation felt. My ex-wife, Deb, had gotten pregnant once, but her body had rejected the fetus. She'd never really been the same after that, truth be told. And by the time she had seemed to return to a version of her normal self, she'd asked for a divorce.

Jack's body was rigid. "Where was the arm found yesterday?" As always, his focus was solely on the case. While he was a person who sheltered his emotions quite well, he usually could muster some empathy.

"Ah, yes, right out there." Pike pointed toward a boat in the water, about halfway out from the riverbank. A diver surfaced next to it. "The arm was lodged in some mud and sticking out above the surface."

To be out that far, either the limb had been dumped from a boat, had come down the river and settled here, or our unsub had a good throwing arm. If we could determine which, it would give us some helpful insight into our unsub.

The investigation by Savannah PD had dismissed the idea of the murders taking place on plantation property, though. But if our unsub had chosen here as the dump site, it would tell us how organized he was, whether he assumed risk or preferred isolation.

"Are the gates normally left open for the public?" I asked. "It seems rather remote back here, but is there much traffic?"

Pike wasn't wearing sunglasses, and he squinted in the bright sunshine. "It's not an overly busy place, and they close at night."

"But could a person come down the river to the plantation on a boat at night after hours?" I asked.

Pike curled his lips and bobbed his head. "Yeah, I suppose that's possible."

"I want the parts of the river going through the property under surveillance. Twenty-four seven," Jack directed, drawing Pike's gaze to him.

"I'll make sure that happens."

"And make sure the officers are hidden so if our unsub is brazen enough to return—"

Pike nodded. "Not our first rodeo."

"And make sure the search for more remains continues during daylight hours."

"Those are already their orders." Pike put his hands on his hips. "The community has gotten wind of yesterday's finding, and on top of last week's discovery, let's just say people are panicking. Somehow a local news station found out that the FBI was being brought in. Don't ask me how."

While I probably should have, I didn't really care. My senses were too busy taking in the crime scene: marshland, relative seclusion, an arm and leg discovered last week, an arm yesterday. Aside from the human remains that had been found here, the property had a serene feeling to it, a sense of peace. There was a tangible quality to the air, though—or maybe it was the presence of law enforcement and crime scene investigators—that made it impossible to deny that death had touched the place.

"What else can you tell us about the limbs that were recovered?" Paige asked.

The lieutenant cleared his throat. "Well, both arms didn't have hands, and the leg didn't have a foot. We found incision marks indicating the hands and foot had been intentionally cut off."

"Our killer could have taken them for trophies or to make identification impossible," I suggested.

Pike gave a small nod and continued. "And while we know the hands and foot were removed, it's not as clear how the appendages separated from the torso. It would be something we'd need the medical examiner to clarify."

Jack's brow furrowed, and I could tell his mind was racing through the possibilities.

"But," Pike continued, "all the limbs have one thing in common: muscle tissue remained, even though the skin had been removed."

"It is possible that the skin was also taken as a trophy," Zach speculated.

"We could be looking for a hunter or a sexual sadist," Jack said.

Hunters were typically identified by the type of weapon they used—a hunting knife, rifle, or crossbow, for example—and they tended to dispose of their victims' bodies in remote, isolated areas. A sexual sadist, on the other hand, got off on the torture and pain. But we'd need to gather more facts before we could build any sort of profile on our unsub. Even knowing more about the victims themselves would help. Was the killer choosing people he or she was acquainted with? Were the victims of a certain gender, age group, occupation? The list went on and on. From there, we could more easily speculate on our killer's motive and what they had to gain.

"Any IDs on the victims yet?" I asked.

Pike shook his head. "Not yet, but they're working on it. I'm not sure when we'll know."

I looked at Jack. I didn't know all the steps involved with processing DNA, but it could take weeks, if not months, to go through the system. Things could be sped up if the government was willing to foot the bill for a private laboratory, which was costly and would still take days. Oftentimes this was approved for cases involving serial murder, but primarily when we had seemingly solid evidence that we believed would lead us to the killer.

Jack gave a small shake of his head, as if he'd read my mind and dismissed the private laboratory.

"Anyone reported missing from the area recently?" Zach asked.

"No." Pike's single word was heavy with discouragement.

"It could be that the victims aren't being missed by anyone." Zach's realistic yet sad summation was also a possibility.

"The ones from last week were all Caucasian males in their mid- to late twenties," Pike offered next.

"What about the arm from yesterday?" Jack asked.

"It was male. I called in a friend and colleague to get us more information. She's an anthropologist, and she'll take a look at it as she had the other remains, but she won't get to it until much later today."

"She?" Paige queried.

"Shirley Moody. She's one of the best in the field but from out of town."

Jack nodded his acknowledgment. "What can you tell us about the guy who found the arm yesterday?"

"Name's Jonathan Tucker. He works at the plantation, and we took his statement, of course," Pike began. "His record is clean, and he seems like a down-to-earth guy. He's got two young girls and his wife died a couple years back. He seemed really shaken up by all this."

"What about Wesley Graham?" Jack asked.

"The man who found the remains last week? Nice guy. He's single and proud of it. Never been married. No record, either. But he didn't seem too upset by the whole situation."

So far we weren't getting much more out of Pike than we had his detective's reports. Graham didn't work for the plantation, and the file noted that his reason for coming to the plantation was to de-stress.

"This site attracts tourists and locals," Pike said. "People like to surround themselves in nature. Personally, I could live without mosquitoes." He swatted near his face as if to emphasize his point. "I know you'll probably want to pay Tucker and Graham visits yourselves, but—" Pike made a show of extending his arm and bending it to consult his watch "—right now, I've got you an appointment with the owner of the plantation. We should probably get moving toward the main house."

"Lieutenant!" A female investigator shouted as she waded through the water toward the riverbank in a hurry. She was holding a clear plastic evidence bag.

"We found a cell phone," she called out as she reached us.

Pike looked at the investigator skeptically. "Where?"

Her eyes dipped to the ground, but she regrouped herself quickly. "It was near where the arm was found."

"And it took a day to find it?" Pike raised his eyebrows.

She squared her shoulders but shrank somewhat under the lieutenant's gaze. "It was in a tangle of weeds, but it could have just come to rest there in recent currents."

It seemed Pike was a hard one to please, and he reminded me of the way I used to view Jack—an unforgiving perfectionist. And while Pike might not be impressed, I was pleased. That phone could lead us to a killer.

Also available from
International Bestselling Author
Carolyn Arnold

REMNANTS

Book 6 in the Brandon Fisher FBI series

He wrenches at the chains on his wrists and ankles—to no avail. Tears stream down his cheeks as his captor comes at him all dressed in black, chanting and mumbling incoherently, a large knife in his hands…

When multiple body parts are recovered from the Little Ogeechee River in Savannah, Georgia, local law enforcement calls in the FBI. Special Agent Brandon Fisher and his team with the Behavioral Analysis Unit set out to investigate, but with the remains pointing to three separate victims, this isn't going to be an open-and-shut case.

With no quick means of identifying the deceased, building a profile of this serial killer is more challenging than usual. Why are these victims being selected? Where are they are targeted? Why are their limbs being severed and their bodies mutilated?

The questions compound as the body count continues to rise, and when a torso painted blue and missing its heart is found, the case takes an even darker turn. The FBI will need to convince the Deep South to give up her secrets if they're going to catch the killer. After all, one thing is clear: the killing isn't going to stop until they figure it all out. And they are running out of time…

Available from popular book retailers or
at CarolynArnold.net

CAROLYN ARNOLD is an international bestselling and award-winning author, as well as a speaker, teacher, and inspirational mentor. She has several continuing fiction series and has many published books. Her genre diversity offers her readers everything from cozy to hard-boiled mysteries, and thrillers to action adventures. Her crime fiction series have been praised by those in law enforcement as being accurate and entertaining. This led to her adopting the trademark: POLICE PROCEDURALS RESPECTED BY LAW ENFORCEMENT™.

Carolyn was born in a small town and enjoys spending time outdoors, but she also loves the lights of a big city. Grounded by her roots and lifted by her dreams, her overactive imagination insists that she tell her stories. Her intention is to touch the hearts of millions with her books, to entertain, inspire, and empower.

She currently lives near London, Ontario, Canada with her husband and two beagles.

CONNECT ONLINE
CarolynArnold.net
Facebook.com/AuthorCarolynArnold
Twitter.com/Carolyn_Arnold

And don't forget to sign up for her newsletter for up-to-date information on release and special offers at CarolynArnold.net/Newsletters.

Printed in the USA
CPSIA information can be obtained
at www.ICGtesting.com
LVHW092053171123
764248LV00043B/1623/J